The Magpie

Bridge

鵲
橋

Liu Hong was born and grew up in China. She came to England as a student in 1989, and now lives in Wessex with her husband and a young daughter.

Also by Liu Hong

Startling Moon

The Magpie Bridge

Liu Hong

review

First published in 2003
by REVIEW

An imprint of Headline Book Publishing

10 9 8 7 6 5 4 3 2 1

Cataloguing in Publication Data
is available from the British Library.

ISBN 0 7472 7088 0

Typeset in Meridien by
Letterpart Limited, Reigate, Surrey

Printed and bound in Great Britain by
Clays Ltd, St Ives plc

Headline Book Publishing
A division of Hodder Headline
338 Euston Road
London NW1 3BH

www.reviewbooks.co.uk
www.hodderheadline.com

To Lucy and Susie for Huda and beyond
To the Aitchisons and Cannons for England

Remembering Tian Jingyu (1914–1999)

ACKNOWLEDGEMENTS

I thank all at Review and Toby Eady Associates for their professionalism, and my family and friends for their help and encouragement.

In particular, I thank my agent, Jessica Woollard, and my editor, Mary-Anne Harrington. This book would not have been possible without their dedication and inspiration.

I thank Irene Andreae, Terry Pevvy, Hilary Whyte and Peter and the late Agnes Stein, for letting me glimpse their gardens.

Thanks also to Dr Glen Bowman, Jon Cannon, Hugh Desaram, Professor Roy Ellen, David Heath, Laurent Jean-Pierre, Professor Chen Junyu, Susie Jolly, Billie Lee, Lin Lengshi, Ian Leese, Professor Wang Liyun, Simon Long, Jackie Macbeth, Joy Newton, Jack Oliver, Hazel Orme, Craig and Julia Orr, Dr Zhao Shiwei, Neil Taylor, Susie Whimster and Fang Yingji, for their generosity, advice and support.

'If the affections are mutual and everlasting, does it matter
that they cannot be together in everyday life?'

from 'The Magpie Bridge'

兩情若是久長時
又豈在朝朝暮暮

The Story of the Magpie Bridge

O nce upon a time a poor shepherd fell in love with a fairy, the seventh daughter of the Emperor of Heaven, and she with him. They lived for seven happy years in secret and had a baby together. But when the Empress found out, she was furious and came down from heaven to snatch the girl back. The shepherd pursued them with their child in a shoulder pole but the Empress took off her hairpin and threw it into the poor boy's path and a river emerged separating him from the girl – the Milky Way or, as we call it in China, the Silver River. But the lovers' plight moved the magpies, who could not bear to see them apart. On the seventh day of the seventh month each year, they cluster together to form a bridge to link heaven and earth so that the shepherd can climb up it to meet his beloved. That's why we call the magpie the happiness bird.

1: *Yu Shui* – Rainwater

19 February

Tie Mei

I'm coming, Jiaojiao, your scent alone guides me.

Where am I? An island, green like an enclosed garden. So many lights. I head for dark lanes, familiar, comforting. Why has she chosen this place? Words are written back to front, women wear short skirts that bare their legs in the freezing wind. Foreign devils are everywhere, tall and arrogant. Only a drunkard acknowledges me. He staggers, gesticulating. His friend laughs, unaware of me. I would have taught them a lesson, but I am startled by a cry.

I follow the sound. Under a faintly lit street-lamp I see a little girl who sits all alone sobbing. She leans against a brick wall by an entrance with stairs leading underground. 'Mummy, Mummy,' she cries, and looks up, but I don't stay. I had a soft heart once, but now it's as frozen as the Moon Lady's. I step over the crying child. Stupid of me, of course, to be fooled so easily: my own little treasure is no longer such a child.

When I first went to live with Jiaojiao, she was not much older than five, crying for the mother who had abandoned her, but only in her dreams, never in front of me. She was tough then. I wonder how much she resembles her mother now.

Up the hill through the fog, I approach the grand red-brick house, fronted by a lawn, boxed in by hedges. I can smell something, not her scent but something else familiar,

3

something floral. Is there a garden? I find it at the back of the house. Curved twisted lines, branches tangled together like confused thoughts. A wild, free garden like my own. How unexpected.

The scent plays tricks: it comes and goes with the night wind. Then suddenly, I see it, the Mei tree, standing at the edge of the garden by the half-collapsed brick wall.

I go to it slowly, carefully, not knowing what to make of it. A slender trunk, small pink flowers shivering on its bare branches, petals opening like a pretty girl's mouth. This is the tree I'm named after; it is what I am about. 'Remember what Mei stands for. Be pure, brave and resilient. You are the blossom that braves the cold.' My mother's words come back to me even now.

But what is this tree of my motherland doing here, looking sad and lonely as if it also knows that it does not belong? For a moment I am taken back to my garden – my one true happiness – which I had deserted. The Mei trees there have all gone wild, and sparrows make their nests in my precious rosebushes. We desert our gardens eventually, abandon them when the garden inside us dies, through heartbreak, through carelessness. The garden inside me died a long while ago.

Dogs in the neighbourhood bark and I am reminded of why I'm here. I head for the house, filled with apprehension by the unexpected discovery of the Mei tree. I touch the door, which opens with a creak, then stand still, overwhelmed by a sense of hostility. As I have expected I do not feel welcome here – but where is she? Which room in this maze-like building does she sleep in? I have only her scent to guide me. Silently I make my way upstairs to a room that feels like hers.

A shapeless person lies fast asleep in bed. This cannot be her. Confused, I edge nearer to see a foreign woman with long hair draped over the sheet; a wireless on the table next to her murmurs words I cannot understand. As I am about to leave, something next to it catches my eyes: something solid, round, is caught in the moonlight and, for a moment, I see my face reflected back.

How can it be? What luck is it to find this heirloom

4

alongside my precious girl? In seeking one I have discovered the other. So close to my fulfilment, I stand, frozen like a puppet, not knowing what to do next.

Something stirs: a cat emerges from the sleeping woman's bed, ears flattened, tail erect. Shining in the dark, its green eyes somehow echo the greenness of my treasure on the table.

The woman on the bed does not stir. I spit at the cat and sweep past it, up another flight of stairs to be enveloped by the scent of my dear girl, which has brought me at last to her. Gazing down, I take in her sleeping face and whisper, 'Jiaojiao, wake up.'

Jiao Mei

'Jiaojiao, wake up. I need to talk to you.'

A voice whispered my name, a strong fragrance woke me. I rubbed my eyes, still sleepy, swallowed, put a hand to my pounding heart. Without moving from my futon, which occupied much of the small attic room, I scanned around me. Nowadays when I woke up, I spent the first few moments looking for the self I had lost during sleep.

Someone was sitting on the heap of clothes on the small wooden chair next to my head. I blinked and the figure seemed to dissolve. But then the voice came again, more clearly, a woman's voice. This time I realised she was speaking in my native tongue, Mandarin.

'I need to talk to you, something very important.'

I looked at the clock by my bedside: 1.15 a.m. A cold winter's night, but the small sash window was open. Even in winter, I liked to let the air in. Often I would be woken by the conversations of night drifters, otherworldly sounds in English, a language now familiar by day but which still eluded me at night.

I had dreamed of my mother again. We were in our house in Beijing; for some reason I hadn't been sent to nursery. Mama and I were playing in the courtyard waiting for Baba to come home. The late-summer afternoon sun shone on us; the hens ran around in the background. The big pagoda tree in the middle of the yard, heavy with white flowers, drooped in the afternoon heat. Street pedlars' voices called enticingly in their provincial accents from just outside the gate; I smelt their delicious popcorn and ran to Mama and begged. As dreams went, this was so real: I could see the dust in the air caught in the sunbeam, and how happily my mother smiled. 'You can have whatever you want, my dear,' she said, as she opened the gate to let the man in. He carried a shoulder pole with all my favourite sweets in two baskets: blood-red dates, golden peanuts, yellow and white popcorn, sugar-glazed haws, roast pine-nuts. 'Whatever you want, my precious.' She nudged me towards the man. Incredulous, I held back, picking one thing up and putting it down again, just to prolong the pleasure.

The pedlar's face had been hidden in the shadow of the straw hat. When he looked up, he broke into a cruel grin. I screamed – I was sure I screamed – but my mother just smiled indulgently. She did not seem to have heard me. I lost my voice as terror seized me.

I knew why that man had come. He had come to take her away from me.

I had woken to find myself speaking English. 'Mama, Mama?' Someone had called me 'Jiaojiao', my nickname, known only to my family. It could only be her. But the soft English voices from the street nudged me closer to the surface of wakefulness and I remembered that this could not be: my mother was back in China, and had remarried now. She hadn't been in touch since I had left.

'Don't you know how to show respect? Don't you recognise me?' the woman demanded. I staggered to my feet, still only half awake, clutching the duvet around me.

She was dappled by the moonlight sieved through the cracks of the tall trees, waving outside the window, but I could see that she was pale. What a peculiar face: perfectly formed, fine features, no wrinkles, almost too perfect. She was dressed in a long creamy silk robe, glistening with golden threads, which looked heavy on her fragile frame. It was odd, the contrast between her authoritative voice and her ethereal body: she had the furtive look of someone on the run, as if she shouldn't be there. Her speech puzzled me especially: it sounded dated and pretentious, like something from Peking opera.

Did I recognise her? No. She was like a black-and-white photo of a person, conjuring a vague impression of a long-lost memory. 'Who are you? Why are you here?' I asked, stepping towards the window. The air was icy cold, full of a suffocating sweet fragrance. I wanted to escape.

She sat up in the chair and glanced round my small room imperiously. 'Do you not know? You are pregnant with the foreign devil's child. I have come to help you.'

I looked down at my belly, flat and smooth, a lake without a ripple. I said nothing.

'You can't ignore it. You are feeling sick. It's called *haixi*: fearing the happiness. Your due date is around Big Snow Day, and it's a boy,' she said, somewhat disdainfully.

I closed my eyes. Downstairs, the radio buzzed. I was standing in my nightdress at one in the morning, speaking Mandarin to a visitor who was telling me that I was pregnant. Had I gone mad? 'Leave now or else . . .' I thought desperately '. . . I'll call Barbara.' I stamped my feet, cold and numb. Barbara, no doubt asleep in her bedroom a storey below me, would barely hurt a fly, but she would have to do.

'You will do no such thing. Is that how you treat your grandmother, your father's mother?'

'You are lying. I have no grandmother. She is dead.'

The words had hardly left my mouth before a hard lump rose in my throat. I ran to the bathroom and threw up. I turned the light on, let the tap run, and stared at myself in the mirror. What was wrong with me? I rinsed my mouth and coughed before I went back to my bedroom.

She was gone.

I woke again to the downstairs radio, and the sound of Barbara pacing about. A night of bad dreams. I yawned and peered out of the window. The fog had cleared to reveal another wet day, reassuringly like so many others I had experienced since coming to England six months ago. Such a lot of rain. No wonder it felt a long time already.

Lying back I faced the photos of my family I had Blu-tacked on to the wall. The nearest one was of me, my parents and Nainai, my grandmother, taken in black-and-white then coloured, a typical sixties studio shot. I was sitting on Nainai's lap, my parents standing behind us. Everyone was smiling. Nainai didn't look that old and my mother wore her pretty floral shirt. All our lips were painted red, which looked odd on everyone except Mama.

Why was it always my mother I dreamed of, when it was my father who had died, nearly seven years ago? Perhaps, I wondered, putting a finger to his face – an act of intimacy I would never have permitted myself in real life – it was because I had been able to say goodbye to him: I had half expected his death after he'd been diagnosed with cancer. With my mother, well, I had never got over the fact that she could leave us in such a cold-blooded way, and for someone so undeserving, so inferior to Baba.

And that other dream, so vivid, of the woman who had called herself my grandmother! She was nothing like her, although she did remind me of someone I had once known. And how strange that she had addressed me by my childhood nickname – no one had called me Jiaojiao in years. Impatiently I threw off the duvet, jumped up, drew the curtains and pushed the window wide open. The fresh air of the day drove away the thoughts of the night. My head became clearer: I'd been overtiring myself. All the late-night reading was unsettling.

By the time I got downstairs I felt almost normal. Barbara was still in her pyjamas, the dragon-patterned pair that her brother had given her for Christmas, which she didn't like but wore none the less. One of her hands clutched casually at the front so I knew she still hadn't found the belt. Her hair was tangled and she looked as if she'd slept late again.

She yawned and waved at me with her free hand. 'Want a coffee? Don't you just love that smell!'

'OK,' I responded. Usually I had tea, but coffee seemed like a good idea this morning.

She leaned forward to examine me. 'Not slept well? You look a bit tired.'

'Bad dreams,' I said, sitting down.

'Thought so. I heard you calling out in your sleep again.' She poured me coffee. 'In Chinese. You were dreaming in Mandarin. You must be homesick.'

'Do you think so?' My eye was drawn to her hand, and I noticed how dry the skin had become. When I had first met her, so many years ago, she had taken such care of her hands, always applying creams and lotions, but now that she was older – or, at least, recently – she didn't bother.

Laughing, she leaned forward again and kissed my cheek. 'Yes, you are – I think you're pining, poor girl.'

I gulped down the coffee. I wished she'd stay close like this, just for today, with her soft voice, her warm dry hands. I needed her to banish the strangeness of last night – the icy fragrance that was unsettling me still. But I didn't know how to return her affection. I wouldn't dare to kiss her. Such a strange, foreign custom. I kissed my boyfriend, Ken, but that was different.

The moment had passed. She pattered away, barefoot, to fetch sugar and came back to sit next to me again. I watched her pretty painted toes. Did she not feel cold? I knew better than to ask, and returned to the subject of my dream. 'What was I saying, Barbara? You must have heard.'

'Oh, Jiao Mei, my Chinese isn't what it was, though I've been trying to work it out. I think you've been saying the same words, over and over, these last few nights. It's definitely Chinese, I'm just not sure of the sounds. Oh, Oscar.' She bent down and I saw the cat arch his head and circle her ankle, his tail proudly erect. She scratched his chin and a loud purr rose up. 'Puss, you're okay now. It's been a funny night, hasn't it? Has that black cat next door been bothering you again?'

His thick ginger fur puffed up with pleasure, he strode towards me, hoping for more admiration. I stood up abruptly to refill my cup – I like cats at a distance, but can't bear them touching me, and I was decidedly jumpy that morning. As I went to open the fridge door, Barbara called, 'Is that anything important? I found it under the cooker last night. Anything to do with your new man?'

'Oh, it must be one of Ken's doodles.' I stared at the bit of scrap paper pinned to the bottom corner of the fridge door by a magnet in the shape of a frog. I had been with Ken for barely four months but I knew his doodles: it was he who had taught me the word. This one consisted of what looked to me like a series of question marks. 'He must have left it last time he was here,' I murmured. That had been about three weeks ago, the first time he had come round for the evening. 'I'll keep it for him. You never know, it might be to do with something he is designing now.' Ken was an architect.

Barbara poured herself more coffee and inhaled deeply. 'Oh, I could live on that smell alone.' I smiled, Barbara and her nose: Bill, her boyfriend, had once said it was sharper than a dog's. 'And how is Ken?' she enquired, smiling.

'Fine,' I responded, uncomfortable with her curiosity.

She cocked her head to one side expectantly. I returned her smile, but remained silent. I couldn't tell her more: the relationship was still so new, and confusing at times. 'Some cereal?' She stood up.

'No.' I shook my head. I had always professed to like cereals, as I had embraced everything else English since I got here – the butter, the cream tea, Jane Austen, the rain – but today I felt I could not swallow a mouthful of that dry bird food. I craved something pungent, something Chinese: some salty hundred-year-old eggs. When Xiao Lin, my Chinese friend, came here, usually when Barbara had gone to stay with Bill, she sometimes brought me those eggs. And meat. Barbara was a vegetarian, had been for as long as I had known her. She did not even add salt to her cooking. When we ate together we did not make a sound and it felt as if I was eating silks, beautiful flavourless things. It seemed wrong to make noises, as I did in China, when I wanted to show how I enjoyed the food.

10

When I left she was still sipping coffee. This would be one of her painting days. She was a librarian, but spent much of her time in the studio. She used to paint quite a lot, Bill told me, but since I'd been around all she seemed to do was stare into space.

The front lawn was wet as I stepped on it. The grey shed to my right, where Bill's tools were kept, was locked like a mouth clamped shut. Through the window, which was wiped clean as a mirror, I could see the spade hanging in its usual place; next to it would be the fork, then the rake, all carefully wiped clean after use. Neatly arranged, they looked like props rather than tools. Bill treated them, like his lawns, with the greatest respect and care. It upset him if they were left outside, or put away in the wrong place, just as Barbara would be angry when Bill accidentally trimmed off one of her prized roses. All growing things delighted Barbara, but Bill's preoccupation was his lawns. I shared his reverence, but less, perhaps, from a longing for order than from a sense of discipline – I had been fined for stepping on the grass in China. When I first arrived in England, I marvelled at being encouraged to walk across lawns. In China, earth was precious: lawns were only found in parks, and it was forbidden to step on them.

There was a time when even flower-beds were used for cabbages in the north. Why grow daffodils when you can plant food for the masses? Nobody could dispute that, and nobody dared to: if you did, you were labelled a rightist and sent to the remote countryside for hard labour, like my father had been. Something pulled inside me at the thought of him and I brushed it away – I should not think of the past so often.

The cobbled path led towards the tube station. Hampstead, posed as if for a postcard. I hugged my raincoat tightly around me to keep out the English rain, drizzle pitter-pattering like the soft murmurs you heard in the tea-shops. In China when it rained people scattered and you didn't see a soul in the street; here, people unfurled their umbrellas and continued on their way.

I found myself thinking of my grandmother and her stories.

I would have good fortune, she always used to assure me. 'Wherever you go, you will always encounter a noble person, a *guiren*, who will watch over you and ensure you turn ill-luck into good.'

I had reproached her: 'How can you say that, when my own mother deserted me?' But as Nainai liked to say, 'Fate is a mysterious thing.' She had gone on to tell me the story of the old man who lost his horse. When people came to comfort him he replied, 'How do you know this is not a blessing in disguise?' Sure enough, several days later the horse returned with a dozen others, but when people came to congratulate the old man he said, 'How do you know this is not a misfortune in disguise?' Some days later, thieves broke in and stole the horses. The old man tried to fight them off, and was injured.

On and on the story went, until my head spun. I was sick of the old man: he couldn't make up his mind as to whether or not he was lucky. Reluctantly I concluded, with Nainai, that no situation was wholly good or bad.

As the packed lift descended, I contemplated the bad luck I'd had since my parents had separated, and Baba had died. What good could possibly come of that, Nainai? I thought, a little rebelliously. I imagined her nodding at me, considering her response.

Again, the image of the woman I had seen by my bedside last night surfaced. I stared into the face of a girl in a mini-skirt, who glanced up from her novel, and experienced a flash of panic. Had my mother been thinking of me? What if something were to happen to her? Then I would really be an orphan, truly alone in the world. I preferred not to contemplate it. In any case, since she'd remarried, I suspected her thoughts rarely turned to me. I gripped the handrail harder.

So far, Barbara had been my one piece of undeniable good fortune. Ten months ago, she had arrived in Beijing with her plan for me to return to London with her and study at university. As my colleagues at the middle school where I had taught put it, my pie had fallen from heaven.

I had hardly recognised her then: it had been nearly six years since we had met and both of us had changed so much in that time. She had looked just like one of those plump middle-aged foreign tourists with sunglasses whom the coaches disgorged every day in the centre of Beijing, not the casually dressed student who had had mud-fights with me while my father looked on. It was only when she smiled and her cheeks touched mine that I recognised her. I don't forget smells easily.

So now here I was in her Hampstead home where, in return for free lodging, I did the cleaning once a week. For me, it had proved a good deal. If only she was not so aloof, and I could learn to show my gratitude.

I dozed on the rocking train and thought half-heartedly of the morning's seminar, at which we were expected to debate, to argue with the teacher. This was unheard-of in China: there, you sat and listened, or pretended to. I was good at that. But here there was also the reading list: that week I had five books to get through. All the foreign students complained – one book in a second language was bad enough, but with all that sociological jargon! Most of us would cheat, read the introduction, the conclusion, but never the body of the essay. I didn't like doing it, but often had no choice. Only my friend Taro, the Japanese student, ploughed diligently through all of the reading.

He grinned at me from his place in the overheated lecture room, a couple of seats away. I nodded and smiled back. The grin never left Taro's face, except when he was thinking really hard about something. Our regular lecturer was ill and this lesson was being taken by a young American woman, too nervous about her own performance to notice I wasn't participating. I listened carefully to Sasha, the Russian student with big brown eyes. Older than most of us, she was confident and articulate, and kept interrupting the teacher in her heavy accent.

Afterwards I hurried to the basement – a smoky student common room – and took out the sandwich Barbara had packed for me. When Taro joined me and found me frowning, he smiled. 'Why don't you tell her you don't like cheese?'

'I can't,' I said. 'I just can't. She's been so kind to pack lunch for me, how can I tell her I can't eat it?'

'I understand. It's difficult.' I was grateful for his sympathy.

I went to buy a ham sandwich, and came back to sit next to Taro. We ate in silence. Then his eyes brightened as he remembered something. 'Oh, my wife invites you to come and have dinner with us. I almost forgot.' His wife? He looked about eighteen.

'Yes, I'd love to,' I said, thinking of a home-cooked Japanese meal.

'She said she would cook Sichuan food. That's your home town, isn't it, Sichuan?' I nodded, but my heart sank. I didn't want another foreign 'Sichuan' dish. They were never spicy enough: you needed freshly roasted Sichuan chillies, which were unavailable in England.

All afternoon I felt sleepy. Taro's invitation, kind as it was, made me feel somehow exposed and lonely. It seemed to me that all of my fellow students were here for a purpose. Taro wanted to be a better civil servant; Sasha, unbelievably idealistic, 'wanted to make the world a better place'. I was only here because Barbara had pushed me, to do sociology.

On the tube home I stood holding the handrail. So tired, longing to lean on something. I thought of Ken – warm thoughts. I could, and did, lean on him. Sitting on the tube, my head on his shoulder, listening to the sounds of the carriage, was one of my favourite experiences in London. But I had never told him that – why was I so guarded with him?

Barbara was staring out of the window at the front garden, as if she hadn't moved since I'd left her, although I noticed that she had changed into her artist's smock, so paint-spattered that you could barely tell its original colour – the rainbow dress, we called it. I turned the light on, and she blinked as if I had woken her from a dream. 'Mei, I think I might have gone mad.'

'What do you mean?'

'I kept seeing someone coming up the path, but when I went out to check, they'd disappeared.'

I peered into the darkness outside. The fog had come back, but there was no one to be seen. 'But you know why they're here.' They came all the time to read the blue plaque on the front of the house, with the name of a famous linguist on it. The bolder ones would come right up and have a good look at the house, too.

'No, it's not that, it's an oddly dressed woman, Oriental, I think. I can't see very clearly, with the fog, but there's something strange about her . . . I find her a little menacing.'

Menacing. I remembered the sparkle in the eyes of the woman in my dream. It was how Oscar looked when he was ready to pounce on an unsuspecting bird. I bit my lip. Could we both be dreaming? I did not say anything – I did not want to make it more real by talking about it, but inside me the strange woman's message surfaced again. I wasn't pregnant, was I? I shook my head and talked instead of supper.

Barbara cooked a delicious mushroom soup with plenty of garlic and nutmeg. I could never get enough garlic, but nutmeg was new to me. Too much, she said, was bitter, but the right amount made the soup special. Despite the abundance of milk in it – so alien to a Chinese stomach – her mushroom soup was one of my favourite dishes. Other people's was not the same. The secret? 'I taste all my cooking.' Barbara prided herself on her palate.

I lingered downstairs longer than usual, sensing that she wanted company. She kept suggesting cups of tea, trying to draw me into a conversation about the book on rock gardens she'd been reading. The phone rang and she dashed to it. From her tone I guessed it was her brother, Ted, who lived in Sussex, by the sea. They often talked on the phone, and she always sounded relaxed and girlish.

When she finished, silence bounced back into the house, which felt bigger and emptier. The sound of her turning a page cut the atmosphere sharply.

'So, did you paint today?' I asked.

'I pottered around, really. Took Oscar to the vet so he could treat that wound he had from scrapping with the black cat – the fighting's getting a bit vicious. I did some dusting . . . That reminds me. I noticed something in your room. Have you started wearing perfume? Did Ken give you some?'

'No?'

'That's odd. I could swear I smelt a strong fragrance, floral, and it's only in your room. My nose is never wrong. Besides,' she bent down to stroke Oscar, who had padded in silently from upstairs, 'Oscar smelt it, too, didn't you, Oscar?' She turned to me again. 'He hissed and growled and wouldn't go into your room – I don't think he approved.'

'Could it be a flower? My bedroom window is always open – there must be some blossom nearby.'

Barbara was unconvinced. 'In February? I don't think so.'

'Well.' I shrugged my shoulders and buried myself in the Weber book I was reading.

Neither of us spoke for a long time.

'*Wuthering Heights* is on at the Everyman tonight.' Barbara rustled her book. 'Why don't you ring Ken and go to see it with him? Laurence Olivier is in it, so it should be good.'

I ignored her, and stared at Ken's question marks on the fridge. What did they represent? He could express his thoughts easily, almost carelessly. Mine were all hidden inside me. I had half expected him to call – we hadn't spoken for about a week, not since Valentine's night.

Surrounded by the flowers, the wine and the card Ken had made with the Chinese character for love, with one dot extra where the heart symbol was, we had made love. It was the first time we had not used protection. I had told him it would be all right as I had just finished my period.

2: *Jing Zhe* – Startled Insects Awake From Their Hibernation

6 March

Jiao Mei

B efore I opened my eyes I smelt her – fuller, stronger, fresher this time.

'Well, have you thought about it?'

I won't open my eyes. I won't. It might still be a dream. I had been thinking far too much lately. Of ghosts, my late grandmother – and, oddly, my first boyfriend, Jieming. Ghosts and my grandmother were closely connected: so many of her stories were about ghosts – the female ghost who lured lonely scholars into her grave, the grateful ghost who showered gold on those who had helped him when alive. When we were indoors, she'd turn off the light and her voice rang out in the darkness – an otherworldly sound that both attracted and frightened me, like now. How many nights of my childhood had been spent listening to that voice, which lulled me to sleep? How often since then had I recalled it at times of illness and weakness? 'There were eighteen layers of hell and the Goddess Queen of the West resided in Mount Kunlun where she welcomed in the good dead . . .' It was as if even when she was alive she had been preparing for the other world, its protocols and hierarchies, and its famed Soup of Confusing the Souls: 'When you drink it, which you must, you will forget everything about this life.'

The voice drew me back from my thoughts: 'Are you listening? I'm asking if you have thought of your pregnancy.'

Pregnancy? There had been a scare with Jieming, which had worried him more than me. Concerned for my honour, he had promised to marry me if anything went wrong. Perhaps I had been hoping for a more passionate proposal, and it was soon impossible to ignore the cracks that appeared in our relationship. I read Jieming's letter, announcing his engagement to a girl from his village, beside my father's hospital bed. When I looked up again a nurse passed me the consent form to sign for Baba's operation. Under the bright fluorescent light in the hospital corridor I practised my signature on Jieming's letter, over and over again with the black pen. Then I picked up the consent form and banished all lingering attachment to him.

The sensation of cool air on my skin forced me to open my eyes, and I stared into the furious face of the scented woman, smooth, young and expressionless. Last time I had seen her she had seemed more distant, as if I had been watching her through a veil. Today that veil had been torn away. I considered reaching out to touch her, but was taken aback by her words: 'Don't pretend to be asleep, I know you're awake. I know what you're thinking of.'

'Why ask me, then?' I glared at her.

She ignored my question and went on. 'I am your grandmother.' She raised her voice, as if she'd read my thoughts. 'You didn't know me in my youth, but has it ever occurred to you that once I was young? In my youth they said my beauty drowned the fish and caused envious swallows to drop dead from the sky.'

I laughed nervously, astonished by the old-fashioned expressions she used, but she continued: 'You don't want to be pregnant, not when you are unmarried and carrying a foreign devil's child.'

I might as well have been told off by a fussy 'aunt' from the Neighbourhood Committee: in my childhood, this vigilant group had watched our every move to report any wrongdoing to the police. 'What if I am? It's not the end of the world,' I sneered.

My left cheek suddenly stung with cold. 'How can you say

such a thing? What about your reputation?'

She was not the first to remind me of it. Not long after I had started seeing Ken, another Chinese girl had come up to me in the library. After a brief exchange of pleasantries she had come straight to the point: 'I feel obliged to advise you that people have been talking behind your back. Think about your reputation. We are Chinese. We don't sleep with foreigners.'

I had wanted to slap her – just as now I wanted to strike the woman before me, with her painted face. 'To hell with reputation, it's none of your business.'

Her scent intensified, surrounding me. Her voice exploded in my ears like thunder. 'Have you forgotten how your great-grandmother died? Have you no respect for your ancestors?' She stepped back a pace and glared at me. 'If you really feel no shame, then you are no granddaughter of mine. I shan't come again.'

Her scent became overpowering and my eyes closed under a heavy weight. As in a nightmare I struggled to breathe. After a few minutes when I opened my eyes and gulped down some air, she was gone.

When I left the house Barbara was still in bed. I stepped out into rain. Whatever was going on? The woman had seemed to know so much about me and my family: 'Have you forgotten how your great-grandmother died?' she said. Had she been referring to the story of the mirror? And hadn't my great-grandmother died of an incurable disease? That was what grandmother had told me.

I remembered her last visit a fortnight ago – I had been able to dismiss her more easily then, but her anger made her real. No, these were not just dreams: a dream would not leave a trail of scent so strong that it lingered even now, stinging my eyes. And yet my grandmother had died peacefully in her sleep.

I knew death: I'd watched my father dying, sat holding his hands when his eyes were closed and he lay there in front of me, gone for ever. I had realised he would die long before he had from the smell of decay on his breath – something in him had been dying already. I'd seen Nainai die, too, and that had been easier to accept.

Both of her visits had fallen on dates that had been ingrained in my mind since I was small: they were among the twenty-four days in each year around which the peasants based their cycle of planting and harvesting, following the traditional calendar. A gardener, my father had adhered to their fortnightly intervals. Significant dates were always remembered in this way. Instead of saying 'Monday next week', he would say, 'Two days after the day of the Frost Descent.' Nainai, with her amazing memory, had made the twenty-four two-syllable names into a song that rhymed, so it was easy for me to remember. I can still recite these old sayings that predicted the weather and diseases: '*Dahan bu han, ren ma bu an,*' Nainai used to say: 'If it is not cold on the day of the Big Chill, many people and cattle will be ill.'

'Why, Nainai?' I had asked, thinking her a witch.

'I'm not sure, really,' she'd say slowly, 'but if it's not cold on the day of the Big Chill, then the natural cycles are out of balance, which does not augur well.'

I knew better now: it was because the temperature had not sunk low enough to kill off all the germs. My teacher at school had explained it to me. There was nothing mysterious about it: science could explain everything. 'Your *nainai* is spreading superstition,' the teacher had said.

Nainai had been like a mother to me. As gentle as the spring wind, she had never raised her voice. Her face was old and wrinkled, but kind, and she was the one who told me to forgive those who bullied me at school: 'Think of it as though you'd been bitten by wild dogs,' she urged. 'Dogs will bite, but it doesn't mean you bite them back. You are human, superior to them.' How could I reconcile her mild, philosophical nature with that of the hot-blooded young woman who claimed to know all about me and my family? Why had she come to me now?

Pregnancy, she had said.

It was too much to take in at once. I gave up with a headache.

At college I was greeted by Taro: 'Mei, my wife wanted to know if you enjoyed the dinner she cooked last weekend.'

'Of course. It was delicious, my first real Japanese meal.' I wasn't being polite, the food *had* been lovely, as had their company.

'She said it was a shame you talked her out of cooking Sichuan-style for you.'

'Oh, it's nice to try something new. I don't really miss it, not that much.' I wished Taro did not always look so earnest. I knew I should invite them back but I had to choose a date when Barbara and Bill were away, so I left it.

Later, sitting in the library, I lifted my head to yawn and saw him walk past, his wife by his side, a petite, well-dressed figure, apparently even younger than him. She had with her a basket of goodies. They made me envious. Ken and I were much less cosy, our relationship so new.

Academically it wasn't a fruitful day, so I left early. In Hampstead, the front door was open and the house seemed empty, but as I went in I heard scuffles and curses in the back garden, as if a fight was in progress. I ran outside. Barbara, her hair tied back with a rubber band, was battling against an overhanging branch with a pair of shears. Littered around her were piles of dark greens and dead browns, from which bright yellow daffodils poked out.

She stopped, breathless. The branch she was clutching bounced back, arching over her head. She sighed. 'I had to do it, otherwise my rose won't be able to breathe.' She straightened up and pointed at the carpet of soiled pink blossoms beneath a slender tree near the half-collapsed wall. 'Isn't it a shame? The blossom's over. I hardly come into the garden these days. Did you see it in flower?'

I stared at the tree and couldn't believe my eyes. 'But that's a Mei tree,' I stuttered, surprised and delighted. 'What's it doing here? I wouldn't have thought it could grow in England.'

'*Prunus.*' She smiled at me. 'That's the Latin name for it, *Prunus mume*. We call it Japanese apricot. I planted it when I came back from China, but it's never blossomed before.'

I looked down at the fallen petals, then up at the branches, some still bearing the pretty little pink blossoms. I thought of a Chinese watercolour painting. Bamboo and Mei are easy to draw because their lines are so distinct; I began to sketch them in my head, like I had as a child, and thought again of Nainai.

I bent down to pick up a blossom and smoothed it in my hands: five petals of happiness. How extraordinary that Barbara should plant this particular tree, the one after which I was named. I brought the petals closer to my face and inhaled. A strange sensation flowed through me: a long-lost fragrance . . . but I had smelt it recently.

Suddenly Barbara exclaimed, 'That's it! That's the fragrance in your bedroom. There, I told you I wasn't dreaming. How odd, though, that I could smell it all the way up there.' I turned to see her sniffing the blossom too.

Maybe that explained it: the fragrance, so strong and once so well known to me, had reminded me of my grandmother, who then appeared in my dream. Suddenly the last few weeks' confusion was explained, and I felt an immense weight lift from my shoulders. Then I heard Barbara speak again: 'It's a miracle it's blossomed, I've never even bothered to water it. I wonder what woke it up. Perhaps it's something to do with the year – which is it?'

'Sheep – and you did right not to water it. Mei hate too much moisture.'

'Goodness me, are you sure? It's my year, which means . . . it's yours, too. You're two cycles younger than me. That's twenty-four years.'

'How do you know that?'

'Yuan Shui told me. He said he was destined to be linked with Sheep women. All the women in his life, you, me, your mother, we're all sheepish women, ha. What was he?'

'Don't you know? You seem to know about everyone else.' I kicked a stone at my feet.

'Now I remember. He was an Ox. I've never met anyone so stubborn.'

That was Baba all right. So stubborn he would rather lose

22

my mother than try to win her back. So stubborn that he would rather be sent to the countryside than apologise. All he had to do was confess, they said, but he claimed he had nothing to confess.

'It didn't get him anywhere, did it?' She was staring at the scattered petals.

He had become a downtrodden gardener in a small public park on land that had belonged to his ancestors. He died a 'Model Worker', though. But I didn't want to discuss the past, had no desire to talk about my father. I changed the subject. 'Barbara, you have to wear a red belt, you know, to ward off evil spirits.'

'Oh, yes. I'd forgotten that too – so we're both especially susceptible to illness and disasters, are we, because it's our year?'

'Don't be pessimistic . . . but this is a critical year for us Sheep. It will either make us or ruin us. How dramatic that sounds!' I said. Her eyes twinkled. 'Wear a red belt, just in case. Anyway,' I laughed, 'you need one for your pyjamas.'

She took off her gloves and rubbed her hands together. 'You're right, but you mustn't forget, either.'

Before I could say any more, she was striding across to the space before the pavilion Bill had built, studying it, measuring it with her feet. 'What's going to happen there?' I asked.

'I'm going to dig a pond – actually, Bill is. He's meant to be here today – which reminds me, when's Ken coming next? He's very welcome to help out.'

'This weekend, I think, but I'm not sure. He said he'd be busy before the Easter holiday.'

'Oh, well, we can't depend on men, can we? They always promise but never deliver. Let's go in and have a coffee. I'm knackered.'

Inside it was darker. For a while the dewy wetness of the garden lingered on us, fresh. She went straight for the kettle. 'I'll just have instant, I suppose,' she murmured, a dark silhouette against the window by the sink. I switched on the light, which banished the atmosphere of the garden.

I felt lost for a moment. I hated the sudden change of light:

outside it was much more gradual. I stared through the window at the darkening sky, the pale wooden pavilion, so new it looked like a toy. Next to it, tiny bamboo bushes waved in the wind. In the miniature of the window this scene reminded me of home, a shed, really, that my father and I had shared in the People's Park, where bamboo sang in the breeze, and there was another pavilion in the distance. Suddenly I was struck by the contrast in size between the house I lived in now and the shed of my memory. In China, confined spaces and constant physical contact meant we were used to being self-contained, to keeping our thoughts and feelings locked away in our heads. In the small home I had shared with my father, I had felt safe thinking of Mama, although he sat but a breath away from me. Somehow I didn't feel so safe here with my thoughts. The high ceilings and large rooms seemed to amplify them, echo them even.

My eyes drifted back to the window. Today was the first time I had looked at the pavilion through it. I understood the effect Barbara probably wanted to achieve, but to me it had failed. The pavilion looked out of place, contrived, the new wood and the stumpy bamboo an awkward attempt to recall China. Perhaps she wanted to re-create the place where she had known my father. But there was nothing to go back to except our memories.

'Here is your tea, without milk.' She put a cup in front of me, her fingers stained with paint and still smelling of earth and leaves. She sat down with a mug of coffee, and stretched back on her chair. 'Do you like the bamboo?' She had followed my gaze.

'They're small.' There were miniature bamboo with fancy names in China, but I had never liked them; the wild variety in the wood near my home had always been luxuriant and overgrown.

'I know,' she sighed. 'They just remind me of the real thing. The green colour, the sound they made when the wind blew. And they were big and solid, planted square like pillars to support a palace.'

I sipped my tea and didn't say anything. She leaned

forward. 'Don't you miss the bamboo, the sound it makes, the feel of its cool leaves on your hands?'

And the stool I sat on, the chopsticks I used, the mat I slept on, the shutters I pulled down to shelter from the strong sunshine – in our home, what hadn't been made of bamboo? 'I don't,' I said shortly. 'But it sounds as if *you* do,' I added, beneath my breath.

The chair I sat on seemed harder than usual. She talked of bamboo and Mei blossom; home had never felt so near – yet so far away.

It was properly dark now but still too early for dinner. She sat with her chin in one hand, silent, gazing out through the window into the darkness. I leafed through a book, unable to take anything in. The tick-tock of the grandfather clock in the corner of the room lulled me, but just as I was on the brink of falling asleep, I remembered the apprehension I had felt when we had first come in from the garden. Her silhouette . . . Why had she suddenly overhauled the neglected garden? Why did I feel there were shadows behind the furniture and whispers behind my back? And what did this all have to do with my mysterious night-time visitor? I was not so sure now that I could simply explain her away as a dream produced by a fragrance.

A gentle thud made me look up. Yawning, Barbara had pushed Oscar off her knees. The cat's tail twitched from left to right as if its owner was trying to decide where to go next. She stooped to stroke him, then turned to me: 'I'll be in my studio for a while.'

I stood up, feeling action was required. I decided to cook: it was a bit early but it was sure to take my mind off things. I deep-fried the hot chillies, watching the shining red change to golden brown, my hands warmed by the wooden handle of the spoon, my face glowing with the heat; the tangy fragrance hurt and soothed like an acupuncture needle. I sneezed and coughed, taking in gulps of chilli smell. When I felt the steam from the rice on my face, I remembered to switch on the fan, but the room was already redolent with spices.

To eat, the dish was less pungent, and for me, a stir-fry

without salt was like taking a bath with clothes on. We ate in silence.

I chewed self-consciously, trying not to make any noise. I thought of things to say but did not know where to begin. I didn't belong here, however much Barbara tried to make me feel at home. The furniture was the wrong shape, the pictures on the walls were full of figures whose expressions I found unfathomable, and the food . . . Mushroom soup aside, I found English food unappetising. Perhaps I *was* homesick.

But where was home? The singles dormitory I had shared with the other girl teachers in Beijing? Or the shed in the small town near Chengdu where my father and I had lived, which no longer existed? After he died the work units had taken it back. The only letter I had from one of his former colleagues had said that the shed had been torn down for safety reasons. When I lived there, it had seemed so solid – I hadn't envied my classmates in their high-rise buildings: we had greenery around us.

At the end of our silent meal the telephone rang. It was Bill. I heard his metallic, leisurely voice, which sounded apologetic. 'He couldn't come. I wish he'd rung earlier,' she said, then put the phone down and headed upstairs without another word.

I collected the plates and noticed what Barbara had left: chewy bits of aubergine, tomato skin and pieces of ginger, my favourites. What a waste. Despite her complaints I never remembered to leave them out and she never learned to love them. I piled the plates by the sink. As I had cooked she would wash up.

Barbara came down with a piece of blood-red silk ribbon. 'Our good-luck belt,' she said, and cut it in half. 'It was Yuan Shui who explained it all to me, the first time I met him, twelve years ago, in your house in the park. Were you thirteen, fourteen?' She stretched out a piece against the light, examined the texture with the look of concentration she usually reserved for her paintings, then thrust it into my hand. 'Something like that. I remember the day well. It was unusually warm for early spring, sunny, a weekday, no tourists, so he had brought out all his pot plants. He'd been itching to do that for a long time.'

My father's potted plants were his treasures. They were usually hidden behind a thick black curtain at the back of the shed near the coal bunker so nobody would spot them. It was so ironic: he was a botanist, living inside a park surrounded by flowers, but his garden had to be portable, so that he could hide it when strangers visited. The problem was that his prize orchids, which had got him into trouble years before, were in the pots. The political atmosphere had relaxed since then, but he could not. He could not bear to be without them, so he had kept them in pots. Usually he would have covered them up before sunset, but that day, when Barbara saw them, he hadn't. Perhaps he had wanted them to get the last of the sun – it was such a bright day.

Barbara put her ribbon on the table, walked to the sink, looked at the plates and turned on the tap. 'And what a display it was. I had got lost in the labyrinth of azaleas, and followed a path that intrigued me. At the end I found your father, his back bent, sweeping. Not your typical Confucian scholar.' She turned off the tap and turned to me, her chest heaving beneath her floral shirt. I wore a jumper and felt chilly: she was hardier than I.

'Baba always swept the path, even though it wasn't part of his job. He couldn't bear untidiness,' I said, and picked up a tea-towel. Cleanliness was important to my father. It was why his favourite flower was the orchid, the cleanest flower with the purest fragrance. It would not tolerate dirty soil, or polluted air, he had told me admiringly.

'He looked guarded when he saw me approach,' she laughed, 'then I introduced myself in Chinese, and he gave me a lovely smile. He told me his name was Yuan Shui, Distant Water, and invited me into his home – so humble, a shed, as you say. I drank hot water from his Thermos, and admired the calligraphy on the wall. He told me he'd written it himself. I thought he lived like a hermit.'

In a sense he *was* a hermit – some days he would not say a word to me. But I remembered the calligraphy well. It was a couplet: *Hai kuo ping yu yue, tian gao ren niao fei.* 'The sea is as wide as a fish can swim, the sky is as high as a bird can fly.' Hardly the words of a man who had turned his back on the world.

Barbara's voice was low now, as if she was talking to herself: 'I was on my second year doing Chinese in nearby Chengdu city, one of the few western students in the country after China had opened up. China disappointed me. All my life I had read about it and dreamed of its palaces, gardens, poetry and scholars with long gowns, and the China I saw was a bit of a let-down.' The clattering of the plates stopped briefly as she looked up at the window.

Scholars with long gowns? I stared at the figure whose back was still turned to me: she looked so middle-aged and ordinary now that it had never occurred to me she might once have had such dreams.

'Instead I found a mass of people, uniformly dressed, who stared, cursed and spat.' She spoke faster now, the words spilling out of her mouth. It wasn't until a few seconds later that the meaning of what she had said sank in and I stopped half-way to the sink with the tea-towel. I threw it into the sink and walked quickly to the other window overlooking the front garden.

After a long pause I heard her voice behind me: 'Sorry, Mei. Did I say something wrong? I just meant masses of people, many people.' She raised her voice and spoke faster, as if she was impatient. 'Anyway, meeting Yuan Shui was a turning-point. I'd never seen so many different orchids. And the things he talked about – his mind, his passion. This was the China I'd come for.'

I turned. How could I not melt at such glowing compliments to my father? We stood at opposite ends of the dining-table, the size of a small boat. She smiled at me. 'I stayed too long for the guide who was accompanying my group. He had gone to alert the local police to hunt for me in the park. When they turned up I had just left Yuan Shui, just in time or there would have been trouble for him.'

I remembered that bit. When the police appeared, my heart had pounded: after all the years of peace and quiet, was he going to be taken away again? But that day he was lucky.

That night, long after the police were gone and the park cleared of tourists, my father did his usual *t'ai chi* practice before he went to bed. There was no heating in the shed, save for a stove, which had been turned down for the night. I huddled inside the quilts and watched him. I had always thought of him as an old man, but that night he looked young. Even then I knew that that had something to do with Barbara.

Our eyes met. The memory had thawed the ice that had come upon us by the sink.

'Extraordinary man, your father.'

It was strange to wear the red belt, stranger still because Barbara was wearing one too. I remembered the way she had cut the ribbon in half, carelessly, as she did most things. Barbara and I, united and disconnected by a red ribbon. Looking at her, I wished I could take them off. Instead of protecting us, I felt somehow that they singled us out, made us vulnerable.

I was tired, and it was not yet nine o'clock. On my way upstairs, I stopped half way. On his previous visit Ken had had a tour of the house and had told me that buildings of this period in this part of London all had this box-shaped space at the turn of the stairs and the window there framed the garden so well. I could see all the plants clearly, prominent among them the revived Mei tree. Now that it was dark, the trees' outlines were more distinct than those of the plants on the ground. There were bigger trees in the garden – an old apple tree stood diagonally at the far end in the corner, assured, solid. But it was the fragility of the Mei that struck me. It looked shabbier than it did in China, where it would have been covered with snow at this time of year. It hardly ever snowed in London, apparently, and that was fine with me.

I continued upstairs, my footsteps dragging. So tired. I lay down and closed my eyes. As the noise of traffic died away, I thought I could make out the voice I'd been craving all day, a voice that was old, slow and magnetic, which drew all the children from the yard to beg: 'Tell us another story, Nainai.'

'Which one shall I tell today? Now, let's see . . . a short one or a long one?' said the voice, kindly. Time seemed to stand still as she spoke.

'A long one,' I murmured.

'The mirror story, then,' said the voice, whose caress alone would soothe my childhood troubles.

'Once upon a time in the Qing dynasty – the last imperial dynasty in China – there lived an old craftsman and his daughter in the garden city of Suzhou in the south. The old man made the most beautiful wood-carvings for an aristocratic family, who allowed them to live in their much admired garden. Over the years the garden became famous for two things: its exquisite carvings and its prized green-calyx Mei trees. The rich man guarded his treasures jealously and would not allow anyone near his blossoms or his talented craftsman, for fear they would steal them.

'The old man's wife had died in childbirth, so he had raised their daughter as a boy and taught her all his skills. In no time at all, she was almost as good as he was. He loved the Mei blossom passionately and he called his daughter Mei after it. From a young age, she was told how special the beauty of Mei was, that it was a flower of five petals, each of which represented a kind of happiness: joy, luck, smoothness, peace and prosperity. True happiness could only be attained when all five were fulfilled.

'One day, the garden that was closed for ever to the outside world had a surprise visitor. The emperor of China had come down from his capital in the north to collect the rare southern blossoms for his summer palace on the outskirts of Beijing. When he saw the beautiful wooden carvings on the rich man's doors and windows he fell in love with them and demanded that the craftsman be brought to him. The old man and his daughter knelt before the emperor, trembling, for they were just ordinary folk and revered him as if he were a god. Besides, the daughter was dressed as a man, and, in those days, that was a serious offence.

'But all the emperor said was how delighted he was with

30

their carving and how he would like them to come back to the north with him to work on his summer palace.

'An emperor's request was not to be refused, so the old man and his daughter packed their things, said goodbye to their old master and travelled the grand canal to the north. The emperor's convoy was huge, and the old man and his daughter enjoyed the journey, which took them to parts of China they had never dreamed of visiting. But the new food and the harsh northern climate affected the old man's health so badly that he died of pneumonia just before they arrived in Beijing. Before he died he left the girl their family treasure, which he'd carried with him since leaving his home town of Sichuan as a young man: a round bronze mirror decorated with Mei blossoms and a dancing dragon. He told his daughter that she should look after it and defend it as if it was her own life. "It is a magic mirror that will bring you good fortune," he said.

'All the new scenery lost its appeal as the girl wept for her father and grew homesick for the south. She became thin and sad and refused to eat.

'When the emperor heard of this, he took pity on her and, believing her to be a man, promised to find a suitable young woman to console her. She dared not tell him that she was a woman, for fear she would be punished. Now that her father was dead, no one else knew her secret.

'Days turned into weeks but finally they arrived in Beijing. She was taken straight to the emperor's summer palace, where she wondered at the heavenly sight of the most beautiful garden she'd ever seen, hundreds of times bigger than her father's, and much more sophisticated. The emperor had not forgotten his promise. The girl he had chosen was the daughter of his favourite gardener, a Manchu. It was a rare honour indeed as, at this time – at the end of the Qing dynasty, the last days of feudal China – the Manchus were the royal race.

'There was no one to advise the girl what to do. On the wedding day, after all the guests had gone, the bride, Yulan, a beautiful girl with rosy cheeks and big feet – Manchu women did not bind their feet – strode over to her groom with a bowl to wash him. She discovered his ears were pierced, and Mei could not hide any longer. She fell down at Yulan's feet, confessed to her and asked for her forgiveness.

'At first Yulan was furious and threatened to tell the emperor, but Mei's tears softened her. She relented and eventually promised to help. But what were they to do? Neither woman slept that night. When dawn broke, Mei brought out her bronze mirror so that she could do her hair, and Yulan let out a cry: "Thank heaven! Now we are saved." She explained that she had a twin brother, who, when he was small, was told by a Buddhist monk that he would marry a woman who carried a bronze mirror. "And here you are." Yulan smiled. "You must marry my twin brother – he looks just like me. If we dressed the same even our parents could not tell us apart."

'When the twin brother and Mei met, they couldn't take their eyes off each other – it was as if they had known each other all their lives. They thanked heaven for their strange yet happy union, and attributed their good fortune to the magic of the bronze mirror.

'One late spring day, when Wubao, the young man, learned that the emperor had gone hunting further north, he took Mei to visit some other parts of the gigantic garden. He told her it was called the Garden of Divinity and Brightness, the Yuan Ming Yuan. Every year after the Spring Festival the emperor came to live there with his royal concubines and stayed until the First Day of Winter, when they went back to the Forbidden City.

'It was the biggest garden you could ever imagine, filled with lakes, palaces, exotic animals and plants from all over the empire. The wooden buildings were adorned with majestic creatures, elegant bridges led on to winding paths, which opened up to fountains and waterfalls. Pine trees stood upright on hills, bamboo sang in the wind, willows bent to the water and the fragrance of lotus blossoms rose from the lakes. The garden was surrounded by long walls, guarded by armed eunuchs – eunuchs and gardeners were the only men the emperor allowed to enter. He did not want anyone else to look upon his beautiful concubines.

'Soon Mei's feet hurt from so much walking. It was not possible to visit everything – it was said even the emperor had not seen all of the sights. But how happy she was to be working in such a heavenly place with the man she loved.

'They returned to their part of the garden, on the north-eastern edge, where they saw a cluster of giant stone buildings whose style bewildered Mei. She was told they were western, built with the help of big-nose foreigners – the French Jesuits who spoke Chinese. They were strange-looking, taller than Chinese buildings, and no one apart from the emperor had ever been inside. It was said there was even a mosque amid the complex built for the emperor's favourite *uigur* concubine, who sat and prayed to her god, different from ours.

'During the day, Mei and her husband worked alongside each other, she on the wooden doors and ceilings. She carved animals, fantastic dragons and curled grasses, dancing phoenix and haughty cranes. She carved insects: dragonflies, crickets, bees and long-horned grasshoppers. She carved flowers: peony, lotus, passion-flower, peach blossom. Above all, she carved Mei blossoms, her favourite.

'He planted the real flowers. In front of their little wooden house he planted all her favourites, flowers of the south that cured her homesickness with their delicate fragrances: sweet-scented osmanthus, gardenia, jasmine. He planted her favourite variety of Mei tree. In deep winter when it snowed the almost transparent pale green of the blossom appeared as if heaven sent.

'All who came to their little garden were jealous, all who saw her carvings were rapturous. They were a perfect pair indeed, creating a garden inside a garden, beauty within beauty. How could they not be fulfilled?

'In the evenings they sat opposite each other and played chess in the candlelight. Sometimes the wind carried to them the giggling of the concubines in the nearby Yellow Flower Maze, so-called because concubines with yellow silk lotus blossoms on their heads fought to find their way out. It was a romantic spectacle for the emperor, who sipped his tea in the pavilion above and smiled.

'On festive nights the pleasures intensified. The heady scents of food and incense, the chanting of the monks, their clattering bells, the golden dragons and dancing phoenix firework displays that lit up the sky made the lucky couple feel transported to another, more magical world.

'Soon they had a baby, and Yulan moved in to help look after her. When the little girl was five, rumours of foreign invasions reached them: blond-haired English and French whose guns overpowered our soldiers, armed only with knives and arrows. Wubao trained with all the other gardeners and eunuchs to defend the garden and the women stayed at home and prayed at the little temple of Guanyin, the goddess of Mercy.

'One autumn day they saw black smoke in the distance, heading their way. The wind carried the scent of burnt wood, the cries of people and animals. Wubao armed himself, patted his little girl, waved goodbye to the women and joined the eunuchs to fight off the invaders. They were outnumbered by the foreign devils, but in Wubao's heart he was defending not just the emperor's pleasure ground but his home, the paradise he had built with his beloved.

'The women prayed all day at the temple, but bad news began to arrive. They learned that the emperor had escaped to the north and, in shame, the chief minister in charge of the garden had drowned himself in the Happiness Sea, the biggest lake in the garden. They continued their prayers, but soon they heard gunfire, and the news they'd been dreading came in: Wubao and all the eunuchs defending the garden gates had been killed.

'The Summer Palace was wrapped in choking smoke. Most of the buildings in the gardens were made of wood and burned easily. With tears in her eyes, clutching her little girl, Mei watched her flowers wither and her carvings turn to ash. She wanted to avenge her husband's death, but Yulan said, "Your little girl needs you, now."

'The three joined the exodus thronging away from the

smoke and fire, which chased them like a ferocious dragon ridden by the foreigners with deafening guns. Yulan ran faster, slung the little girl on to her shoulders and had soon left Mei behind.

'Mei's feet hurt: she had never had to run so fast or for so long. She stopped beneath a Mei tree to catch her breath.

'When she looked up again a foreign devil wearing a red uniform stood in front of her. She sprang to her feet but it was too late. He snatched from her the parcel she was carrying and Mei's belongings fell out. A shining object caught his eyes. The bronze mirror. He grabbed it.

'Enraged, Mei flew at him. She was small and frail, but anger and grief gave her strength and she used her teeth as a weapon, sank them deep into the foreign devil's flesh. He let out a cry. Furious, he raised his other hand, the one with the gun, and pointed it at her. He fired, and she collapsed on to the ground, bleeding from her chest.

'The devil took the mirror and rode away. As she lay dying, Mei turned to her daughter and Yulan, who had come back to look for her. "Don't weep," she said. "I'm going to join Wubao. Look after my little girl, and tell her to avenge us." Looking up she cursed aloud: "Heaven above be my witness, I wish misfortune on the devil who took my mirror, stained with my blood. I wish misfortune on all into whose hands it falls, until it is returned to our family."

'That little girl was my grandmother, your great-great-grandmother, and the year her parents died was 1860.'

Tie Mei

R eputation! What did I care for *that*? Was I trying to shackle her as I, too, had been shackled? Had I not done enough damage with all those stories I'd told her about the value of obedience, the virtue of submission? What use had any of it been to me?

I had been afraid – how curious that I should fear this when even hell's fire could not prevent me from coming to her – that we might not be as close as we had once been. I was unsure of myself: a mere fragrance, a ghost from her past. Could this new life mean more to her than our old bond? She lived in a foreign woman's house, was pregnant with a foreigner's child: had she forgotten the mirror story?

Poor girl. How pale she was, unhappy and deceived. Motherless, like me, she needed guidance as much as I had. Was she five or six when her mother, Orchid, left her? I remembered her then, a willowy child, whose resemblance to her mother made her father weep. Oh, the two of them were good at pretending, Jiaojiao behaving as though she never mourned her mother, even though her pain was written all over her face. She was a gourd, with a smooth exterior and a deep hollow within, where many things were hidden. But even a gourd could take only so much: after a while there would be a burst of tears and she would rest her little head on my lap, let me stroke her hair and tell her stories.

My Jiaojiao, I will rescue you again. You are all I have. Come back to my garden with me. We'll never be parted again.

3: *Chun Fen* – Spring Equinox

21 March

Jiao Mei

At Boots I picked up a packet of Tampax with the pregnancy testing kit, just in case – and to confuse the checkout girl. I felt like a magnet to the scents in the shop, drawing them to me. My nose sniffed out their artificiality in them and my stomach twisted. One caused acid to spurt into my mouth. It brought with it the memory of my father's hospital bed, the scent they used to cover his smell. I waved my hands about my face, longing to get out of the thick atmosphere of chemicals.

'Mmm.' The checkout girl shook her head as she scanned my purchases.

'For a friend.' I pulled my hair down to hide my face – I hadn't washed it that morning.

Outside I took a deep breath. These days, my body didn't seem to belong to me but to someone with an extraordinary sensitivity to scents. The air smelt of rain, wind and the dust from the traffic. I gulped it down eagerly. The black smoke from car exhausts satisfied me especially. Plain bad chemicals, but there was something honest about them that my body accepted.

The fresh air made me even hungrier – that was the other thing, my insatiable appetite. I had noticed lately the speed with which hunger gathered, what a short temper it had. The moment food crossed my mind, I was ravenous, the desire to eat stronger than thirst, as primitive as living. And it was always a particular food I craved. What did I want now? Not fish – definitely not that. The fishmonger's was set back from the high street, hidden behind a fruit shop. I did want something savoury though, something I could swallow quickly – the urge was unbearable. I settled for crisps. I clutched the packet, and breathed in the sharp smell. Deep inside me, the hunger beast opened its mouth and eagerly swallowed the lot. I licked my salty fingers.

There had been an old, faint painting of the 'Greedy Beast' on a wall in the courtyard that had belonged to my grand-parents; since the revolution it had been a pigsty. Blue-white curls of cloud surrounded a beast with a fish's body and a lion's head. Its mouth was wide open. The painting was meant to represent greed, the beast in all of us that had to be suppressed. The Red Guards had tried to deface it with knives, and had daubed a red, tightly clenched fist over it, but the picture was still traceable. It was an attractive animal, with its giant horns and green and white curves. I fell in love with it, rather than despising it.

The beast in me was too real to be attractive; it alarmed me. I had to obey it, and now it said, 'To bed, to sleep.' I felt so tired: a weight had anchored itself inside me.

Out of habit, I paused beneath the terracotta-brick building at the corner on the crossroads. It was a regular rendezvous spot for Ken and me. I looked up: 3.45 p.m. 'Fanciful mock-Venetian.' Ken's voice echoed in my ears. I had to hurry. Ken was coming round: I should cook him something nice to eat.

The house echoed my every move. Strange scents sprang at me from different angles. The oak table in the middle of the room gave off a murky, warm aroma; nearer to the cooker a strong odour of grease hit me, as if years of cooking had concentrated into a large ball. The dead flower in the vase on the oval telephone table gave off a sweet, stale but comforting odour. The dust from the brown carpets leading upstairs made me cough. My whole sensory world had changed. I remembered briefly the story of the boy who acquired a pair of ears that enabled him to understand the language of the animals. I had been given the nose of a dog, and the stomach of a pig.

Pig. I laughed, and the sound echoed in the little box space looking out over the back garden. Dandelions already. Barbara would say how pretty they were, but Bill would be furious. There was never a single dandelion in his front garden and he was on red alert when any appeared in Barbara's. They would spread, he said, as if dandelions were chicken-pox. I smiled secretly at the prospect of his distress. When it came to their garden war, I was all for Barbara.

I paused at her bedroom door. There was a faint smell of cigarettes. Bill never smoked indoors, but the smell lingered wherever he had been. Usually I liked it, but today it was revolting, metal against metal. The clash pierced my stomach.

I covered my nose, entered, opened the window and gulped fresh air. I turned to Barbara's bare dressing-table. A circular metal object the size of a small plate lay beside her small mirror. I picked it up. There was a thick ridge round the outside edge. I rubbed the uneven surface but couldn't figure out what the pattern was. It must have been a picture once, but now it looked as if it had been buried for a century or more. Dark green patches dotted the surface like the shadows of trees in a deep lake. I could not guess at its function. I turned it over to look at the other side, but its metallic smell forced me to put it down.

Oscar lay curled on her pyjamas – so this was where he went nowadays. His favourite daytime sleeping place had been the sunny patch in my bedroom where he could lie undisturbed, but he had not been there for quite a while. He rolled over, and the red silk belt was revealed. So she wasn't wearing it. I bundled up Barbara's pyjamas, put them on a chair and headed for the door, then changed my mind. I listened for a sound, but the house was as quiet as its scents were loud.

I lifted the bedcover and saw a strand of brown hair, startling and lonely. I imagined her lying there, alone too. On impulse, I crawled into the bed and waited to get warm. Oscar purred louder.

From Barbara's bed, I watched the tree waving outside. The first time I had met her I had been thirteen. It was late March, a month or so into the school term, and I'd walked through the park in the soft spring wind. I'd been happy that day, looking forward to cooking for my father, which I had wanted to do for a long time. I had resolved to make more of an effort to look after him. Nearer to the house I smelt food – not the usual boiled cabbage and potatoes he cooked for dinner: although he was Sichuanese, his cooking was stubbornly northern and he liked to boil things rather than stir-fry. I puzzled over the smell: it wasn't Sichuanese either. It wasn't spicy, or thick and heavy, but fresh, like the fragrance of the lotus blossom. Then I heard laughter. Through the open window I saw a tall foreign woman with pale skin and brown hair sitting on my bed, with its pink and blue peony-patterned cover. My father was standing next to her, showing her something. I'd never seen his back so straight or his face so soft and smiling. My heart pounded: it was the woman the police had been after, the woman who made him seem young.

'Baba,' I called, deliberately lingering at the door.

She jumped off my bed. 'Hello,' she said – she saw me before he did. I ignored her, hesitated, then charged in. Curious, uncertain, I stared at my father. I was almost as tall as him – I took after my mother, who was a tall northerner. He seemed at a loss: we hardly ever had visitors, let alone foreign, female ones who sat on my bed as if they had known us for years.

Finally he seemed to gather himself and, avoiding my eyes, turned to the foreign woman. 'My daughter Jiao Mei.'

She strode over: 'Jiao Mei – Proud Mei?' Baba nodded. 'What a wonderful name! I am Barbara,' she said, in passable Chinese. She was simply dressed in a red shirt and a loose pair of grey trousers. Her lips touched both of my cheeks. The kiss had been a surprise: it was such an unexpected gesture of greeting. Others had held my hands, rubbed them as they talked to me, sometimes affectionate, but always casual. Her touches felt intimate. My father never kissed me – at least, not since I'd reached adolescence.

I didn't say much: any woman close to my father was my sworn enemy. I knew they wanted to replace my mother, and snatch him away from me. I spent the rest of the evening doing my best to create an awkward atmosphere, pestering him with maths problems that I could easily have solved by myself. To her queries and helpful suggestions I responded in monosyllables.

When evening came and she still did not show any sign of leaving, I became even more hostile. 'You must be hungry,' she said, when I had finished my homework.

'No,' I replied immediately.

'Come and have some of the food Barbara has made for us.' My father pointed at the pot on the stove. I approached slowly, feigning lack of interest, though inwardly curious about what this foreigner would cook. I knew from the smell that it was lotus root, but when I lifted the lid I frowned. A big lump of peeled root, not even cut up, lay floppily submerged in water, with a dash of cooking oil floating on the surface. I dipped in a finger and tasted the water.

'I've prepared a sauce,' she said enthusiastically. I decided there and then that I wasn't hungry. That was not how food should smell and look, as far as I was concerned. I turned back to her, feeling triumphant: if she was a bad cook, that was one up to me in our battle for my father.

I gathered later on that she had come to see him often since that first day when the police had been, always during the day when I was at school. After we had met she came almost every day. Whenever we met, she always kissed me.

That was when I began to store smells. And around that time my periods started. A summer of smells, of blood, intimacy, confusion, dreams. Hiding my sanitary pads from my father.

One day when he wasn't at home I searched his big square cabinet, which was usually locked. Curiosity got the better of shame. My father had always been a mystery and, as an adolescent, I was desperate to discover his secrets. Here was my chance. I dug my fingers deeper, and each time a layer of shirts was revealed, the strong smell of camphor balls wafted up to me. To know him, I would have to dig deeper, through the layers of shirts and underwear. At the bottom of the cabinet I found the camphor balls in a sealed plastic bag, one crushed inside, like white pills, and underneath a bulging brown envelope.

I seized it, untied the white cotton thread that bound it and pulled out a yellowed, musty-smelling thin booklet: *Manual for the Newly Married*. There was also a packet of condoms. It had been opened.

I didn't know then what they were. I looked at them suspiciously, surgical-looking balloons, and realised vaguely that they were something private. I read the manual and, trembling, felt the condoms through their packet with disgust. Then, startled by the sound of the wind, I put everything back, replacing the layers of carefully folded shirts, until finally I had buried the smell of camphor too.

Buried, but not forgotten. Every so often I remembered the smell – the first time I made love with Jieming, when I saw my father and Barbara together, their bodies touching gently. I hadn't thought of it for a long time since, though, and was surprised by how vividly it had all come back to me: the picture of a young girl discovering her father's sexuality, associated for ever with the smell of camphor.

Hunger drove me off Barbara's bed and down the stairs to the kitchen. The plastic Boots shopping-bag lay on the table. I picked it up, then put it down again – there would be time, plenty of time.

When the first whiff of hot vapour rose from the frying-pan I had to switch off the cooker and open the windows. There would be no stir-fry. Sorry, Ken.

Every avenue to the outside world was open, the door and all the windows; the house, cooled by the wind, floated in the night. I sat in the darkness for a long time. The moment I heard footsteps, I switched on the light. In the few seconds before they reached the door I closed my eyes and listened to the familiar, reassuring sound: solid, unhurried. It was Ken.

With his arrival the air around me seemed to move faster. Time started like a machine newly oiled. Now I would have to face him without the cover of darkness. I took the flowers from him. He had brought tulips, not my favourite: a flower without scent is a fake, a song without a tune. I sighed secretly: he doesn't know me yet. But I welcomed the cold touch of his hands, the crisp wrapping paper that smelt of its print and the fresh air. We kissed.

'So, we're all by ourselves tonight.'

'Looks like it. She won't be back until next week.'

He looked at me. 'Why do you look so thin? My God, you're ill.'

'I'm not. I just feel a bit sick.'

'Is it something you've eaten?'

'Maybe. Are you hungry?'

'I'm starving. Where's my Chinese banquet?'

'I'm afraid it's . . . not very exciting.'

'Your food is always exciting.'

When I put the plates on the table he fell silent. 'Well, I warned you, didn't I? No stir-fries today,' I said.

'Mei, is today a special day?'

'What do you mean?'

'I don't know. Is it a Chinese festival, a kind of fasting day?'

Boiled cabbage, boiled carrots, boiled potatoes, cold ham and some warm rice from last night. This was almost like Barbara's food: the plain English food I used to scorn.

'Something's wrong. What is it?'

I stood up slowly to fetch the test stick, which I had left by the cooker. The air was close. 'It's positive,' I said calmly.

'Positive?'

'Yes. I'm pregnant.'

Silence. I was surprised. I had almost wanted him to exclaim, 'But you can't be!' so that I could tell him I didn't believe it either. But as the moments passed I wasn't sure I could say the things I'd planned.

Finally he spoke: 'How long?'

'Only a month, I think.'

The conversation was making me feel sick. I put some cold cabbage on top of my warm bowl of rice. Ken stared at me.

'Would you like some cabbage?' I was still the hostess, however reluctant my guest.

'No.'

I started eating, couldn't wait.

He continued to stare at me. 'Mei, are you all right? This doesn't make sense. This isn't like you.'

'Of course it all makes sense. I'm going to have a baby.'

He stood up, went to the window and tried to close it.

'Don't, please, I need fresh air.'

'But I'm freezing.'

'I need the fresh air, otherwise I feel sick.' There was no way I'd allow the window to be shut until the room was cleared of the nauseating smell.

He stayed at the window and was silent. I decided to go upstairs to light a fire – the heating was on, but the house was never really warm. 'You can shut the windows when I've gone,' I called to him. He didn't answer.

I lay down on the rug in front of the fire. The smell of burning wood was reassuring. The room was dark, except for the flickering flames. I pulled a blanket around me and dozed, my back to the fire. I'd stayed at Ken's overnight but this was our first night together here. Somehow this felt more serious. I was still uneasy about sleeping with him. Although none of my family was here to check on me, something nagged deep inside.

'But think of your reputation,' my grandmother's ghost had admonished me. 'Remember who you are! We Chinese don't sleep with men before we are married. Look at you, pregnant with this foreigner's child.' The young woman was so much fiercer, so much more critical, than the grandmother I remembered.

I turned on to my side. Did she have a point? Did that meddlesome Chinese girl at my college have a point? Why did I have to conform to Ken's culture and sleep with him? Why couldn't he conform to mine? But Nainai had only met her husband once before she was married. I knew I could not live like that, and when Jieming and I had begun to sleep together, *I* had told *him* not to worry about what people might say.

A cold hand – Ken's were always cold – and the hot steam from a cup of Earl Grey woke me. I rubbed my eyes. 'What time is it?'

'Nearly midnight.'

'What have you been doing downstairs all this time?'

'I made some food, ate it, and thought about things. And I shut the windows and washed up.'

'Thank you.'

'Nice of you to say that for once.'

'You're always nagging me about that.'

'Well, it doesn't hurt to be polite.'

This was absurd: we were arguing about etiquette when I'd just told him I was pregnant. 'We don't say thank you to people we are close to. The fewer thank-yous you get, the closer you are. My parents never said thank you to each other, except when they were being ironic.'

Ken gave me an odd smile. 'So, does that mean we're close?'

Yes. But close enough to have a baby together? I sat up and sipped my tea. The wind blew outside; next to me the fire crackled.

'Such a big house. Does Barbara live here by herself?' he asked, making conversation.

'Mostly. Sometimes Bill comes to stay the night.'

'Is she . . . easy to live with?'

'That's an odd question.'

'Well, do you get on with her?'

'Of course. I've known her for years, although she's different here in England from how she was in China.'

Ken looked puzzled. 'Different?'

'I don't know . . . It's as if there are two Barbaras. There she was trying to act Chinese, but here she seems as English as can be.'

'It's generous of her to let you stay, though.'

'Oh, I'm grateful to her, of course I am, and for getting me to England.'

'Do you thank her?'

'Sometimes, but perhaps you're right. Maybe I ought to thank her more.' I met his eyes for the first time. It was as hard for me to thank Barbara as it was to talk of love with Ken – especially in a language that was not my own.

The wind was getting stronger and I shivered. Ken wrapped the blanket round my shoulders. I started to speak, but he put his hands on my waist and whispered, 'Don't say thank you to me again.'

I leaned forward and we kissed.

I was still in Ken's arms when the fragrance woke me. I debated whether or not to open my eyes: to open them was to acknowledge the existence of a world I did not care for, to be taken away from the warmth of the man whose breath mingled with mine, but the fragrance drew me, powerful beyond reason, appealing to the sense that was most alive in me. To resist it was to resist living; to resist it was to resist being myself. My eyes opened.

And there she stood, the familiar shape in a long robe. I untangled myself from Ken's embrace and followed her to my bedroom upstairs. She stopped by the window, and turned to me. Moonlight shone through her body and my heart was stirred. How rare an opportunity to see your grandmother in her youth! How could I doubt my senses when they saw, smelt and felt her so truthfully? 'Nainai,' I whispered, as tears ran down my face.

Tie Mei

At last she called me 'Nainai'. And what a welcome sound it was. Now I was truly back in the world.

Jiaojiao in the flesh. I saw her clearly this time. How tall and upright she held herself. Square broad shoulders and big bones, her hair cut short like a boy's, showing off her round ears like a pair of coins. Her smile lit her face and tears flowed down her cheeks. She was the pear blossom with a pearl of spring rain, the sight of which had refreshed and delighted me in my beloved garden. She opened her arms to me. Uncertain of the gesture, I stepped aside, and caught a whiff of something alien – the smell of the foreign man with her.

'You came at last. I was worried you might not.' She followed me. For a moment, her height startled me. Her arms still extended, she whispered: 'Is this . . . really you?'

Was this really her? Could I be sure she wasn't another of the images I conjured to comfort myself? I cannot touch her, embrace her. 'Yes, it is I,' I said, hearing the hollowness in my voice. It took so much courage from both of us to witness, to sustain this; we were so close, yet so distant, like flowers in a mirror, the moon in water. I felt part of me return to life, a part of me I had tried to suppress, the soft part whose only outlet in all those years had been my garden. Here she was before me: my little girl, my flesh and blood.

She knelt on her mattress, her size no longer intimidating. My eyes were drawn to the photographs on the wall behind her. 'You,' she said, touching a picture in which I wore a traditional buttoned blue jacket, all wrinkles and smiles, with her sitting on my lap. Now that image of me was more substantial than I was.

'Look at you,' I said. 'Big girl now.'

Something in what I said seemed to break the spell. Suddenly she was matter-of-fact and familiar. 'I feel so sick.'

'So?' But I liked her weakness: I wanted to encourage her to confide in me. 'I need to think, Nainai. You see, I've only just told Ken . . . my boyfriend. We haven't had time to think things through yet.'

We? What was all this about? *We* had always been she and I. Since her mother left I had been a mother to her. And now she knew the truth, shouldn't she listen to me as she always had in the old days, then do something about it?

'My child, you need to think quickly. Otherwise it will be messy.'

'I know.' She nodded.

I was dismayed. She wasn't asking me to make the decision for her but addressing me as an equal, a friend. She was no longer the small girl who had cried on my lap: she was a grown-up woman with her own secret.

Silence. The wind whistled and she shivered; her shadow moved under the moonlight as if with an identity of its own. Suddenly there was such a distance between us. There were so many things about her that I didn't recognise – the way she tapped her fingers unconsciously on the floor, so careless and foreign. I thought of a story I told her. It was about a man from Handan, who thought the way people walked in another city was more beautiful than it was in his own so he tried to copy it. He failed and in the end he had to give up. But he had forgotten how he had originally walked and had to crawl home. We used to laugh about the man together, but now I can't share that memory with her: she'd be insulted.

'The wind,' I started.

'I don't want to talk about the weather,' she muttered, and stood up to push open the window. She leaned out and ran her hands through her hair, as if to bathe her head in the fresh air, then turned to me: 'I smell you, but I can't touch you. I see you, but I can't explain to others what I've seen. What's happening to me?'

I stood behind her and glimpsed cars, smoke, drunkards, the heaving mass of the city from whose clasp I had sought sanctuary in her strange, bare room. In the distance, above the tree-tops, the sky was turning pink with the promise of dawn. It was the signal for my retreat. 'Morning so soon?' I whispered.

She laughed. 'That's London, it's never dark.' Then she faced me. 'But before you go, you must tell me why you are here.'

'Don't you know? You called me, in your dream.'

Her eyes were very wide. 'And where did you come from?'

'My garden.' My beloved garden, the cool freshness of the

little stream . . . I smelt it then. I never seemed to leave it – the scents stayed with me wherever I went.

'A garden? Where?'

'In my youth, in Sichuan.' It was springtime, always spring-time. Peach blossom, pear blossom, apple blossom, the feel of the soft moist wind . . . Why had I ever left it?

She looked confused. 'You used to tell me . . .' She closed her eyes. 'Do you remember what you used to tell me? The Platform of Farewell where you watch the living for the last time? Then the bridge over the River of Helplessness, the devils who drag you to the Hell Court guarded by the twin devils, Cow Head and Horse Face. Then the Mirror of Reality, which shows your good and bad deeds. And, of course, the Soup of Confusing the Souls. Did you not drink it?'

I was shocked to hear my own story on her lips. Had I *really* told her all that?

'Tell me, tell me.' Her voice was impatient.

For once I was tongue-tied. The screech of a car gave way to drunken shouting, then silence. Everything was still, hold-ing its breath. I didn't know where to begin.

One thing I *could* tell her: 'I didn't drink the soup,' I said. 'I refused it because I didn't want to forget.'

'But how? And what didn't you want to forget?' she whispered.

I had told her too many stories and too few truths. How was I to explain? 'It's as unfair a world over there as it is here,' I said, picturing the sneering Lord of Death. 'My mother had always told me there was justice in death. She believed it, I know. But even Mother, the purest, kindest woman . . .' I couldn't finish my sentence, remembering how she might still suffer. 'Your ancestors who died defending our country, was there any reward for them? No. And my parents-in-law, the cruel couple, were not punished.'

Her eyes were glued on me; she hung on my every word. Poor child. I could imagine what was going through her mind. She had always been a greedy listener, and now she had to know the whole story. 'I will tell you everything,' I said softly. 'It's time you knew.' But where should I begin? So many different threads were knotted together in my mind.

Suddenly it came to me. 'Do you remember the Monkey King? That's who I'm like now, in my world. I was a rebel.'

'The Monkey King!' Her eyes lit up. He had been one of her favourites, the monkey who, not content with mortal life, went in search of immortality and created havoc in heaven. Then, he conquered the underworld. The Lord of Death trembled at the mention of his name.

The flicker of brightness vanished and her face was grave again. 'But, Nainai, if you didn't drink the soup, what happened?'

I was unable to meet her gaze, but my silence confirmed what she suspected. The look on her face, though, convinced me that my suffering had not been in vain. 'Nainai, poor, brave Nainai,' she murmured.

Hell fire, my rite of passage. It had cleansed me of filial piety and chastity, had turned to ashes that weakness. I rose from it with a hardened heart.

'Do you remember what happened to the Monkey King when they caught him and sent him to the flaming furnace to be punished? Instead of burning to ashes he gained an invincible body and a pair of eyes that could withstand even heavenly fire. Instead of destroying him they made him stronger – and that,' I laughed, 'is what happened to me.'

In death I had become the woman I should have been in life. Souls gathered around me: I was respected, admired, even feared. I became a leader. I started to plot my revenge.

This felt so right – this was what I had come for. So good to have her back, so good to be together again.

Then a murmur interrupted us, the sleepy voice of the young devil calling her name from downstairs.

Never had I seen a face change so quickly. All trace of concern for me vanished like a wind. There was first a look of surprise, then softness as his voice became clearer, then such happiness that I felt empty and defeated. I'd thought I had her.

I saw the pinkness of the sky spreading fast. Now it really was time for me to return to my world, just as she had been called back to hers.

As his heavy footsteps approached the door, I fled.

4: *Qing Ming* – Clear and Bright

5 April

Jiao Mei

Every Qing Ming day after I was six Nainai told me the mirror story. She told me other stories at other times but only the mirror story on Qing Ming, the Day of the Dead, when we honour our ancestors. It was her way of remembering, I think, but I didn't appreciate that then. It wasn't my favourite story either: it was heavy, and boring at times, unlike her other ghost stories, which were magical and sometimes funny. She usually had some sewing or mending in her hands and her voice would be soft. There was never any mention of revenge, and I often interrupted her with irritating questions: 'Why should women bind their feet? Who is a concubine? What is a curse?'

Once, Nainai had shown me her bound feet. She had been reluctant, and flashed them at me after my constant pestering. It had been shocking, though: the feet I saw did not resemble flesh, they were like the dead branches of a tree, lifeless.

The night of the Qing Ming we would burn papers, secretly, as we shared the yard with three other families. Nainai said there used to be symbolic money you could buy in shops to send to the other world, but this had been outlawed so we made do with homemade notes. Nainai's were covered with words she wrote and pictures she drew: mirrors, flowers, fish, words such as 'peace' and 'prosperity'. She wrote like a pupil, diligently, carefully. She said, red-faced, that it was because she had only learned to read and write as a grown-up. 'Make sure you become a scholar while you are still young,' she said. 'That way you will never be bullied.'

After the burning Nainai would pretend that we'd baked some potatoes to explain away the smoke, and brought some out to share with the other families. Curiously enough they all seemed to be baking potatoes in their fires too.

I thought of this as I sat on the tube on my way to Chinatown. Qing Ming, Clear and Bright. Today's weather was neither. A gale was blowing and the whole of Chinatown shook like a flimsy film set. Chinatown reminded me of scenes from old movies I had seen as a child. In them dark red lanterns illuminated figures whose pale, remote faces indicated they had been drugged with the poison of feudalism. We were meant to contrast them with ourselves in the present, bright and cheerful, with the rosy-cheeked, positive images from the propaganda posters, books and films. These thin-faced Cantonese lived in the old society and longed for us to liberate them, we were told.

Ken always suggested a trip to Chinatown when he reckoned I was homesick, but each time I came here, I felt more alienated than I had before, for here were people who looked like me but spoke a language I didn't understand – Mandarin and Cantonese couldn't be more different. And, try as I might, I couldn't shake off the impression I'd gained from those films.

But now I was choosing to walk into that old movie – into the shop, the only shop in London probably, where I could buy paper money to burn for the dead. Today I was remembering my father and Nainai. My thoughts turned again, as they had over the previous weeks, to what Nainai had told me happened to her after she died. How could Nainai have been to hell? She who was gentle and cultured, who wouldn't even step on an ant when she was alive.

A smell distracted me. I stood outside a window and watched a big pot of meat boiling – duck? I remembered it well. I pictured my father, nodding humbly to a man in another room while I was stealing a piece from a boiling pot, burning my hand and mouth. I hadn't had meat for a month.

When we got home my father smelt it, even though I had washed my mouth – he'd never eaten meat. Stony-faced, he ordered me to go back to the man and apologise. I refused, so he starved me for a day, and gave me the only thrashing I'd had since my mother left us. Now I understood the humiliation he must have felt: that I had stolen at a house where he was being criticised. He had hit me because I had made him lose face, but at the time I had felt so wronged. I never ate duck after that – indeed, I hardly ate meat at all – and I think the incident sparked off the distrust of my father and the whole adult world he represented.

I sat down with a bowl of vegetarian noodle soup. I had a good appetite for the food I liked: eating for two. Would it be a boy or a girl? Would it have Ken's nose? I hadn't seen much of him lately.

Ken had seen and heard nothing that night. All he had said when he'd pushed open my bedroom door was 'It's chilly in here. What are you doing?'

I felt torn. Part of me wanted him to 'see' Nainai as clearly as I did, but I was scared that if I told him my secret I might lose him. Surely he would think I was mad.

After my announcement he had stayed the whole weekend, and cooked for me. I hadn't known he could cook so well. He couldn't do stir-fries, but he made stews, slow to cook and delicious. We went for walks on Hampstead Heath and talked about everything except the matter that dominated our thoughts. He spoke about his work, about an Oriental-style bridge he had been asked to design for a park in the Midlands. I understood his silence, but wished he would break it.

Then he rang last week to say he was spending Easter with his widowed mother and would not be coming to Hampstead. 'You will have Barbara, won't you? Make sure she cooks for you.'

Coward. He did not want the baby, he did not love me, and he did not want me to stay in England.

I spent the Easter weekend fidgeting, unable to answer

Barbara's questions: 'Why are you eating all the time? Why won't you cook? Why have you bought so many crisps? What smell?' She was making mushroom soup, the smell of garlic stealing out of the door as I approached. I was overwhelmed by the fragrance of lilies. When I saw Bill in an armchair I knew he had bought them – her favourite white regal lilies.

'Hello.' Bill waved a newspaper at me.

'Hello.' I went to the flowers, couldn't resist feasting on the scent. 'How wonderful to have such scent in April.'

'Do you think so?' Barbara turned to me. 'I can hardly smell it. It's the way they grow flowers, these days – they look nice but don't smell as they should.'

Bill frowned, but didn't say anything. Barbara wasn't the most diplomatic woman – but to disparage such exuberant fragrance? I glanced at her, but she had turned back to the cooker.

I sat down opposite Bill on a low stool and put my shopping on the floor. He looked up from his paper. 'How are you?' I asked.

'Tired. Barbara slave-drove me for her pond.' He sighed proudly.

'Is it filled with fish?'

'Not yet,' Barbara said. 'We have to wait a few days for the water to settle. I've been thinking we could find some frogs for it.'

'I've been to Chinatown,' I said.

Barbara turned and noticed the bag. 'What did you buy? Chinese sweets?'

'Paper money.'

'What for?'

'Today is Qing Ming.'

'The Day of the Dead,' she exclaimed. 'Do you know about Qing Ming, Bill?'

Grudgingly, Bill looked up again. 'No.'

'Tell him about it,' Barbara encouraged me.

'Qing Ming is the day you remember your ancestors. I am remembering my late father and grandmother.'

'How fascinating,' he said.

I met his cool blue gaze and, as usual, glanced away. When I looked up again his eyes were still on me, expressionless. Was he expecting me to say more? Somehow to explain it was to trivialise it. 'There's not much more to tell. You burn papers, you wish them well in the other world. That's it.'

'Oh, you must tell him more or he'll find out for himself and become a great bore on the subject,' Barbara mocked.

'I've visited Hong Kong, you know.' Finally, Bill dropped his paper and stood up. 'There they observe the traditions strictly.'

'Of course they do,' I responded sharply. 'That's the old China, fossilised.'

'What do you have against tradition?' he asked.

'It's backward-looking and superstitious.'

'So what are you doing now with that paper money?'

I bit my lip and Bill smiled smugly: *he* would never allow himself such an inconsistency. He often caught me out like this.

'We have a tradition in our family.' Barbara had rescued me. 'All through my childhood Dad dressed up as Father Christmas on Christmas Eve. I believed he *was* Father Christmas until I was about eight. After that he did it for show and we joked about it but he still dressed up. It would have felt wrong if he hadn't.'

'How much nutmeg are you putting in?' Having won the argument Bill deserted the battleground. He went over to Barbara and stood behind her, his arms round her. She leaned back and they kissed quickly. 'You must do something about your dandelions,' he went on.

'What do you mean, "my dandelions"?' Barbara protested.

I buried myself in the newspaper Bill had been reading, relieved that I was no longer the focus of attention.

'Where's Ken?' Barbara asked. 'He's very late.' The soup was ready, and she licked the big wooden spoon with which she'd been stirring it. He was supposed to be here for dinner.

'Must have been delayed,' I murmured and blushed.

Barbara was not satisfied. 'He should have called.'

We waited another half-hour and then we began to eat.

The soup tasted bitter – too much nutmeg. Bill grimaced, and I saw that he had noticed it too.

When Bill was making the coffee I went upstairs to my room and ate the two buns I had bought in Chinatown – I was still hungry. But how was Barbara to know it – or that I didn't like cheese sandwiches – if I didn't tell her? I dropped hints, but she never picked them up. I rolled the bun wrapping into a tight ball and threw it into the bin. Now my hunger was satisfied and I had saved my hostess from embarrassment.

I came down to see Barbara ensconced in the armchair by the phone with a coffee mug in her hand. Bill had opened an atlas of China and was consulting a chart at the back. 'Here,' he gestured for me to come closer, 'it says that Qing Ming . . .'

To Bill every question must have an answer, and he would delight in finding and sharing it. When he talked like this I felt light-hearted and safe. He drew me to him as if we were conspirators. We pored over maps and consulted dates. If only my seminars at the university were so involving. Bill wasn't the most expressive of men, but sometimes he could charm the 'water to flow upwards' and 'flowers to fall from the sky', as my grandmother used to say. Perhaps that was why Barbara loved him. How flattering to have such a silent and elusive man take an interest in you.

But some part of me wouldn't join in today. I was distracted and looked at the other two anew: Bill's childish enthusiasm, Barbara's pensiveness – her hands were busy knitting and her eyes were on us but her thoughts were further away than the places marked on the maps. All of this was familiar, but something was different. Me. I was a woman with a secret, a sophistication that made them seem innocent.

When Bill paused during a lengthy paragraph he was reading, Barbara spoke: 'I hope Ken is all right. It's . . . unlike him not to ring.' She looked at me. I didn't say anything.

After a moment she put down her knitting. 'When is your exam, Mei?'

'In June,' I said. I didn't need reminding.

'We must think of what you want to do afterwards. When

does your visa expire?' I spilled my tea on the map and exclaimed loudly. In the clean-up that ensued, I managed to evade her question. I didn't want to answer it.

'I wonder what happened to Ken, though? It's annoying, isn't it, when people promise something but don't follow it through?'

I had promised to visit England for a year, then go back to serve my country. My visa expired in September, three months after the exam. I had pledged not to impinge on my hosts.

Did Barbara not want me here? How would she react if I told her that I was carrying a baby? Did I want to tell her the truth? Why was there such a distance between us?

It had not always been like this. For the first six months, I had plunged myself into my new life as if I had always led it and it had always been there waiting for me. I had seemed to fit in well. Family mysteries and nicknames were explained to me; birthdays and Christmas were one big party after another. I had been vain, swimming through the parties like an exotic fish. Sleek, aloof, I acted as if I did not have a past, or as if it was richer than it had been with the food rationing and the fear of my father's being taken away from me. In no time at all I had learned how people, especially men, expected a Chinese girl to smile and charm, and obliged. It made life easier but left me even more confused as to who I was.

Finally, homesickness had set in. Perhaps it *was* time to return to China. But how could I go home with a growing belly? Soon the loose jumper I was wearing wouldn't conceal the lump beneath it. I didn't want to think about that.

It was the contradiction in Barbara that exasperated me. She had brought me here. Nobody, not even my parents, had done for me what she had: surely, if she hadn't cared, she would not have sponsored my studies, and installed me in her home. But if she really was concerned, she would have been helping me plan my future, not enquiring about it as if she were a mere acquaintance.

What she had done meant so much – yet she had allowed me to show little gratitude. The Chinese in me wanted us to be closer, and the English in her pushed us apart. But if I tried to get closer, as I wanted to, might it not seem as though I expected her to do more for me? I was afraid to risk it.

I looked up for her face, full of words I couldn't say, but instead met Bill's penetrating gaze.

There was a knock. I glanced at the clock: a quarter to eleven. Barbara yawned. 'Who can that be? It's late.' She went to the door.

Ken burst in, as if delivered by the wind. Barbara stepped back. 'Hello, Ken. It's . . . a surprise to see you. We wondered where you'd been. I'm afraid there's no food left.'

My stomach twisted. Since I had been pregnant I seemed to experience emotions in my belly, rather than in my mind.

'Don't worry about me. I hope you're feeding Mei well,' he said.

'Yes.' Barbara frowned, annoyed by his lateness, and the silly remark. She went back to her seat and resumed knitting. 'Believe me, she's well fed.'

Ken was looking at me strangely – he'd realised that I hadn't told Barbara. He walked past her to me. 'I'm glad, because you're feeding two,' he said, and patted my belly gently. 'She's carrying our baby.'

It was an uncharacteristically dramatic gesture and we were all stunned. Bill dropped the atlas and Barbara her knitting. They collided as they stood up to congratulate us, their reactions betraying that they were not sure of the right response. My stomach tightened, then relaxed, and I stood there like a log. 'You should have told us,' Barbara said, beaming and blushing, as if she were the expectant mother.

'She didn't know for sure until . . . last week,' Ken answered, on my behalf.

'How are you feeling?' Barbara asked.

'Fine, sickish when I'm hungry.'

'Now I know why.' She nodded emphatically, and turned to hug Bill.

With Ken's arms round me I was the centre of attention, but somehow I felt at a distance. 'Our baby,' he had said. I smelt alcohol as he whispered, 'Sorry I wasn't here earlier. I was . . . down at the pub. I thought I needed a drink before coming here but ended up staying later than I meant. Oh, Jiao Mei, it's good to be with you.' He squeezed me tightly. 'Our baby,' he whispered again, and I felt as if my heart had dropped to its usual place.

I should have felt proud, happy, but . . . 'Sorry, people,' I said, disentangling myself from Ken, 'I have to go and burn the papers.'

'Listen to that wind! Perhaps you shouldn't go out,' Barbara said, concerned. Bill muttered something to Ken, who came over and draped his jacket over me.

I couldn't get away from him, from them all, fast enough. The more understanding he seemed, the more they fussed over me, the more unbearable it was. To follow through what I had started I needed to be strong, not weak. I welcomed the cold wind as I wrestled to shut the door. I could think of nowhere more appropriate to light the papers than beneath the Mei tree, and I headed for it, past the big hollow in front of it that was the newly dug pond.

The Mei tree danced frantically in the wind. I put my arms round its trunk, feeling its rough support, using it to steady myself. I shook my head to rid myself of thoughts of the present, of the people whose language I now spoke, and tried to focus on the dead I'd left behind. It had been on a windy day like this that I had come home from school to find my father sitting alone on his bed in Beijing. 'Close the door behind you,' he had said gently. I noticed the quiet, and his red eyes, as if he'd been rubbing them. 'Your mother has left us,' he said simply. The wind was howling outside, but inside we heard only the sound of her absence. She must have tidied the house before she left, because the room seemed very bare.

So she had left us, but in a way she never did. Every little thing reminded us of her. A missing button, the flavour of a dish now that my father was the cook, a gust of wind and those long nights. It was as if she left tiny thorns in our flesh that pricked every so often, triggered by a sound or a smell. We could never get rid of them, and in a way we never wanted to. I knew my father felt them more than I did.

Soon after, Nainai came to live with us. She mended socks and patched the quilts my mother had started but not finished. At first I had resisted her, then accepted and came to love her. She won me over with her stories, which drew not only me but all the other children in the yard – nine of us. There was no television then and Nainai's bedtime story was the best treat of my childhood. There were five years of story-telling in which I learned and grew up.

When I started school she became almost humble. She treated my books with reverence and often stood over me as I did my homework. Some of it she could follow, but not all. To be a scholar was, for her, the ultimate aspiration. Every Chinese family wanted this for their children, but my grandmother's desire was stronger than most. I could sulk, be naughty and messy, but as long as I brought home good academic results, she treated me like a princess. I much preferred her stories to my textbooks, but to please her I tried to do well. It wasn't hard in those days, anyway, and she was happy. Why was she so keen on study? I asked her once or twice, and she'd say I wouldn't understand until I was older. I'm still not sure I do, or at least not why she valued printed words over her traditional wisdom.

Eventually Nainai grew homesick. She complained about the weather and said her old bones were melting: she needed to go back to Sichuan to die. No one took her seriously, not even my father. But at her insistence he asked to be transferred back to his hometown. It was two years before permission was granted, but by then it was too late for her: she had died, 'not used to the water and earth', as she kept saying. It was strange that she identified with the south: she had been born and brought up in the north and didn't leave it until she was twenty. But in Sichuan, in her youth, she had once had a garden, and she had loved flowers. Perhaps that was why.

My father was sent back to his ancestral home, a small town on the edge of Chengdu. His family had owned the land where the People's Park now stood; after the liberation, it had been taken over by the government and returned to the people. There would be no housing for him, he had been told. He was not deterred: he said he would build a shed on the land of his ancestors. The authorities agreed, not believing that he would succeed, because he was not strong. But he did. After that he changed: the man Barbara had glimpsed sweeping was nothing like the willow of a man with whom I had grown up in Beijing.

When the train entered the Qin-ling mountains, leaving behind the Northern Plain, my father had seemed relaxed and happy for the first time on that long journey. He had entered the kingdom where he had grown up. He held me briefly and whispered, 'Home.'

Now, lighting the fire was no easy task. I had to plant my feet firmly on the papers to stop them blowing away. At last when the fire spread, they sprang into the air, carried off by the wind before the flames had turned them to ash. The smell of burnt paper made my eyes water. The red flames enhanced the greyness around me.

I was between worlds.

'Nainai,' I murmured, 'please forgive me.' I needed her more than ever, but she was also the last person in whom I could confide. Which would hurt her most? That I had allowed myself to become pregnant by Ken, or my reluctance to go back to China – to her? Oh, Nainai, I have failed you.

I closed my eyes, feeling the branches of the tree buffeting me, like an impatient child. As the fire died, I felt a chill take hold within me and shivered.

Then, out of the howling of the wind, I heard another voice, vague at first but familiar as it grew stronger. It seemed to come from the Mei tree. I opened my eyes and saw a shadow emerge, smelt the familiar fragrance.

Nainai looked different out here. Her shape was less distinguishable, her body swayed in the wind, lacking solidity, but her manner was confident, as if she was in a place where she belonged. Yet it was a shock to see her in the open air. I couldn't pretend any more that it was a dream.

'Thank you for remembering me today, and for your gift.' She sounded pleased. I could not see her face clearly: there was no moon tonight. 'But you know I don't need it. I can look after myself.' She laughed like a little girl.

My teeth were chattering, not just from the chill, but there was no point in holding back. 'Nainai, we have decided to keep the child.'

'Do you know what you are doing?'

'Yes.'

'Does he . . . ?'

'I think so – he called it *our* child,' I said, and wanted to say it again. It seemed so right. *Our child.*

'He's got you, this pale-faced devil. He's taken advantage of you and you're glad.'

'Nainai, please. I lied to *him* so that I could get pregnant. Now do you see?'

'But why ever would you want to do such a thing?'

She seemed angry now, but I was defiant. 'Because I want to stay here. I don't want to go back.'

Silence. I had thought that she would be disgusted and upset, but I had not expected silence. Slowly I looked up at her. She was staring past me, and I followed her gaze. Ken was standing by the door, a jumper in his hand, his face illuminated by the porch light, which had come on automatically. 'Are you all right, Jiao Mei?' he shouted, hesitating to come over.

I had to tell him, now. But it was hard to condemn myself – before we had begun to enjoy together the new life I'd so hoped for. I drew nearer to him. 'I'm all right, Ken. But . . . you should know that I lied about the date of my period.'

Those were the hardest words I'd ever had to say in English.

Tie Mei

When the young man had gone she turned to me as if she would devour me. She shouted something in the language I shouldn't have been able to understand but which

I felt, somehow, that I did, then spoke again in Chinese: 'Look what you've made me say! Wretched ghost, I wish you'd never come!' She kicked at a bit of half-burned paper, which flew into the air, where it was snatched by the wind and gone. In a flash she was gone too.

She had wounded me with those words. She had hurt me where the devils in hell could not. She wished I'd never come. I turned to go, but something held me, a voice within me: 'Stay,' it said. 'Don't be angry with her. She's just a child, she didn't mean it.'

It was a desolate night in that garden, such a wind, full of sorrow, wailing like a child. But it wasn't the wind, or a child; it was her, sitting on the step just outside the door, her shoulders heaving. She was a five-year-old again.

'Nainai,' I heard her say, 'please come back, I'm sorry.' She looked up and around but didn't see me. 'Please come back. He's gone, he's gone . . .'

The wind subsided. How quickly things changed: now she was all mine. I'd won. I should be generous. I must let her mourn him, my poor girl.

'Nainai,' she shouted when she finally saw me, 'I know you won't desert me.'

I stood over her, feeling the urge to take her into my arms and rock her, like I used to. Instead I motioned her to follow me, pointing to the pavilion. It smelt of new paint, which I didn't like, but it was a shelter for her. We sat opposite each other in silence. Pain pierced me to the core: the words she had said flooded back to me. It had not occurred to me that she might not want me: my love for her had been the only comfort in the darkness I'd been through. Reputation be damned! It was the shift in her allegiance that hurt.

'Jiaojiao, why do you want to stay here?' I asked.

'I've been asking myself the same question,' she said.

'What do you have here that you don't at home? There's so little fun that even a dog would be bored.'

'It's true . . . I'm not always happy here. I hate the weather and people staring at me. Sometimes I'm desperate to leave.

But whenever I decide to go home, something stops me.'

'You mean the young man you are . . . involved with?'

My impatience must have shown, and she looked at me apologetically. 'Nainai, I can't explain. I feel alive here. I look forward to a future here. Isn't that enough?'

'But at what cost?'

She lowered her head. 'I didn't think.' After a few moments' silence, she looked up. 'Nainai, don't be too hard on me. You've acted without thinking, haven't you?'

There was a naughty twinkle in her eye. She was using her charm on me, but I never could resist it. 'Jiaojiao,' I said, holding her gaze, 'do you remember, last time, I spoke to you of my mother?' This was the time to explain how it had all begun, the story behind my quest for revenge.

She nodded. I watched her, big feet and hands, trusting eyes. But this time I was not telling a story, only the truth. 'Before I knew you, Jiaojiao, I had a bitter life, so bitter that *huanglian* would have tasted sweet. All those who were close to me, my mother, my lover and my child, were taken from me brutally.'

'She didn't die of an illness then, as you told me?'

'No. She died when she was two months pregnant, like you now,' I said softly, and saw the alarm in her eyes.

I began, 'My mother, your great-grandmother, died on my wedding day, when I was nineteen, and she was thirty-nine. She died for her reputation. That was how she had brought me up and, as you see, I suffered for it.

'I grew up in the north-east. My family had been quite well off when my father was alive. We had a maid. Then the Japanese came and they divided the town into two parts. The occupied land where they lived was clean and tidy. Not many Chinese lived there. At first we lived in the Japanese part, but Father started to visit the opium houses. He gambled and soon had lost all our money. We had to move house several times to flee his creditors.

'We ended up at the cheap end of the town. There was an atmosphere about it, and the smell of opium in the lanes from the rows of opium houses – brothels where pretty girls wearing Qipao dress, cheongsams, with slits to the top of their thighs, lay in dimly lit smoky rooms with men. I knew about the opium houses because I was sent there to look for Father – Mother could not bear to go herself. Each time I came back, she made me describe everything I had seen, the smell, the light, the girls and the way my father lay. She'd sit there saying nothing, but the colour of her face kept changing, and her shoulders heaved.

'After Father died we were even poorer. We moved again to a tiny house in the same area. Mother hated the sight of the opium houses and I felt sorry for her – we had to live among them. "If only we had a little more money," she would sigh. Even on the sunniest days our door was always shut with a forbidding sign above it, "Decent residential area, strictly no entrance", which seemed only to arouse curiosity. Men pretended to have lost their way and slipped into the yard, peering into our rooms through the holes they pinched in the paper windows. Mother, dressed always in black like a hawk, would scold them and chase them out with a broom. "Pretty Widow", they called her, their arms over their heads to protect themselves from the blows, their eyes throwing back longing glances.

' "One day soon we'll find you a good family," Mother would say to me, breathless from the chase, "and we'll leave here. We have our reputation to think of."

'She was an exemplary widow. Since Father died, she'd never worn makeup, always dressed in black or blue. The only moments of vanity she permitted herself were when she stared into her treasured old bronze mirror, after she'd cleaned it. Then she would fiddle with her hair, and her delicate fingers would trace the pattern of Mei leaves on the back.

'The mirror was her pride and joy. A family heirloom – the mirror from my story. How it had returned to us was a mystery. According to my mother, her own mother, the little girl in the story, had searched all her life for it and the thief, but to no avail. She had died urging my mother to find them. One dark night shortly after her mother's death, my mother was sitting on her own when a man in a black robe and mask slipped into her house soundlessly, dropped a wrapped parcel, then left as quickly as he had come. Inside, she found the mirror. There was no letter of explanation. It was as if the man had risen from the earth, then returned to it. She checked the door and it was locked.

'Mother thought it was a gift, a bequest from her dead mother – that was the only way she could explain it. All our good fortune came from that mirror, she often told me, and from early on, I treated it with respect and awe. She hardly ever let me touch it. Small people's souls were not complete, she said, so I should not look at myself too much in its polished surface. But on some rare occasions I was allowed a glimpse over her shoulder. It was then that I realised how beautiful she was. I could find all sorts of faults with my own face: nose too big and crooked, lips too wide, eyes too long and narrow, but with Mother, everything seemed perfectly proportioned.

'In the spring after my eighteenth birthday, matchmaker women with long smoking pipes began to drop in to our household, their voices like broken gongs. Their colourful dresses and language spiced up our austere little room. The air was thick with strong smells – from their armpits, their cheap face powder, and their breath, a mixture of tobacco and spring onion. With dread and excitement, I sat away from them sewing a shirt, watching.

'One matchmaker sat cross-legged on our bed and kept her eyes on me through the smoke. Mother brought her tea. The woman coughed, picked up a teacup and gulped a mouthful. "Tie Mei," Mother called, and I approached. The matchmaker examined me as I stared at her powdered face, the freshly picked flowers in her hair, and her hand, like Mother's wind-dried meat. "Show me your sewing, my dear," she said. When I came back with it she felt my hands. "As tender as freshly made tofu."

'Mother smiled indulgently. Several men were presented. One was thin and small, like a sugar cane with its juice sucked out, standing there as if the wind would blow him away. He was so nervous and boyish that I giggled behind the curtain. Another man wore a long grey gown, so old he could have been my grandfather. He cleared his throat before he came in and ceremoniously removed his hat. Through the crack in the curtain I saw his thick dark eyebrows and shuddered. He had presence: he was an undertaker.

' "What about him?" Mother asked when he was gone. I shook my head. I'd rather have died than let him touch me. During the afternoon siesta I dreamed of a wedding with him and woke up screaming. Mother held and soothed me: "No, no." She shook her head. "You always dream the opposite of what you get. So, let's see, instead of an old man in a grey gown, you will have a handsome young man perhaps wearing glasses because he is learned, but tall and upright. This man, whom you've never met, will adore you. He will take such delight in you that he will treat you like a flower."

'That night when Mother lit the incense for her prayers to Guanyin, the goddess of Mercy, I knelt down next to her. "Please give me a good-looking man," I said, "gentle and cultured, like the ones I read about in books. Please make him poor. Let him be a student, so he will be modest and good-tempered." I knew this would not be what Mother prayed for and I wondered which of us Guanyin would listen to.

'A few weeks went by and Mother went to the countryside to visit her cousin. The night before she left, she couldn't find the mirror and she was very upset. It was usually kept on the dark red oval table just beneath her altar for Guanyin, next to the candles. We searched everywhere without success. She left reluctantly, after making me promise to search for it again.

'When she came back, her appearance shocked me. She had been away only for a few days but she had aged so much. She was thin, there were bloody scratches on her face and her eyes stared as if her soul had gone from her body. "What happened, Mother?" I asked, but she wouldn't answer. Instead she asked me whether I'd found the mirror. "No," I replied. "I've searched everywhere." Her face turned grey and she looked so desolate that I rushed to her side and took her hands in mine. "It's just a mirror," I tried to comfort her. But she screamed at me, the first time she'd done so. It was our family treasure, our good fortune depended upon it.

'A few days later, all of this was forgotten when another matchmaker came, with a man who seemed perfect for me. The day was bright and the air sweet with peach blossom. He was tall, had big bright eyes, with glasses, and wore a modern western suit. I was told he worked as a teacher.

'I remember exactly what I wore that day, a sky-blue cotton top and a pair of purple silk embroidered shoes, which were rather loose – the result of a battle of wills between my grandmother and my mother. Mother had wanted my feet wrapped small so that I could be presented as a suitably conservative, old-fashioned girl; but my grandmother, a Manchu, had wanted me to be able to roam free. The battle raged throughout my childhood. During the day my mother bound my feet but at night my grandmother unwrapped them. By the time the fashion had changed and my mother agreed for my feet to be freed, the bones were damaged and floppy but my feet were still bigger than those of other girls my age from similar families.

'Once the young man's brief visit was over, the matchmaker brought in a giggling woman of around forty. I was using an old iron on my mother's shirt. She kept glancing at me and my feet.

'The next day the young man came back with a new iron, a present from the giggling woman, who was his mother. He asked my mother if he could have a word with me alone. She left without a word. He looked at me and I saw how delicate his skin was, almost like a girl's. "I am from a big family, and my parents are not very strong. They need looking after. You will have to work hard if you come into my family." Not a word about us. In those days you did not talk about love. I blushed and said I had been spoiled, that I was not very good at housework, which I did not mean and knew he did not believe.

'That night after Mother's prayer she came to my bed and smoothed my hair. I had not joined her because my happiness was complete and there was nothing else I wanted. "But, Mother," I said breathlessly, "I'm worried . . ." '

' "What, my precious?"

' "That he is better-looking than me, that they will despise me for being less good-looking than he is."

' "Silly child, you are the beautiful one. You are my beautiful Mei flower, how can you doubt that?" She pulled me to her prayer mat. "Kneel down and thank Guanyin for your good fortune. She granted your wish. Thank her." I knelt and thanked Guanyin for my handsome man.

'On getting up, I found Mother sitting on a corner of the bed wiping away tears with the front of her jacket. What about her? I felt helpless as terror seized me. I had always taken her for granted, she was like part of me, but soon we had to separate. I felt like a young horse galloping on a strange mountain road. I had been carefree, enjoying the movement, when suddenly a chasm had opened. How could Mother manage without me? It was against custom for her to live with me once I was married.

' "My dear, let me tell you more about your new family," she said. "It is a big family, and your mother-in-law is clever but rather strict and severe. I know you are happy with the man, but . . ." She looked at me. "If . . . however badly they treat you, be good in yourself and Guanyin will reward you, in the next life if not this. I . . . will not be with you for long. Remember how I brought you up. You must show your in-laws what a good girl you are. Remember your reputation."

'In my happiness I did not take these ominous words to heart. I thought Mother was sad because we were to part. I told her that however unreasonable my in-laws were, they would not stop us seeing each other. She sighed but didn't say any more.

'Over the next few months Mother prepared for my wedding. She turned the whole house upside-down looking for her mirror, which she said she must find. That was the most important dowry she could leave me. Without it, she feared I would not have a happy life. I helped her half-heartedly. I was young, focusing on the future. What was an old mirror to me? It did not turn up, and she would often stare blankly into space, or at me. Again, I attributed this to my imminent departure and did my best to comfort her.

'The day before the wedding, a "complete" woman, one whose immediate family were all living – parents, husband, children – came to help me shave off all the tiny hairs on my face. Mother sat jealously nearby to wait on us – as a widow she could not perform this task. The woman, stern-faced, used a thin piece of thread to pull out the hairs and pluck my eyebrows. When I winced with the pain, I was told this was the price I had to pay to be fit for my future husband. When the ordeal was over, the woman put down her tools, and sighed. "From now on, your face is marked. You cannot be looked upon by strangers before your husband sees you."

'My wedding day was bright and sunny. Crowds of women dropped in, like actresses in a play. First a hairdresser came. She swirled my hair up high and pinned it into a bun. Mother watched from the other side of the bed. There was an invisible gulf between us that, as the day went on, grew wider and wider. She was in the background hovering to help, but she never came near. When the "phoenix crown" with its colourful glass jewels arrived – hired from a nearby theatre – she rushed out to fetch it, and was scolded by an aunt for handling it. "Remember, you're a widow, you'll bring your daughter bad luck." Mother winced and withdrew.

'When I put the heavy crown on my head, it felt like a sign that my innocent girlhood was over. Before I rose to go out I looked for Mother and saw her coming from the kitchen with a steaming bowl. A fussy aunt was pulling at her jacket, scolding her, reminding her yet again how unlucky this would be for me. But Mother freed herself with such a determined look on her face that all around stepped back as she held the bowl in front of me: "This is the last meal I will cook for you," she said. It was an omelette. For a whole day I was to live on eggs. It was the traditional meal for brides, who were not allowed to leave their room, even to go to the toilet.

'As I ate the omelette, Mother put a hand on my shoulder and her tears fell. Her face wrinkled and she stared at me as if she was going to swallow me. I sobbed. An aunt, who had been helping me, supporting the crown, chided, "Not now, finish your omelette first. Then cry – cry loudly so that people can hear you."

'Crying was part of the ritual, the last tears a girl shed before she left her old home. The aunts started a chorus of weeping, but it was my mother's silent tears that moved me. I was dragged out into the sunshine, amid deafening firecrackers, to the waiting *jiao* – the sedan chair.

'There were two *jiao*s. One, I had been told, contained my future husband, whom I was not to look at. The other contained a little boy, a symbol of my future role as a mother. Two women helped me into the one with the child, who was bribed with sweets to get out. Ahead of us I could hear the *suona* horns. I recognised the men who blew them – they were the group the townsfolk hired for funerals – and the message in the tune: they were sending someone on a journey from which they would never return.

'I sat in a red world – my own red dress, the red velvet interior of the *jiao*, the red handkerchief covering my face. I could hardly see, only smell and hear. The trumpeters took me through mountains and valleys, whispers of water and birds. When they stopped occasionally and joked among themselves, I heard voices of people commenting on the entourage. I smelt dust, food and my own sweat. My hands ached from having to support the heavy crown and my back hurt from sitting upright.

'When the men carrying the *jiao* stumbled, I swallowed the dumpling – I had been given it before I got in. "Keep it in your mouth and do not swallow it until you get to your husband's house," a voice had warned. I had obeyed the instruction, without comprehending its significance. What now? Was it a bad omen? Before I had time to ponder the *jiao* shook violently from side to side. In the hot, steamy interior it felt like an earthquake, but I remembered Mother's words: "When the carriers jostle you, lean to one side, and that will stop them." I did so and they stopped. I thanked Mother silently. The thought of her gave me strength, which I needed.

'I was exhausted when we reached my in-laws' home. It might have been a tiger's den and I would have happily crawled into it. But they made me wait half an hour – another ritual, to test my patience. When, finally, a hand raised the curtain, a hot cloud of dust and food smells were upon me and I blinked in the bright afternoon sun. I stepped on to something soft, a dazzling spread of red carpet, then entered a dark hall. Too exhausted now to care what was happening around me, I did as I was told. "First bow to heaven and earth." I bowed. "Second bow to your seniors." I bowed. "Third bow to each other." I bowed. "And now to your new room."

'In the new room someone – there was always someone who knew exactly what to do – took my shoes off and for the first time that day I was able to rest. The crown was removed. I sat cross-legged on a bed littered with small lumpy objects: I felt them with my hands and brought them to my nose to smell them. They were nut and dates, objects whose names punned on fertility: "Nuts, *huasheng*, give birth", "Dates, *zhao zi*, give birth early to a son". "You can swallow your dumpling now." A voice startled me. I swallowed hard to show I had done as I was told.

'When the evening light was turned on I was changed into a thinner jacket and was made to sit there again like a doll. I could hear the noise of the banquet – children screaming, adults chatting, glasses clicking. The smell of food made my mouth water. Once in a while the curtain of the room was raised and I would feel the stares of a curious guest. I felt like a prop in a play. I thought of Mother and felt her distance from me.

'I must have fallen into a kind of trance. Cool air hit my face as the veil – through which I had only glimpsed the world all day – was pulled off me. The smooth jade face of my husband appeared, blushing, smiling, smelling of alcohol. "I've brought you an egg," he said, picking up my hand and putting it into it. "Are you tired?" I nodded, feeling as if I had known him all my life, although this was only the second time I'd seen him.

'He sat down next to me. I put the egg into my mouth and chewed. A woman appeared behind him, my mother-in-law: "Is it raw?" she asked sternly.

'I was puzzled. "No," I said, too hungry to care anyway.

' "No," the woman seemed angry, "say 'raw'." Suddenly I understood. It was another pun for "give birth". I obliged, and her face relaxed.

'When she had gone my husband picked up my hand and smoothed it. I pretended not to notice and carried on eating my egg, trying to maintain a dignified face.

' "Gluing up already, are they?" A giggle and a loud whisper from beneath the window made us jump and he withdrew his hand quickly. We were being watched. This was the last and most trying of the rituals: disturbing the bridal couple. Guests would wait outside the window peeping in on our most intimate moments and commenting loudly, as if they were watching a show. My husband went out and soon I heard him joking with the people outside. I gathered from their conversation that they were mostly his colleagues – fellow teachers from his school. They were a much more civilised crowd than average, educated, and I felt reassured.

'It was well past midnight when my husband came back. I sat up, rubbing my eyes. I had been dozing. I wanted to turn off the light to sleep, but it had to be kept on all night. I could not bear to take off my clothes in that brightness, knowing that people could see me. "Relax," he murmured. "They have all gone. Are you still hungry?" I shook my head. It was very quiet now and I could hear my own heartbeat. He came closer. "How tired you are!" he said. "You've had a long day." We looked at each other. I felt his kindness in those words, and leaned closer to him.

'You will know what happened next, and my mother had

prepared me for it. I had thought I would be scared but I felt comforted and not so lonely. It hurt a little, but I had thought it would be worse.

'The next morning no one disturbed us. We lay there watching the sunlight on the floor, gradually filling the room with its warmth. I did not want to stir and held him down when he tried to get up. Already I felt my power over him and his over me. It was as if we were bound by a mystical thread.

'Mother had told me once that that was what happened to the perfect couple. The old man in the moon had a piece of red string. He searched all over the world for the perfect man and woman and when he found them, wherever they were, he would string them together. One might live near the East Sea and the other in the Western Hills, "but so long as you are right for each other, the old man in the moon will find you and string you together. This is how a perfect match is made, you must not try, you have to trust the old man in the moon."

'Were we the perfect couple? I had thought we were but, then, I didn't know any better. I didn't know any other men. He was gentle and kind to me, the first stranger I had met whom I liked, and I thought that that was love. All anyone asked was that we were compatible, that our families matched. I thought myself lucky – I might have ended up with the undertaker if my mother had wanted more money.

'In the late afternoon we heard the clatter of pots and pans from the other rooms and women shouting. We were playing chess together and drinking yellow wine. He had wanted to put the light on but I stopped him. I'd had enough of being exposed to light and stares the previous day. I enjoyed the darkness. We carried on with the chess. I took one of his horses and was teasing him about it when we heard heavy footsteps coming from the other room. "Wen Ting, Wen Ting, come out." A loud woman's voice called my husband's name. He jumped up and put on his outer garments. "Yes, Mother, I'm coming." He slipped on his shoes and rushed out.

'I heard a brief exchange of words and a long silence. Then the footsteps strode away. I waited in the semi-darkness, soaking in my happiness, our warmth. I had no idea how short-lived that happiness was to be.

'Eventually when I looked up he was hovering by the door. He came closer, his face in the shadow. "I'm afraid there is bad news. Your mother . . . she died."

'The darkness around me sharpened. I fell down like a feather. "She hanged herself after you'd gone."

'Words of comfort from my husband mingled with shouts of abuse from my mother-in-law and many of my new relatives, who only the previous day had smiled in welcome. The machine of scandal hissed around me. "She should have killed herself earlier rather than bringing this shame on her daughter"; "I'd always known there was something under-neath that self-righteous white face. She was not known as 'Pretty Widow' for nothing."

'In my grief I fought them, my voice coarse from shouting. Reputation: my mother had died to protect it, yet her name was stained.

'For days I lay in bed. One night I had been dreaming of my mother in her blue dress, standing in my new room, in the moonlight. When I woke, she was gone, and a piece of my heart was cut out of me. I howled with the pain and my husband woke up. "Mei, you have come back. Thank good-ness." He put his arms round me and I sobbed. I turned on the light and read the letter he gave me, which she had left for me. I can recite it because I read it so many times.

Tie Mei

It happened about three months ago when I went to visit my cousin in the countryside. You must remember – the night before I left we lost the mirror. I had an uneasy feeling in my heart and I knew something bad would happen. I shouldn't have gone. Many people had warned me against the Japanese, and I wish I had heeded their words. We were sitting there chatting when I heard screams. My cousin, who was old, put black ashes on her face to make herself look even less attractive, and pushed me into a hiding-place – a gap in a thick wall between two rooms, near the kitchen fire. But the men had a dog, which sniffed me out. They were beasts – no, beasts are better than they were. When they had gone my cousin gave me new clothes.

I didn't know where I was going, and when I saw the river I wanted to jump in, but I thought of you. I kept thinking, This is not true, it's a nightmare. Then I pinched myself, and I knew it was not a dream. My cousin had tried to comfort me by saying, "At least you were not a virgin." But I had been a widow for thirteen years.

When I started to feel sick I knew I was pregnant. There was nothing I could do but wait. Now you are married, I can go.

Don't be sad, Tie Mei. It is my fate that I should suffer in this life, but I know that in the next I will be compensated. I have kept an impeccable reputation.

My only regret is the mirror, which I had meant to leave you as your dowry. Find it, because so much of your good fortune depends on it. I will not be at peace until you do.

'There! Reputation and the return of the mirror. My mother's dying wish. It must be hard for you, living now, to understand what respectability meant to women then. Mother would have had no other choice. She had been raped by an enemy soldier so she would have been despised and spat upon, a fate worse than death. Her experience showed me the unfairness of double standards, but it was not until I fell in love with a man other than my husband that I started to resent them, and realised how damaging they could be. That was why I hurried to you when I knew of your pregnancy. I could not bear anything to happen to you.

'But what I did when I saw you was wrong. I should not have talked of your reputation. I was so afraid you would reject me that I resorted to the old ways. I thought that you would listen to me then. I know now that the tie between us is stronger than that. We are family, flesh and blood.'

Our eyes met and her soft look made me melt inside. I

almost forgot what I was going to say next, but the words slipped out of my mouth: like my love for her, my desire for justice sprang from the deepest part of me. 'But you see, Jiaojiao, don't you, how heavily it lay upon my conscience that I should find the mirror and avenge my mother and our ancestors? You see, don't you, why I flare up when justice is denied us, even in death, when the Lord of Hell said he would not listen to the words of a disgraced woman? You see, don't you, why I had to seek justice for myself?'

'Nainai,' she said, 'you are a heroine.'

5: *Gu Yu* – Grain Rain

20 April

Jiao Mei

'So you're going to keep the baby?'
'Yes.'
'Even though Ken has left you?'
'Yes.'

We sat in the shade of the pavilion, out of the sun. Xiao Lin was eating sunflower seeds. The black of the shell contrasted with the white of her teeth, which were sharp, like her. 'The bastard.' She spat out the words along with the shells. 'This is turning into a Chinese garden. Did Barbara do it all?'

'We helped, but she did most of it. Ever since her accident, she's been keener than ever.'

'What accident?'

'Didn't I tell you? She collapsed suddenly, while she was weeding. Fatigue, they said.'

Xiao Lin nodded. 'And how is she now.'

'Fine. But Bill said she mustn't over-exert herself.'

'Perhaps she shouldn't garden if she's been ill. It's hard work,' Xiao Lin said, tapping the wicker chair with her painted fingernails. The idea of her dirtying them in soil made me laugh.

'We told her so but she wouldn't listen.' I paused. I remembered Barbara's collapse vividly. It had happened the day after Nainai's last visit, when she had told me of the death of my great-grandmother. The night before, Bill said she had complained of a severe headache.

Today Bill had taken Barbara out for lunch and we had turned the kitchen upside-down, emptying several spice jars. Xiao Lin, also from Sichuan, cooked spicy aubergines, which made my mouth water. Then we remembered I was not to have spicy food. To compensate, she stir-fried some cabbage. She had looked up, her forehead damp with sweat. 'You're still so thin, even though you've been eating like a pig. Where has all the food gone?'

'In here.' I patted my lower belly.

She shook her head. 'You're tough. If I were you I'd be losing sleep.'

'How do you know I'm not worried?' What would she say if I told her about Nainai's ghost? 'How are things with Andy?' I asked.

'Oh, I was about to tell you. We're going to get married.'

'Really? He's finally got round to proposing, has he?'

She rolled her eyes at me. Andy was thirty years older than Xiao Lin, besotted with her youth but mindful of her appetite for spending his money. 'We can't afford a big wedding, though. He says he's poor because all his money goes on maintaining his divorced wife and their children.'

'So you're not going to stop working?'

'You bet I am, as soon as we're married. I can't bear my boss.' Xiao Lin worked in a Chinese restaurant whose owner was just like one of the exploiting landlords in the films we had grown up with. 'He watches me all the time and I feel like a robot.' Xiao Lin rubbed her eyes. She came back from the restaurant most nights after midnight and slept through the morning. To her, early afternoon was breakfast time. 'Think how lucky you are. No rent to pay, doing a degree. And don't worry about Ken, he'll come round – it's his flesh and blood after all.'

'I don't think so.'

'You mean . . .'

'No, no! Of course it's his child, but . . . he never wanted it.'

'Neither did you. It was an accident, and accidents happen,

though I do know girls who skip pills or fake the dates so they can get pregnant.'

I didn't want to think of myself as that sort of girl. I bit my lip and said nothing.

She studied me and lowered her voice: 'You didn't, did you?'

I nodded slowly.

She chuckled. 'Hey, I didn't know you had it in you. Well done.' She gave me a wink. 'Although,' she smiled, 'if I were you, I wouldn't tell him. Why make things more complicated? Don't worry about Ken, he'll come round,' she said again and beamed. 'I told Andy I was a virgin when I first met him, and he believed me.'

'But what about your little girl?'

'I told him the truth later. But I got him hooked first.'

I felt sick again. 'I have to lie down, Xiao Lin. I'm not feeling well.'

As she left I noticed her strong perfume. Was that what had made me feel ill? She always wore it to cover the smell of cooking that clung to her from the restaurant kitchen. Xiao Lin reminded me of a hedgehog, prickly outside but soft within. I had seen her with men, flirting outrageously: she was acting – she knew it and I knew it, but I wondered if the men did. Englishmen expected Chinese girls to behave in a certain way and you soon learned to manipulate it.

She had complimented me on my toughness, but really she was the hard one: an abortion and two failed marriages, with a six-year-old daughter who lived in China with her grandparents. Although she had lived in England for some years, she still worked in a restaurant. Compared to her I lived like a princess, and I was grateful that she remained a close friend.

I sat down slowly in front of the open window, watching the rays of sunshine leaking through on to the table. The Chinese and the English reacted differently to sunshine: if you were soaking in it, like a thirsty man running for water, you were English; if you withdrew to the shade, you were Chinese. There was too much sun in China, land of dust and light.

At this time of year the sun would be warm, not too hot. The ground would be covered by the white blossom from the pagoda trees. You wouldn't see children on the ground, they were all up in the trees, gathering it from the branches. All the blossom in the neighbourhood would be rationed. I had melted the little flowers one by one in my mouth. They felt cool, then soft down my throat like the stream of a scented fountain. That was in the north, in Beijing, before Mother left us and Father died. I had been in Paradise. Flowers tasted sweeter then.

I walked out into the garden again. Xiao Lin was right: the garden *was* becoming Chinese. The pavilion had blended in. Rain and wind had softened its colour, and climbing roses had attached themselves to it as if to a tree. The pond was filled with waterlilies and goldfish; at the edge of the garden the branches of the Mei tree swayed. Tiny green leaves were showing, and new buds were appearing on the apple tree.

Everywhere the earth was freshly dug, dead roots withering in the sun. Bright pink and yellow tulips stood cheerfully, defying the decay around them. I bent to smell the fresh, sun-baked soil. My father had bent down like this on our first spring in the People's Park. He had picked up a lump of earth and held it to my face: 'This used to belong to us, all the land you see around you.' He waved to take in the whole park. 'Our family, our ancestors.'

Why was Barbara defying the doctor's advice and wearing herself out to create a bit of China that made me pine still more for home? Why the hurry? Perhaps it was just spring. But her collapse had worried me. She had always been so fit.

A frog leaped and snapped me out of my thoughts, leaving me with a feeling of vague apprehension. I saw spawn in the pond. A cat from nowhere was fishing it out of the water and licking it. I shooed it away and sat down on the steps leading to the pond.

Clumps of frog spawn, and a clump inside me, conceived in deceit. I remembered the look on Ken's face. It was the most despicable thing I'd ever done, and I'd done it to him. Everything had been going so well between us, and I had tried to be honest. With him I did not act 'Chinese', I did not pretend, I was myself and we understood each other, or so I thought.

It was not too late to get rid of it. Its father did not want it, and I did not want it.

I thought of Nainai's story of her mother. My life must seem such a muddle to her. She hadn't said it, but perhaps she was secretly willing me to get rid of the baby. How angry it must make her to see me carrying a foreigner's child.

But Nainai was not the reason I wanted to get rid of the baby. I knew, in my heart, that it was all to do with Ken. I'd wronged him and the only way of rectifying it was to undo what I'd done.

I thought of Taro. 'You look pale,' he had said, regarding me with concern. 'Too many cheese sandwiches for Easter?' We had both laughed. I had felt suddenly light-hearted, relieved that I was closer to him again – even after Nainai's story. Now I had two versions of my great-grandmother's death, one told in life, the other in death, by the same woman.

'She died of an incurable disease, my little Jiaojiao, and it was all over very soon.'

'What sort of disease, Nainai?'

'You wouldn't understand, you are too young. Anyway, it's all fate . . .'

The disease was too vague to picture – but the sight of a terrified Chinese woman being dragged off to a dark corner by a Japanese soldier was one I had seen in many movies.

But Taro's smile banished it. He had an uncle who'd been in the army during the war, who was now a member of the Chinese–Japanese friendship association. We didn't dwell on old horror stories: we swapped notes on our seminars.

I smelt cigarette smoke. 'Ha, the expectant mother.' Bill's voice.

I winced. 'Where's Barbara?' I asked, directing the conversation away from me.

'Gone for a lie-down.' He sat next to me on a rock, the cigarette in his mouth.

'How is she?'

'All right.' As usual Bill did not want to discuss her – it was as if he was reluctant to share her with me. Whenever Barbara and I reminisced, which was often and at her initiative, I felt resentment in Bill's silence. As if he'd read my mind, he added, 'She seems to want to spend all her time in the past, these days. Let's hope it's just a phase.'

He flicked cigarette ash. 'Look at this mess!' He sounded exasperated. 'I'd lend her a hand, but she won't let me.'

I leaped to Barbara's defence. 'But she likes the garden this way.'

'You women, you're all the same, you don't understand. Gardening is . . .' he hesitated, groping for a word. Then his eyes lit up. '. . . a responsibility. You can't do whatever you fancy. Take that tree,' he pointed to the Mei behind us, 'that *Prunus*, for example. Barbara decided to chop it down a few years ago and I stopped her. Now it lives and blossoms.'

He had surprised me: why would he have wanted to preserve it? He liked to weed and uproot.

'I knew she'd regret it if she chopped it down,' he went on. 'Apparently it's an important tree in Oriental culture.'

'Yes, it blossoms in deep winter when all the cowardly blossoms hide. We say it represents defiance of adversity.'

'And such beauty. What a refined, sophisticated shape.'

Only a man like Bill would love a plant for its sophistication. Funny – the man who was accusing Barbara of dwelling in the past was responsible for the survival of the tree that reminded her constantly of China. But Bill was full of contradictions. He dropped the cigarette end. 'That's what I think. Better leave it to nature. But what about you? How do you feel?' He turned to me.

'Quite sick and confused. I don't know if I can go through with it.'

He tapped the bark of the tree. 'Don't be silly. Women do it all the time, of course you can.'

There was something brutal in his words that should have warned me not to pursue the subject, but I went on, 'It's not the birth I'm worried about, it's the responsibility. I'm not sure we are . . . Ken is ready.' Did they know we had fallen out? I didn't think so. With everything that had happened to Barbara lately it was unlikely that they had noticed.

'Oh, yes?' He raised his eyebrow. 'He doesn't know how lucky he is.' Belatedly, I realised how insensitive my remark had been. Barbara couldn't have a baby: it was a problem in their otherwise happy relationship – Bill desperately wanted a child. 'He's a nice lad, I like him. I'm sure if you're . . . straight with him, he'll understand.'

'Straight?'

'Tell him what you want, don't beat about the bush.' He was avoiding my eyes. 'Of course, you don't need to worry about anything now. Nobody would turn you away now you're having a baby.'

He had caught me out again, and this time I had no defence. How could he assume that that was what I had wanted all along – to stay here? And how infuriating that he was right. My stomach twisted as if it had been dipped in the cold water of the pond. 'What if there is no baby? What if I don't want the baby?' I asked.

He raised his eyebrows. 'Really? I wouldn't do that if I were you. Let things be. We're only human, we mustn't interfere with nature. Although sometimes nature has its own schemes of which we humans are ignorant.'

Bill's preaching about letting nature take its course was the last straw, and the contradiction snapped me out of my guilt. I even managed to laugh. He stood up and stretched out a hand. 'You shouldn't sit out in the cold like this, not in your condition.' He hauled me up, and smiled.

Why was I so reluctant to admit to Barbara, never mind Bill, that I wanted desperately to stay here?

Because I feared I might not be welcomed.

The house was quiet and dark, a refuge. When I tiptoed past Barbara's room she called, 'Mei, is that you? Come in a second.'

The room was a mess and smelt of dry dust, which made me cough. Oscar purred from beneath a heap of her clothes. She was going through some old photographs. 'Living in the past', as Bill put it. 'Come and look at this.' It was a portrait of my father drawn on a thin piece of damp-smelling paper headed 'Xiyu County People's Park'. 'Do you remember it?' she asked.

I did. It was early in their relationship, shortly after I'd first met her. She hadn't won me over, but I was intrigued by her. She had said she wanted to do a portrait of my father, and made him sit outside in our only armchair. The slanted sunlight of the late afternoon leaking through the trees caught the small insects in its beams. I sat on my bed, watching them through the window, feeling her power over him.

Barbara stared at him, then dropped her eyes to the paper. There were photographs of him in the house, formal ones in which he smiled handsomely like a film star, or the revolutionary heroes who had a clear conscience and led poor but deserving lives. All the photos we had of him were perfect. The imperfect ones had been discarded. Suddenly it had occurred to me that he might be vain. Sitting there, he smiled like his photograph.

Barbara's fingers smoothed the edge of the paper. Why was she dredging through the past? It had brought a flush to her cheek. No wonder Bill was concerned. The uneasiness I had felt earlier in the garden returned.

'What do you think? Does it look like him?'

I looked down at the portrait. The long, narrow eyes, high cheekbones, tightly shut mouth, his hands. The hands were the best bit, I thought. The hands were really him. He could hide other things, but not his hands. They were big, disproportionate to his height. But they were not fleshy: his knuckles were like the knots on an old tree. The portrait was different from the formal photographs, somehow less grand, troubled, more real.

I remembered the soft glow on her face as she worked at it. I had thought then, admiringly, that she had a typical foreigner's skin, smooth and radiant. But now I know it was because she was young and in love. She had worn her peach shirt and chatted casually with him. 'What would you do if you were not doing what you do now?' I remembered her asking. He had sneered without moving, for fear of spoiling the perfect image he believed he was projecting: 'The county government asked me to be their propaganda cadre, but I said I'd rather be a gardener.'

Somehow this had stayed with me as it must have with Barbara, for now she said gently: 'While he was sitting there, he told me his life's ambition.'

Would he have been happier as a government adviser? It was hard to say. More and more nowadays I realised how little I had known of the man I called Baba. After my mother left him, he had not lived in the same world as me. He took refuge in the glories of the past, withdrawing from the world around him; he imagined himself to be like the wise hermit who scorned the snobbery of the world, who drank morning dew and ate the herbs he gathered. He kept himself apart from the politics of the day, but read ancient literature and history with passion. This Barbara saw as idealism, which she embraced.

But there were two kinds of hermit: the one who refused to come out of the hermitage – even when the emperor burned down the woods in which he lived in a futile attempt to drive him out so he could appoint him minister – and the other, like the poet Su-shi, who 'retired' to the hills, playing for time, waiting to be invited back to power by a more enlightened ruler who would appreciate his talent.

Which one was Baba?

'It was the gardener in him I liked most.' She smiled at the portrait, then put it down. 'Have you been out in the garden? It's a lovely day.'

'Yes. Bill was there. He told me it was he who had saved the Mei tree from being chopped down. Is that true?'

Her eyes dimmed. 'It's odd. Of all the plants in my garden, that was the only one that made me feel . . . that I didn't want it. I have no idea why, it just made me feel uneasy. It's . . . nerves. Bill had read a book on bonsai and recognised it. But I would never have got round to chopping it down, you know me. I still wonder, though, why it's flowered so suddenly after all these years.'

There were colourful plant catalogues on her dressing-table

and the curious saucer-sized object I had seen before. 'What is that?' I asked.

'It's from my late aunt's collection of Chinese antiques. It arrived a few months ago after they auctioned her things. She left it to me with some other bits and pieces in her will. Quite a pretty thing, isn't it? It's a bronze mirror.'

'Can I look?'

'Of course.'

I looked at the smooth side. It was green and rusty. A window would have given a better reflection of me. 'Did you say it's a mirror?'

'In the old days they polished them, didn't they? There were tradesmen who made a living polishing bronze mirrors. Now that it's an antique, nobody dares to touch it because it will lose its value. I don't think this one is particularly precious. It's not very old, probably a Qing. Aunt Ruth's family had been in the East for quite a while. I'd not given the mirror much thought – it was her big porcelain vase that I'd set my heart on, but she didn't leave it to me.'

Her voice was near me, her face next to mine. I was reminded of my father's smell.

'But green is not the natural colour of bronze, is it?'

'No, but this was unearthed such a long time ago, maybe from a tomb. The oxygen in the air turns it green.'

I picked up the mirror and turned it over.

'There's a dragon, did you see? With big teeth and a long spiky tail. And something on the edge, like a vine.' Her voice was elsewhere in the room, but I wasn't listening. I felt the five petals. I remembered the curse of the mirror.

Tie Mei

S he lay curled like a baby in its mother's womb. She was tired all the time.

I lay like that when I was pregnant. It was a relatively happy time for me. My husband spoiled me and did everything to make me happy.

Not my mother-in-law.

I called her Niang, Mother, as was the custom, but it was difficult to love her as one. She was a domineering woman, and very young, about half my father-in-law's age. The year I was pregnant, she conceived too. My husband was their eldest child and only son; they had three daughters, but they wanted another son.

They were an unkind couple. Although they had a maid, my mother-in-law expected me to wait on her, even though I was carrying a child. In freezing weather I was made to go outside and fetch water for her and my father-in-law, then boil it so that it was ready for them when they woke. During the day I cooked all the meals and ate last, if there was anything left. 'I have to eat well and a lot,' she said, showing off her belly, while I swallowed my tears and feared for the little life inside me. I knew if I did not eat enough the child would not live. Once she caught me eating furtively in the kitchen and dragged me by the hair to bang my head on the wall so that the food fell out of my mouth. At night she'd shout for me several times to get up and fetch things, or make her cups of tea.

It was a miracle that my baby did not die. In the early months, I cried every night from exhaustion, my husband crying with me, but because she was his mother, he could do nothing. That what I hated most in him: his weakness.

After the first four months my sickness disappeared, along with the tiredness; I surprised even myself with my good health and happiness, which even my mother-in-law could not subdue. I dreamed of my own family, boy or girl I didn't care.

It was the year of the Ox and I gave birth to a boy, Jiaojiao's father. My mother-in-law had a girl, whom they called La Di (Pulling Out A Brother), after Zhao Di (Waving At A Brother), Huan Di (Calling A Brother) and Yin Di (Attracting A Brother). It made her hate me even more.

She had so much milk her breasts were dripping, but she asked the maid to bring the baby to me to suckle, even

91

though I had pitifully little. I used to pinch her baby as punishment for depriving my own of his food. My nipples were sore after her voracious suckling and my own baby cried from hunger.

Eventually I told my husband. It was the only time I saw him lose his temper. He stood outside his parents' room and shouted, 'Don't push us too much. Those with a wooden head should have heart!' It was brave indeed, but he didn't dare say it to their faces.

After that she stopped sending the baby to me but often cursed outside my room when my husband had gone to work. 'You daughter of a disgraceful woman!' she'd shout, knowing how to wound me most. 'How dare you defy your elders? Is this how that pale-faced woman brought you up? We have our reputation to think of in this family.' I sobbed helplessly inside the room. I could not understand why she hated me so.

Jiaojiao stirred, turned, her hands fell to her belly and a smile lit her face. Things could not be bad if she still smiled like that. I glimpsed my own youth in that smile. Then, I hadn't felt disillusioned with life. But then I thought of Mother, of how different our circumstances were. Jiaojiao had not only wanted to get pregnant, she had planned it. That was hard to swallow. The image of her lover seemed to hover before me.

How this man resembled the other devils I'd seen. I had felt safer since he'd left her, but now, watching her smiling in her dream, I was less secure. What if he came back? I was sure she still cared for him. Impatient, I blew cold air on her face. She opened her eyes, sat up and spoke clearly as if she hadn't been asleep: 'Nainai, I saw a mirror.'

'What mirror?'

'The bronze mirror, I saw it.'

I had wondered when she would come to it. I had been surprised that she hadn't found it sooner.

'Is that the one?' Her voice trembled. 'The curse!' she whispered.

'Yes, the curse.'

'But it can't be true . . . I mean, how ridiculous.' Her eyes regarded me intently. 'Have you known all along?'

'Since the night I found you.'

'Why didn't you tell me?'

'I thought . . .' But there was little point in trying to explain – there was nothing we could do to change this.

She had got out of bed, and as she paced the room I was struck once again by how tall she had become. Her cheeks were red and her eyes flashed. 'Is this another dream? I'm sick of these dreams. Please leave me alone. I could bear being lonely and miserable, but not this, it's too much. What have I done? I was happy that you existed, at least for me, but now . . . Oh, I wish you had never come to me!'

It was the second time she had asked me to leave, but as I turned to go her voice stopped me. 'No, no, let me think. If this is true, you're the only one who can help us.' She stood in my path, almost feverish, her arms reaching after me. 'Please, can't you do something?'

'Do what, my child?'

'Anything! Avert the curse.'

'A curse is a curse. I can't do anything about it. I'm sorry I hadn't realised the Englishwoman meant so much to you.'

'She brought me here, she's my *guiren* – the noble person you told me about!' she pleaded, and added softly to herself, 'She's like a mother to me.'

How many insults could I bear? First my granddaughter had made me forgive her for being pregnant, then she begged me to let her stay in this despicable place, and now she'd adopted an Englishwoman as her mother. Anger rose from deep inside me. 'After all I've told you, you've forgotten about the deaths of your ancestors.'

'You're manipulating me! They are two separate things.'

'For me they are not! Look at you! You feed off a rich Englishwoman and sleep with that dirty foreigner. A monkey would know more shame than you.'

'So I'm shameless,' she said, shrill and sharp. 'Well, I don't care. You're just a ghost.'

It was then that I stormed off.

6: *Li Xia* – Summer Begins

6 May

~~~~~~~~~~~~

Jiao Mei

The mid-morning tube was slow and my carriage was full of young couples and rucksacked tourists with maps, murmuring familiar names to each other: London Bridge, St Paul's and Covent Garden. In happier times Ken had shown me these places. I stared at the floor, feeling out of place.

This morning I'd booked the appointment, and now I was late for my seminar, feeling distinctly odd. The people around me remained indifferent, but the Northern Line was a womb from which I never wanted to emerge. I stared at the tube map and imagined my brain as an even more tangled web of thoughts. Three months: it was hardly anything; it couldn't have feelings; this was the time to do it. The girl opposite placed her hand on the sleeve of the boy sitting next to her, and leaned her head on his shoulder. That could have been us, Ken and I. If only I could speak to him. If only I could gather the courage to explain that my desire to stay here, which had prompted me to make that stupid decision and lie to him, and my feelings for him were two separate things. How could he doubt my love? Talking to him was my only hope, yet I felt too weak to face him. So I would deal with it on my own. I had no option but to end this shame. And then? I didn't know. All I was certain of was the rightness of this decision. Nainai would be pleased, at least – perhaps then she'd help me to do something about the curse.

A curse. It was still so hard to believe in. Perhaps it was my punishment for what I had done to Ken. I'd watched Barbara closely these last two weeks. When we were outside I scanned the street for cars that drove too close to us, for men carrying suspicious parcels with a menacing look in their eyes. I kept reminding her to wear her red belt, despite her protest that I sounded like her mother. But apart from occasional head-aches, she was fine.

The doors closed, and when I looked up again the young couple had got off. An Indian woman now sat opposite me in a bright red and blue silk sari. A man with a huge beard sat next to her, clutching a Sainsbury's shopping-bag, his eyes slanting downwards at the floor. A sombrely dressed long-limbed white girl in a black suit stood by the door swaying to and fro.

At the exit the station staff joked crudely among themselves and waved me through benignly. Posters along the wall promised a West End show, a romantic novel, mouthwatering food. A cynic or a realist would say this new world was as flawed as the one I was so eager to leave behind.

But it was all new to me. I wanted to enter each of the worlds the posters promised. There was no longer persecution at home, no prison awaited me. It was not a flat, a car or a full shopping trolley I was seeking. It was the reward of a new life. My heart lifted briefly as I walked out of the tube into the open air. I had made the right decision about the abortion. I needed to scrub out the past and start afresh.

It was late morning when I arrived at the university and the entrance hall was almost deserted. I was filled with a momen-tary sadness whose cause I could not identify until my eyes drifted to the tubs of plants on both sides of the entrance gate. I thought of my father. For all the distance between us, I was sure he would understand my sadness, he who had never put down roots. Suddenly I saw the point of his mobile garden: rootless, it could never be vulnerable. Rootless himself, he could go anywhere, be whoever he wanted to be. He did not have to depend on anything or anyone. He carried his paradise with him wherever he went, so self-sufficient, so cool and calculating.

I missed the seminars. All afternoon I sat in the library staring at the books I was supposed to read: Giddens, Weber, Bernstein, Durkheim. Would any of them help to solve the puzzles of my life? They looked at the world from a distance, through a mirror, collecting data and samples, studying them. They treated people as statistics, but they harmed no one, and were not hurt in their turn. They were no use to me now.

The tube came as a welcome break. I settled body and mind as though I'd never left it. It was a limbo – perhaps that was why I felt so at home there. One stop to go to my destination. I looked around for an ally, but people were hiding behind their newspapers or staring indifferently ahead. Doubt set in. My potential new beginning was just another day for everyone else. I began to feel more alone than ever.

I was out of the tube and Barbara's house was in sight. I shuddered at the thought of Nainai, and of how heavily the past weighed on me. It was so much a part of me – even this new life couldn't change that.

Tie Mei

I came with trepidation, full of words I had wanted to say to her last time, when she had been rude. How well she seemed: her bony body was becoming smooth and her skin supple; her face glowed, blooming. She was bearing the fruit of her love – the best time in a woman's life. But her words surprised me: 'I'm going to get rid of the baby.'

'*What?*'

'It's wrong. I can't go through with it.'

'But . . .' In my mind was the rosy picture of a fat-cheeked baby calling me 'Tainainai.' 'Surely it's too late.'

'Not if I act quickly. I'm only three months gone.' She looked at me ruefully. 'I thought you'd be pleased. Nainai, please don't make me change my mind again.'

'No, you must think carefully first.' The words spilled out of my mouth.

She looked at me with a mixture of mockery and hurt.

'Listen, child, you've already done something you regret. Don't do something you'll be even sorrier about. What about your plan to stay here? You will lose your chance of it.'

'I'll think of something else.'

She stood where she had stood when she had first called me Nainai, her back to the wall. How tall and grown-up she had seemed then. Now she was behaving as recklessly as a child. Her determination made me shudder. I couldn't rejoice in it. Finally she dropped her eyes, walked over to the open window and leaned on the sill. '*Will* I regret it?' Her child's voice.

'You know you will.'

'Oh, Nainai, there's too much for me to think about – the baby, Ken, and now what you've told me about Barbara. You don't know what I'm going through. I saw Baba die, and part of me died with him. I don't want to go through it again.' She put her fingers in her hair and pulled it – even her gestures were foreign now. 'You don't know what Barbara means to me. I'm not sure I knew until . . .'

Poor girl. She wanted to save the foreign woman but she did not want to offend me – she wouldn't even mention to me that she had lost her lover. But whatever she said or did would upset me. I could see her misery.

'Barbara has been so kind to me, and she loved Baba. You've always taught me that if I was given a drop of water I should return a fountain. How can our family do her harm?'

'If she has the mirror, there is blood on her hands. You know as well as I that I cannot undo a dying woman's curse.'

'Tell me the curse again, Nainai, the exact words.'

'That whoever comes into possession of the mirror will suffer misfortune, until it is returned to its rightful owner.'

'Rightful owner? Is that me?' She brightened.

How quick she was! But I remained silent. I knew what she was thinking, but surely it was too late for that?

'Nainai?'

'Perhaps . . .' I hesitated.

'What?'

'Perhaps your ancestor, who initiated the curse . . . but she has been dead for so long.'

'Find her.'

7: *Xiao Man* – Wheat Seeds Begin to Grow

21 May

Jiao Mei

'Honestly, darling, you've never been to the sea?'
'Never.'

'That's incredible! From what I see on the map, China's got such a long coastline.'

'We didn't travel, not for pleasure – and remember, I am from Sichuan, the most inland province. We have rivers, though, big ones.'

And so many bridges, I must have crossed as many as I had roads, I thought, as I lay in Ken's arms on the beach, the sound of crashing waves in my ears. I stayed still: not a muscle in me wanted to stir and disturb our renewed intimacy. He shifted so that he could look down at me, and moved his hand to stroke my belly. 'I can't remember what you looked like before. This is lovely.'

Like all newly reconciled couples we were tender with each other. A week ago, two days before my abortion appointment, he had turned up at Barbara's. Until then I had thought my heart had hardened – although I had lost count of how many times I had changed my mind. I slammed the door in his face and leaned on the other side of it, tears rolling down my cheeks with relief that he'd come, anger that it had taken him so long and the desire to make him suffer. How long did I stand there? I don't know, but long enough to realise that if I lost him then, I'd lose him for ever. I opened the door, fearing the worst, but was greeted by a face that seemed a reflection of my own: I recognised in it my own turmoil.

We made up. Since then we had spent every night together. 'Our baby,' he said again.

'Thank you,' I said, for want of better words.

'I meant what I said. I don't want you to say that to me.' He told me he was concerned for me, perhaps I was depressed. Shouldn't I see my doctor or a therapist? I laughed it off: everyone knew about pregnancy hormones. I could not bring myself to tell him about the ghost, but I was no longer so alarmed by it. I knew that she was my grandmother. Still, it was good to be away from the big house.

We bought crab sandwiches in the little café by the beach. It was unseasonally warm, everyone told me, smiling, as if they, too, had just been rescued from a crisis.

Ken splashed about. I dipped my feet in the water and flinched. It felt hard and strong, unlike the soft river water I was used to. So, this was the sea, bigger than the river that flowed through my town, bigger than I had ever imagined it to be. Infinite. In my home town the water was mostly still: bogs, ponds, lakes and puddles everywhere when it rained. In high summer the world around us, although liquid, was stagnant. There were rivers, and one was large, the Min, a tributary of the mighty Yangtze, but it did not flow through my town: you have to travel up the valley to follow it, through mountains and more mountains. Its rhythm was irregular, compared to the calm sea, its flow unpredictable. And there were bridges, bridges wherever you looked. The river divided and the bridges connected. It had been my fantasy, since Mama left, that one day a man would build a bridge to rescue me from my unhappiness, to allow me to leave the island I was on.

I watched the surfers coming to shore. You had to trust the sea and give yourself to it to glide like that. I took off my shoes and waded in. I was a baby held by a gentle giant. It felt so good.

At dusk we walked back to the dark green bungalow we had rented for the week. I wanted to tell Ken about my fantasy with the bridge but held back. I had almost lost him so now I was cautious to a fault. Instead I said something irrelevant: 'Could you build a bridge in the sea?'

He didn't blink. 'Well, it has been done, though it's quite a challenge. But it's funny you should say that. You know about this bridge I've been asked to build?'

Vaguely I remembered something in a park. 'The Oriental one?'

'Yes.' He grinned. 'You could be my consultant.'

'Ken, I'm no expert on Chinese architecture.'

'Don't worry, I'm not asking you to tell me how they're built. But you could advise me on the decoration. I like the idea of using lions – that would look authentic, wouldn't it? But how many?'

'I'll think about it. But now explain to me how you set about building a bridge.'

He thought for a moment. 'I'll draw you something when we get in. Safety is paramount, and . . . tolerance.'

'Tolerance? But that means understanding, doesn't it?'

'Well, you could say it means endurance, too.' Ken put his arm round me. 'Tolerance is the margin against which you take into account factors that might affect the performance of the bridge, like wind or earthquake. You have to allow for them to happen.' He paused. 'Like in people.'

'You're talking about us, about forgiveness,' I whispered.

'Understanding is a better word.'

Inside, he tried to light a fire with the driftwood we had collected. 'You'll have to meet my mother soon,' he said, his face glowing in the flames.

'What is she like?' I opened the fridge, scavenging for leftovers from yesterday's dinner which he had cooked. I couldn't stop snacking.

'English people say she is eccentric, but she just doesn't like people to take her for granted.'

'Ken, why are you such a good cook?'

'My mum taught me so that I wouldn't have to rely on a woman.' He grinned.

'Really?'

'But I'm still addicted to your food.' The grin was infectious.

Then he said, 'The only thing I have against Chinese food is that it is too salty. And the MSG, why spoil the dish with that chemical stuff?'

'Surely the whole point about food is to enjoy it at its best. Why shouldn't we make a dish even tastier?' I grew defensive.

'But it spoils it.'

I wasn't going to give in. 'For you, maybe, but for me it adds to the flavour.'

'You're too greedy.' Ah, he was playing.

'You're too austere. You won't be wanting my dinners.'

'I'll eat them even if you put poison in them,' he joked, and we were back to an easy intimacy.

'Do I take it from all these compliments that you'd like me to cook tonight?' I was cleaning the fish in the sink. He chuckled. I would have volunteered anyway. For the last few days I had not felt sick. When the water started boiling I closed my eyes over the steaming fish. It had come from the fisherman in the village, so fresh it smelt fruity. I had added only ginger, spring onion and a drop of soy sauce. All this banter, I thought, as I washed the rice, it was new. Only half an hour ago I had been nervous about what I should and should not say to him, but now I had relaxed. I turned to smile at him, but he was concentrating on the fire. The crisis had brought us closer. The baby inside me, which used to be mine, was now ours.

We left the window open so that we could glimpse the sea while we ate. He washed up and then we sat down to pore over a pile of tourist brochures he had spread across the dining-table. We hadn't been anywhere apart from the beach since our arrival on Sunday evening.

I thought of our conversation about salt. The real reason we indulged in food in China was because we had been scarred by lack of it. My parents remembered famine, what it had tasted like. I had never starved, but I had been haunted by the idea from an early age. You learned to compensate for that, to eat while you could. You might not always be so lucky.

That was the real reason, but could I tell my foreigner that? It was shameful to admit to such poverty. He had never been

to China and consequently he didn't claim to know everything about it. I did not act the role of the pretty Chinese doll,
so my own shortcomings were plain to him, but those of my
nation – I was reluctant to be open about them. It was a
question of dignity.

'There's a swannery near here. Do you like swans?' Ken
was suddenly making plans.

'Of course.'

'And lots of Hardy places we could go to – do you know
Thomas Hardy?'

'I read one book, *Tess*, in Chinese.'

'Here,' Ken exclaimed. 'I must take you to St Catherine's.'

'A church?'

'It's a ruin, a magical place, you'll like it there, and they say
you can pray for a baby boy or a girl.'

'Really? I want a—'

'Sssh.' Ken raised his finger to my lips. 'Keep it to yourself,
or it won't come true. Just tell St Catherine when you're
there.'

'We've never talked about this. What would you like, a boy
or a girl?'

'I don't mind.' Ken shrugged. 'I haven't thought about it –
it's just our baby.'

I sighed. 'You're hopeless.'

He put down the brochure and stretched back to gaze at the
sea. 'We always come here, Mum and I. For me this has been
a more constant place in my life than any of the homes I've
lived in.'

'What do you mean?'

'My dad was in the army. We moved house a lot. After he
died, Mum still couldn't settle. She loves DIY, kept buying and
selling houses. I grew up like a nomad. I think that's why I
became an architect, really. I'm used to seeing houses being
changed and rebuilt.'

'I suppose I'm a fellow nomad, then,' I said. 'I didn't live in
a proper house from the age of eleven. We lived in a shed in
the park. But it didn't make me an architect.'

'It made you my muse.' His eyes focused once more on me.

These last few days I had become so used to this: to lose his attention, even briefly, was painful. 'Are you sure you can't tell me anything about bridges? Your ancestors were pretty good at them.' He was as earnest as a little boy.

'All right, here's a story that every Chinese knows.'

'If it's about a bridge, tell me.'

I told him the story of the Magpie Bridge.

'Slow down a bit, Mei, I can't keep up. So this poor boy was prevented from getting to his beloved by the wicked mother-in-law? And they had a baby?'

'Yes. All happy Chinese stories end with a baby, a son preferably.' I laughed, and flaunted my belly at him. 'But this story goes beyond that. It's about reunion, about what happened after the lovers were separated.'

'That's us, darling.' He winked at me.

I giggled. 'Do you want to hear the end of the story or not?'

'All right.'

'The magpies came to the rescue. They clustered together and formed a bridge so that the shepherd could climb up to meet his beloved. Happiness birds, we call them. They reunited the lovers and allowed them to cross between their worlds.'

He was quiet, but he gazed at me unblinkingly.

'But they could only be together once a year, on the seventh day of the seventh month, I think. I've forgotten. I'll ask Xiao Lin next time I see her.'

'Gosh.' His eyes twinkled. 'I'd better build mine properly.'

Later in bed I smiled to myself when I remembered how Ken's face glowed as I told the story. His enthusiasm had given it freshness, as if it had never been told before.

Tie Mei

A still night, and I was remembering. The feeling of the hot sun on my skin, the taste of a fresh fish, the quick beating of my heart as the sound of my silk dress caused young men to look back in admiration. I was vain then and these were frivolous pleasures, but they meant a lot to me. In the end, they were the only satisfactions I had from that life.

But why had I allowed myself to become distracted from my purpose? The devil must have got into me when I pleaded with her to keep the baby. A fat little bundle who would crawl over and address me as 'Tainainai'. I was a fool if I had been tempted by that. But of course there had been more to it: concern for her. I knew what it was like to lose a baby.

It wasn't like me to be so compromising. Jiaojiao was my blind spot. Her vulnerability disarmed me and now I had to watch her growing big with that foreigner's child. I had to bide my time and take my chances. It wouldn't be easy to get her back, now that she was keeping the baby.

The sight of her naked body sleeping next to the foreign man made my eyes burn. I left in a cold rage, filling the room with my scent.

'Nainai.' I was in a room with a long table that smelt of food when I saw her emerge from the room where I'd been. She wore a long gown, obviously his. Sleep was still with her, her cheeks warm and red. 'I forgot you were coming,' she said, looking guilty. 'How did you find me?'

'Your smell guided me. How did you think I found you in the first place?'

'Forgive me, Nainai,' she whispered weakly, 'for being so impolite.'

As if I was a strict grandmother who cared about rudeness! Her look of guilt touched me, though. I smelt fish, I smelt every ingredient that had gone into the sauce. 'That fish must have tasted good,' I said, relenting.

She smiled. Then her eyes opened wide. 'Do you know what I miss most? Your steamed rice cooked with lotus leaves.'

Small pleasures. I had cooked her that as a treat in Beijing when I could get hold of fresh leaves. In Sichuan, they were everywhere in the lakes. The rice would be stained jade green by the leaves; the parcels melted in the mouth, and it was like swallowing a bit of summer. I sighed. 'What I wouldn't give for a bowl of rice like that?'

She tiptoed closer and sat down next to me, one hand habitually on her belly. A silent moment or two passed before she coughed and said, 'What was it like, carrying Baba?'

'Heavy.'

'And?' There was an expression of peace and tranquillity on her face that had not been there before.

'And I had to run errands for my mother-in-law.'

She closed her eyes. I had told her of how badly my mother-in-law treated me. Then, daughters-in-law had been the lowest in the pecking order. All mothers-in-law took advantage of it, but that woman enjoyed making me suffer. I didn't mind that she was rude to me, but she had insulted my mother and I could not stand that. She had waged a sustained, everyday campaign of small cruelties that had added up to something more.

'But she didn't come to a good end,' I added. 'When the Communists came she was made to sweep the floor wearing one of those newspaper hats that they made denounced landowners wear to humiliate them in front of their former tenants.'

Silence.

I didn't know what to make of her silence. I stared at the cutlery lying on the table like a new chess game I didn't know how to play. Every time I was with her, I learned new things about her, and came away with new tactics to win her back. What was this new calm in her? There was strength in her silence. In her reconciliation with the young devil she had gained a confidence she lacked before. She used to shout and scream at me, and I almost preferred that – I understood her anger and frustration. The hardest thing to swallow was that he seemed to want her, to care for her, and she wanted to be with him. I swallowed my pride. 'Have you met his parents?'

'Not yet. He's only got a widowed mother. But don't worry, we won't live with her.'

'I'm still concerned for you, Mei. I know he cares for you now, but what about later?'

'Who knows about the future? What's the point of thinking so far ahead?'

'You never do think, do you? You have to consider your future. You're all alone here. Can you trust these foreigners?'

'I'll manage.'

She rose, planting her feet on the doorstep – I'd always told her not to do that when she was a child. 'Don't!' I shouted, then stopped myself. Old habits die hard.

She smiled at me mischievously. 'You used to say crows would snatch me away if they caught me on the doorstep, and it always frightened me – like so many other things you told me when I was little. But I'm less afraid now, Nainai. I think it has to do with being a mother. I am not afraid for myself any more.

'Nainai,' she came nearer, 'did you find my ancestor?'

I shook my head.

When I left her the last thing I saw was the vivid green wool with which she was knitting. A jumper for the baby? I was good at that. I was good at sewing too, mending socks, trousers, shirts . . . bruised knees and broken hearts. In that life I was a mender.

It was still early and the sky was dark, not the pink of the London night. Loneliness gripped me as it often did just after I'd been with her – and I was homesick. It was the smell of that fish, the shape of the two young bodies clasped together, their warm flesh, and her pretty young face. I was homesick for my own youth, reminded of my garden in the first few years of my married life.

The first year after my son was born my father-in-law decided to move the whole family from the small northern town where we lived to the south, to Sichuan where the family home was. He had long wanted to do this and the final push came when the headmaster at my husband's school was arrested and executed by the Japanese for 'anti-Japanese propaganda'. They said my husband was next on the list, even though all he did was teach the children poetry about how beautiful our country was.

That journey took the best part of the year. We left the north in the summer, and witnessed such horrors along the way: the Japanese had taken Shanghai, Nanjing, Guangzhou, then Wuhan, raping and massacring along the way. Our own nationalist army withdrew, surrendering our land and people to the invader. Most of the population of China seemed to be on a journey similar to ours. La Di, my husband's youngest sister, grew sick on the way, and died. We slept by the roadside, prey for bandits. Wild dogs fed on the bodies of the dead.

When we arrived, my father-in-law pressed his face to the door-knob of his ancestral home, sobbing and laughing.

Our house was on a large family estate at the edge of a town near Chengdu, where his family had lived for generations. It was reached by a small stone bridge at the end of which was an impressive black-painted gate, carved in red with the characters for the name of the house, in the hand of my husband's great-great-grandfather, who had been an important imperial official. Behind the gate a fan-shaped brick wall greeted guests with a big character of 'Happiness', which I thought ironic. Happiness was the last thing one felt in that oppressive household, even though, after the long, arduous journey, there was in all of us a sense of peace and belonging.

There was an open space immediately after the wall, a *tian jing*, or heavenly well, planted with bamboo; beyond this was the ancestral hall and the sacred altar, where we worshipped my husband's ancestors. Incense was burned and there was always an air of smoky mystery about it. I did not feel comfortable there, and was hardly ever allowed near it, apart from at festival times.

The garden was at the back of the house. At first glance it was a strange place: a huge ginkgo tree grew in the middle. A small bungalow stood next to a neglected well. There were a few plants, a wilderness of weeds, bamboo and a few fruit trees with bare branches. We were told we were to stay in the bungalow, my husband and I.

My mother-in-law did not like to come to our home: it was too bare, somehow unsettling, she said. She even suggested to her maid, who later confided to me, that she thought it was haunted and that those who lived there would fall ill. Rumour in the town had it that its previous mistress had drowned herself in the well, which was why flowers grew around it so abundantly.

My husband started working in the nearby school and I became the gardener. In the far corner facing south I planted Meis, whose winter bloom brightened my days and made me think of my happy girlhood in the north. At the Spring Festival we took large sprigs indoors to let their fragrance scent the rooms. Nearer to our bedroom I planted the Yueji, monthly roses, which bloomed purple from late spring until late summer – they were easy to pick as they had no thorns.

In no time the garden became a paradise. I let the wild bamboos grow and they stood as if guarding the stone wall, but the roses and the Meis were my pride and joy. I looked after them as if they were my children. When spring came I often sat alone in the garden breathing in the fragrance, day-dreaming. Now that my mother-in-law had stopped harassing me, I had more time to reflect.

One day in late spring my husband brought home a colleague, a man whose voice made even the flowers tremble; he dressed so casually that my old-fashioned mother-in-law withdrew indoors in protest. When he caught my eye I stuck my needle into my finger, but did not notice the pain. I was innocent, still looking forward to what life had in store for me.

8: *Mang Zhong* – Wheat Seeds Ready for Harvest

6 June

Jiao Mei

O nly another half-hour to go before I had to finish. The cloud disappeared and a ray of sunlight bathed the room, as if to emphasise the importance of the moment. Outside the traffic flowed; inside the air was static. A sudden flipping of papers, someone felt desperate, but it was not me. This was my final paper. Tomorrow I would be free. No more exams, I had decided. I wasn't a natural student. Sociology is a science, and my response to life was not scientific, especially now.

A young man called Zhang Tie Sheng became a national hero in the seventies for handing in a blank paper after his university entrance exam – he had meant it as a protest, and was hailed in the newspapers as 'a real representative of the proletariat'. He had since been exposed for what he was: a Red Guard who had spent his years idling in the countryside. There was nothing heroic in what he had done: he was simply a bad student.

I thought of him as I left the hall. But there was Ken, holding up a bunch of lilies, to give me a hero's welcome. He'd got the flower right this time but I didn't deserve it. 'I've done badly.' I frowned.

'Sssh,' he said. 'Don't think about it now. I know you've done your best.'

At the noisy Japanese noodle bar, we sat at a long table,

113

served by trendy young people with walkie-talkies at their hips. For a moment I was full of remorse: I hadn't earned this. I hadn't done all I could. In the exam hall I had felt justified, but now I felt regretful. What of Barbara, who had enabled me to study, who had brought me all the way over from China? What about Nainai, who had had such high hopes for me? If I hadn't come here to study, why was I here at all?

But for the time being I wanted to idle, to drift. I wanted to take life by the hand and see where it led me. I knew Ken would understand, but I felt I owed Barbara an explanation.

It had been a bit of a jolt, returning to Hampstead, after the holiday Ken and I had spent together. I was 'jumpy', as Barbara had put it. I noticed the usual creaks and groans of the old house more than before, and my edginess annoyed her. But nothing untoward had happened to Barbara. It had been paranoia on my part.

'My place?' Ken said. I nodded. Tonight it would be good to be away from Hampstead.

We took the bus. I saw London differently with Ken. He was my eyes, and through him buildings came alive with their history. We sat in the front seat on the top floor of the double-decker and sailed into the City, eerily deserted with its neat, high buildings. The contrast of giant glass windows and grand classical pillars set in unpeopled streets was haunting.

Everything that happened here, the coming and going of thousands of workers, the buying and selling of fortunes, the thrill of a successful deal, was represented in these empty, eerily lit buildings. Classical, Gothic, post-modern – Ken pointed at them and named the styles, which sounded foreign and exotic to my ears. I looked at everything with the new eyes of the converted. It was as different a world from mine as could be and my incomprehension was part of its attraction.

Ken rented a room in a house he shared with two students. To the left, their neighbours were an extended Turkish family, who also ran the corner café; to the right, a young English couple were starting a family. The Turkish family's door was always half open, with their four young boys running in and out, mostly on errands to the café round the corner. I loved the smell of food when we walked past. Their door was shut now. I could hear television and laughter, though.

I rang Barbara to let her know I wouldn't be home, and heard Bill's calm voice informing me that she was well and happy – of course she was. I heard the note of weariness in his voice, and put down the receiver, cheered for a moment by the existence of people like Bill, who were immune to 'silly fantasies', as he would put it. It had surprised me that he was there, though – normally he only visited at weekends. Perhaps he found his flat in Edgware too bare and unwelcoming.

Ken's house was peaceful, but not as dark and quiet as Barbara's. Occasionally the sound of a guitar would creep out of one of the students' rooms. Ken had to go to work the next day so he went to bed early. I made a cup of tea and read the messages pinned up on the board: 'Ken's turn to empty the rubbish,' one said. A postcard stuck on the fridge was signed 'Sara', the previous lodger who'd since moved on to live in India.

I sank into the soft old sofa. On the opposite wall there was a framed picture of Buddha and a poster from a temple in India. It was a house I could relax in: here I was just one of many people who passed through, and the mood was less intense than it was in Hampstead where Barbara and I had too much space. Ken liked Hampstead, the area, and Barbara's house: 'It's full of atmosphere,' he said.

Too much atmosphere, I thought.

The phone rang, and I took a message for someone and pinned it on the board. Through the open window I heard the shouts of the boys next door. Two of the Turkish brothers served at the corner café – they did English food and kebabs. Sometimes Ken and I went there for breakfast. The thinner, taller brother was my favourite. He had a gentle smile. Ken said he was a Communist, which made me feel closer to him, as if he was part of my circle, although I had nothing to say about Communism. It was not something I had chosen to believe in: I was born to it. But these people had chosen to be Communist in a non-Communist state, and had been persecuted for it. They had left their homeland and come to settle here, as refugees.

My tea was cold. I poured it away and washed up the mug with the others in the sink. I glanced again at the messages on the noticeboard. I recognised Ken's handwriting, neat and small, the note decorated with one of his doodles.

Tolerance. An architectural term. A bridge had to be built with 'tolerance' so it would withstand impact. How clearly he had described it and how considerate to equate it with 'understanding'.

I was going to be Ken's wife.

The proposal had come on the bus just as we drove past St Paul's. At the threshold between light and darkness, between the City and the East End, he had whispered in my ear, 'When do you think we should get married?'

'Are we to marry?'

'Now that you're carrying my baby, I think yes.'

'Even if . . . even if . . .'

'There is no "if" because that's what we're going to do.' I couldn't say a word so I nodded hard. Ken grabbed my hand. 'So say yes.'

'Yes what?'

'Yes to marrying me.'

'Of course. Yes.'

A middle-aged woman was sitting behind us on the bus, clutching her shopping-bag, dozing, and two young people at the back were buried in conversation. Ken turned round and shouted, 'She said yes!' The young couple looked at us – the man clapped and the girl smiled – but the lone woman frowned. 'We're going to get married,' Ken said to her. She blinked, smiled an embarrassed smile, and shrank back as if she couldn't understand him. 'We're going to get married,' Ken repeated, and the woman turned her face to the window.

The double bed was old – Ken had picked it up from a tip. It creaked as I eased myself on to it.

There was something about the faint hearty laughter of our Turkish neighbour that made me think of my mother. I must write to her, now that I was going to have a baby and marry

Ken. I had her address but had never written to her before. In my childhood I often wrote to her secretly and, when my father or Nainai upset me, planned my escape to see her. I'd spend hours packing my things but even before the next meal I would have made up with Nainai and Baba. On one occasion I almost succeeded in reaching her, but I got off at the wrong bus stop and lost my way. A policeman found me, and escorted me home.

Mama never wrote to me. I'd seen her twice since she left, at my father's funeral, and at the airport when I left China. On both occasions she came with her new husband and spoke to me as if I was a distant cousin. But as I was about to join the queue to check in, she stepped up and grabbed my hands. After she had gone I found a piece of her old jade necklace in my hand, still warm from her body. This was what made me believe that she might like to hear news of my pregnancy. Her new husband, not the one for whom she had left my father, was a silent man, but I believed he treated her well. He was a high-level cadre.

In the darkness I tried to picture her face and could only conjure up a much younger one, the one I saw in photographs of her and my father in the Suzhou gardens, where he had taken her for their honeymoon. They posed beneath a purple haze of wisteria, or in front of bright red azaleas. Mama was always holding an umbrella to shade herself from the sun and her smile was innocent, with no hint of the worry that her face had betrayed when I knew her.

The trouble had begun when I arrived. I had always wondered why my parents had split up. 'Clash of inharmonious characters' was the reason cited in the divorce document. I didn't believe it. I had never seen them quarrel, let alone fight.

I stroked my belly, the baby inside it. Study and academic achievement had never mattered less to me than now. I tried to feel the baby's heartbeat, separate from mine, but Ken's clock ticked louder than the rhythm I was trying to trace. I tried to concentrate. Time slipped away fast. Then slowly but powerfully, as I sank further into darkness, the threat of the curse returned to me. So many ifs ran through my mind: if Nainai hadn't turned up, if Barbara hadn't been given that particular present by her aunt, if my father hadn't met Barbara, if Barbara hadn't arranged for me to come . . .

Tie Mei

S o many different odours. So many people drinking, idling. That house, that room made me feel uneasy, with its huge poster of life-sized people with strange hair and rings in their mouths, ears and noses – it used to be my idea of hell.

Her men were different from mine. In my life I either looked after them or looked up to them. They were never my equals. I looked after my husband and son, I cared for them, but I did not pour out my heart to them. I poured out my heart to Zhi Ying but he did not reciprocate.

I had been proud of my *nuhong*, my embroidery and sewing. In the small town where I grew up, my embroidery was sought after. My mother had taught me to sew and also told me what the symbols stood for. A peach meant love; a fish, prosperity; and a Mei, uprightness, the essential quality in a woman. Now in the south, with a garden of my own, I set aside my embroidery and became a gardener. My fingernails were dirty and my back ached, but tending my plants gave me such pleasure that even my mother-in-law couldn't dampen my spirits.

But I never learned to read – women weren't meant to be educated, although things were changing. I envied those women who could, but my husband never encouraged me; he was old-fashioned in that way.

Then, one day, he brought home a colleague who admired my flowers. It was summer and I brought out chrysanthemum tea to them. They were sitting by my rosebush.

'Sister-in-law, you hide spring here, in your roses,' the visitor said, in a full, low voice. I blushed at his compliment – no one, including my husband, had ever complimented me on my flowers, even though they meant so much to me. I

118

stole a glance at the stranger. He was dressed in a white silk shirt with a button missing at the top. It made him look less scholarly, more like a labourer – it was the sort of thing my mother-in-law hated, but it didn't bother me. He was a little older than us and his forehead was wrinkled while my husband's was as smooth as a baby's. He had a northern accent that made me feel nostalgic. 'I see you are wondering about my accent. I am from the north,' he said.

'Oh, no, I recognised it straight away. We used to live there,' I told him.

'I left my parents there, with the Japanese.' He lowered his head.

I thought of my mother, and my heart warmed to him: it was as if he was my older brother.

'What is your name, sister-in-law?'

'Tie Mei.'

'Which character Tie? Iron or sticky? Can you write it?'

'Your sister-in-law does not know how to write,' my husband cut in. I blushed again, it was something to be ashamed of, but my husband continued proudly, 'She is just a housewife.'

His friend didn't smile with him. 'What does your Tie mean?' he repeated.

'It is iron.'

'Then it is like this. Look.' He dipped his fingers into his tea and wrote on the table. I watched his fingers: they were delicate and beautiful. He asked me why I had been given that name, and I told him it was our family name: all the girls had names ending with Mei. I was touched: my husband had never asked if there was any significance to my name, let alone taught me how to write it.

That night I couldn't sleep. I can't even write my own name, I thought. When my son grows up he will laugh at me for my ignorance. Surely as the wife of a teacher I should be able to read and write. When I thought of that, I became angry with my husband. I nudged him, fast asleep with his mouth open like a frog. 'I want to learn to write,' I whispered in his ear.

He rubbed his eyes and murmured, 'Go on, then, but let me sleep.'

Now Mei stirred and got out of bed. I followed her upstairs to the bathroom. The moonlight was strong and she didn't switch on the light. When she looked at herself in the mirror I went closer. Her eyebrows were drawn together as if something was worrying her. She pushed aside her fringe and I saw her high, wide forehead – a sign of intelligence. 'Do you know, Mei, you are the most learned of our family?' I said to her. For some reason she seemed unhappy about this rather than pleased. I followed her downstairs.

She sat cross-legged on a sofa, which bounced, and looked at me intently. 'Did you . . . ?'

I shook my head. I knew what she meant.

For a while neither of us said anything. A train rattled by, making the air vibrate. 'Nainai, was my study very important to you?'

'I should think it's very important to *you.*'

'Not any more. Since I've been pregnant, I've lost the urge to learn – well, at least from books.'

'How can you say that?' I raised my voice. 'It's the most important thing. Knowledge gives you power, and a woman needs that.'

Again, the gleam of impatience in her eyes. 'There are things I need to learn that aren't in books. I need to do things my way now.' The message was blunt, but her tone was gentle.

'I've learned the hard way. If you'd been through what I had . . .'

'However far I get, it's never enough for you. Just because you couldn't learn when you were young, it doesn't mean it has to be as important to me.'

I turned away from her. There was a poster on the wall behind me that showed three girls of different colours, white, brown and black, their teeth radiant white, their arms round each other's waists. Their vitality oppressed me, as did hers. I felt small and old. Then I heard her voice behind me: 'I'm sorry, Nainai, but please stop criticising me. It has been

wonderful knowing you like this, in your youth, but sometimes you talk like a bitter old woman.' I turned to face her
and her eyes met mine. 'I'd rather you were my friend than
my *nainai*,' she murmured.

She was asking the impossible. I could change my clothes
and even my appearance, but never my heart. I could try to
be young, parts of me *wanted* to be young, but memories
blocked my path like Mount Tai.

I stared at the row of incomprehensible books by the wall.
'Can you imagine the shame of being twenty-one, a mother,
and unable to write my own name?'

'But happiness doesn't depend on that. You'd been happy
before, without being able to write, hadn't you?'

'Content, perhaps, but it's like . . . After I first saw electric
light, I never wanted to go back to darkness.'

I remembered the first time I had had a book of my own to
read. The day after I told my husband I wanted to learn, he
came home with a brand new book and dropped it casually in
front of me. 'For you,' he said, in a self-satisfied way.

'What does it say?' Awed, I smoothed the cover and smelt
the paper.

'*The One Thousand Elementary Words for Women*. Zhi Ying
edited it.' My husband grinned. 'He asked me to give it to
you.'

Zhi Ying taught me, later on, when we were alone, in my
big wild garden, to read the first sentence in his book:
'Women and men are both human.' I remembered the
moment each character made sense to me. 'Look at this,'
he said, pointing to the character for 'human'. 'See how
this stroke curves to the left and the other to the right.
They indicate the legs, for that's what distinguishes humans
from animals – we alone stand upright. You know,' he
looked me in the eye, 'that's what you – we all – have to
do, stand upright, respect ourselves, because we are our
own masters.'

It was a moment I never forgot. 'Do you remember the joys
of reading your first words?' I said to Jiaojiao.

' "Long live Chairman Mao", you mean?' She peered at me.

'That?' I fell silent. Her time and mine, how different they were.

'Nainai, I've written to Mama, telling her about my pregnancy.' Then, more tentatively, she added, 'Would you tell me why Mama and Baba divorced?'

'Clash of characters. That's what it said in the documents, isn't it? It makes sense, his arrogance and her . . .' I hesitated, unable to find a word to describe my daughter-in-law. She was so quiet, so introverted, that I had never got to know her well. I remembered my son begging me to come to their house because he and my daughter-in-law were at loggerheads, and he thought I might be able to help. What a naïve son. When I arrived she had already gone and he never fully explained to me what had happened between them. He can't have been easy to live with: stubborn, self-centred, conceited. But he loved her. I knew the signs.

'Clash of characters? As far as I remember, they were always glued to each other. Baba might have been cold to others, but with Mama . . . Nainai, you said you'd be honest with me now.' She looked at me suspiciously, but I was telling the truth.

'I know no more than that. But had it not been for their divorce, you and I would never have known each other so well. I remember coming to stay with you in Beijing after your mother left, in that courtyard house that you shared with three other families. It was spring and the pagoda tree was shedding its white blossom.'

'When you arrived, wearing a blue top with butterfly buttons, with those delicious nuts in a big sack, the boy opposite our house laughed at you and called you *"tu lao liang"* – silly peasant – and I knocked him down.' She said it proudly, suddenly animated.

The air around us warmed, and we moved closer to each other.

9: *Xia Zhi* – Summer Arrives

22 June

Jiao Mei

After lunch, despite her protests, Bill sent Barbara to bed. But when I came down from my bedroom to make tea I saw her in the garden again, sniffing the roses near the wall by her studio. It was a curious sight: she was so close, eyes closed, that her nose touched the petals, motionless as if she was posing for a photograph. Then she opened her eyes and looked around as if to check that no one was watching. I hastened away from the window.

As I made tea I saw – no, *understood* the whole scenario out there. What I had witnessed was private grief. The expression on her face spoke of a loss she could not put into words: she could not smell her beloved roses at their most fragrant.

There had been hints of this before, a couple of times we had even talked about it, although she had been evasive. And I had been left with lingering hope. But now I had no doubt – I recalled the odd things I had noticed before: when she had used too much nutmeg in the mushroom soup, when she had complained that the lilies lacked fragrance. Scent meant so much to her: it was her reward for gardening and cooking.

I had always imagined the curse would manifest itself in some dramatic event, but lately I had suspected that it would be less crude. It might take the form of illness rather than an accident. But I had no way of proving my suspicion. Anyway, she had seen three different doctors who agreed that the problem was hormonal – she was going through the meno-pause.

I had tried talking to Bill about it. What I had wanted to convey was my feeling that Barbara needed to be protected. But faced with his cold, rational gaze, I could not speak words like 'premonition' and 'nightmare'. He seemed reluctant to talk about Barbara's health with me. It was a matter for the doctors. She can't smell anything? Well, that happens with a cold. Anyway, she'd never mentioned it to him: 'It's her migraines I'm worried about. We're seeing a new doctor who's been highly recommended.'

Headaches, physical pain – he could relate to that, but not to a numbness in the nose.

When Bill had entered the room I was torn between wanting to pull him to the window and point out her distress, and to distract him so that he wouldn't see it. I felt that Barbara needed privacy.

What came out of my mouth was unexpected: 'It's a longing, you know.'

'What?' He frowned and stared at me. Barbara was making her way back to the house.

'I think she's homesick for China,' I said quickly.

'Oh, yes?' From the flash of impatience in his eyes I realised he thought I was talking about my father. Bill knew about him and Barbara: she saw no reason why she should not mention my father to him. Embarrassed, he nodded. 'Well, better get back to the lawn.' He turned and hurried out to the front garden.

I went upstairs with a cookery book I had taken from the shelf by the stove.

When I came down again Barbara was sitting alone with a mug of coffee, her eyes fixed absently ahead of her. She yawned. 'Mei, shall we take a picnic on to the Heath? Bill's gone fishing – he won't be back tonight.'

She strode ahead, clutching a hastily wrapped cheese sand-wich, and was briefly interrupted by a rucksacked tourist asking directions. As she paused I caught up with her. When we turned uphill, I pointed to the glistening white Admiral House, which resembled a ship. 'Ken said the architect probably lived in a plain house himself, like a dentist who never wants to talk about teeth.'

She nodded, but said nothing. As usual, she led the way, up the crossroads by the pond, zigzagging deftly through the busy lunch-time traffic. At the entrance to the path leading down to the Heath she waited for me. I saw her mouth open but couldn't hear what she said as a lorry drove past. 'What did you say?' I asked breathlessly, when I was standing beside her.

'Ken tells you a lot of things, doesn't he? Do you say, "Yes, Ken, yes, Ken," all the time?'

Maybe it was her tone, or the warm air, but something made me want to chase her, and she broke into a run, down to the green embrace of the Heath, down the slope through the wood until we were in the open meadow. At last I caught up with her and pinned her down. Her heart beat against mine, as it had years before, when we were both younger. It had been muddier and hotter then, in the park. It had just rained, the air was damp and I could smell her sweat and saw its tiny pearls on her forehead. That day we had been glad to be away from my father. He had been especially 'scholarly', as Barbara had put it. She had chased me, wrestled me to the ground, and sat on top of me – she was stronger than me then – a childish gleam in her eye. 'I haven't done this for ages, not since I was a girl with my brother. Oh, Mei,' she had said breathlessly.

'I don't have a brother or sister,' I had said.

She had hugged me. 'Don't be sad, little sister. We'll look after each other.'

Barbara's eyes glistened again, beneath me, but the twinkle was weaker now. 'You must meet my brother one day,' she said, and I stood up slowly.

We stopped at a bridge where two lean, tanned cyclists also rested, watching the water. 'Truth be told, Mei,' she turned to me, 'I was joking about you and Ken. Even when I first knew you, you were the most independent Chinese girl I had ever met. You did not giggle and were not afraid to speak your mind. It was refreshing.'

Independent? I had never thought of myself as that, but I knew I had always been a loner and that I had a mind of my own. Independent? I threw stones into the water absent-mindedly.

'I'm glad, really glad, you're staying, Mei. I've always wanted you to, you must know that, but it had to be your decision.'

I carried on throwing stones. I didn't know what to say. But inside some tight knot undid itself – this was what I had wanted to hear. And I longed for her to say it again. I needed to know that I was welcome to stay. Just as it is important in China to urge a guest to eat more and more, it was important for her to press her invitation on me again and again. Stay, please, do stay, you are most welcome. I knew it was a formality and I knew now that in her heart she wanted me to stay, but I still needed her to spell it out, to save my Chinese face.

'Mei, are you listening?' Her face smiled, open like a giant waterlily.

'What?' I stepped back.

'I was saying,' she continued to grin, 'that if you don't stop throwing stones, you'll turn the river into Mount Everest.' Our eyes met, and we burst out laughing.

'Barbara,' I said slowly, rubbing my hands, which were covered in dust from the stones, 'do you mind if I stay here but don't continue with my studies? Because . . .'

'You do whatever you want. It's your life, and I just want you to be happy,' she said. 'But what will you do? You could work as a teacher, or a translator. Or you could be a gardener, like your father. I'm sure you'd be good at that.'

She was so unconcerned about my studies. To think this had bothered me so much! I told her about Ken's proposal.

'Have you set the date for the wedding yet?' she asked.

'No.'

'Do it soon, before the summer ends.'

Suddenly the space around us felt emptier. I looked round:

the cyclists had gone and we were the only two people on the bridge. Why had she said that? What did she know – or was this just enthusiasm? I peered at her face: it was calm, unrevealing. A shadow crossed an otherwise happy moment. During the day I didn't think of Nainai much, even less on a sunny afternoon like this. I shouldn't let it linger.

I said we had to talk about the wedding with Ken's mother, whom he was seeing this weekend. I suspected she was against our marriage.

'Oh, to hell with her! You're perfect for each other.'

When we got to Kenwood she collapsed on to the lawn. 'OK, I'm not going anywhere now.' She lay spreadeagled and closed her eyes. 'Help yourself to the sandwiches,' she murmured, and flung the parcel at me. I caught it, then looked around for a bench. I found one and sat down to watch the kites and children kicking footballs around us.

I stared at the sandwich in my hand. *What about you?* I wanted to shout at her, but it was meant for me: she was used to packing sandwiches for me. Since I'd been pregnant she'd decided I needed to eat constantly, and I did, but not cheese sandwiches. I looked at her and the picture of her sniffing the roses was before my eyes again. I knew now that I would never mention it to anyone, least of all Bill. I turned my face away from her, trying to relax, looking down at the grass beside my feet. I could never lie on it: it was such an English thing – or was it a Barbara thing? – to do. The idea appealed even less now that I was carrying a baby. What if I or the baby caught a chill? And yet, as a girl, I had wrestled in the mud. Barbara had made me do it, lie in the mud and enjoy it. My father had scolded me when he saw us, but she made him relent and smile. I had thought then that that was how English people were, relaxed, natural, unlike the Chinese who hid their feelings and naked bodies. Now, in England, I realised that China had made Barbara relaxed – China was an escape for her. Or perhaps it was simply that she was in love.

A bold squirrel and a scruffy-looking pigeon were eyeing the sandwich in my hand. I stood up, went over to Barbara and touched her arm. She opened her eyes. 'I was wondering, do you know whether it's a boy or a girl?' she asked.

'I don't care. Look, Barbara, I should have told you this a long time ago, but . . .' I pointed at the sandwich in my hand '. . . I don't like cheese, and I don't much like bread either.'

'Don't you? Give them to the birds, then.' She waved vaguely. It had taken courage for me to say it, but my embarrassment hadn't registered with her. I threw the sandwich to the squirrel and the pigeon and was about to go back to the bench when she sat up and said, 'I also wonder who it will look like. Might it resemble Yuan Shui? You can never tell.'

'Or my mother,' I said. 'Some people say I look like her, and I have her height.'

'I've seen photographs of her. She's very beautiful. Is she in touch?'

'No, but I've just posted her a letter.'

'That's good,' she said briefly, then smiled. 'She must miss you. It's odd, isn't it, that I've got you now? But I'm not complaining.' She winked, and I moved closer to her. 'It's a funny thing . . .' her fingers were pulling at the grass '. . . I've been having weird dreams lately. I dreamed I was back in the park with Yuan Shui. You were not there, it was just the two of us alone. He looked different. Not like he did when I knew him, you know, totally different, like he'd . . . changed identity or something, but somehow I knew it was him.' Her eyes glazed over; she was lost to her dream.

I felt a chill creep up my back. 'What were you doing?'

'I was just pottering around, weeding, I suppose, and he was waving to me, but I couldn't hear what he was saying. I got the feeling . . . No, he was waving quite frantically, like you do when you want to warn someone but they can't hear you . . .' She stopped.

'It was just a dream,' I murmured, but something heavy had thudded inside me. Everything around me seemed to shrink and withdraw. Even the grass seemed a fainter green.

'I've had it before. Always it's me and your father, he's waving at me, from far away, and we're always somewhere different in the park.' She laughed. 'Perhaps he wants to see me again, too.'

I could not laugh. I looked up at Barbara, whose cheeks were flushed. It was hard to tell what she was feeling. Alarmed? Pleased? Maybe he had cared for her, after all. Only they knew the truth.

For dinner I cooked the beancurd I had bought in Chinatown, with eggs and plenty of salt. For once Barbara added still more.

The familiar silence descended between us, the sound of knife and fork too audible. Today, though, it was comforting and homely – I was enjoying being at home with her, without Bill. As I thought about her dream I also felt strangely uplifted. I liked the idea of my father being a comfort to her.

And I was going to do my bit. I ate silently and heartily. When my mouth was empty, I said, 'It's going to be my birthday soon, Barbara.'

'Oh, yes?' She turned to me, a bit puzzled, I thought, because I had brought it up. 'Is there anything in particular you wanted as a birthday present?'

'As a matter of fact, yes.' I paused and swallowed. 'There is a bronze mirror that I saw once in your bedroom, I . . . really liked it, and I seem to remember you saying you don't care for it.' I could hardly breathe.

'Well, you shall have it.' She smiled. 'I'm glad you love it. You're right, I've never been fond of it, and it is Chinese, so it would be appropriate for it to go to you. I'm pleased you suggested it.'

It had been so easy. She was used to giving me things.

Tie Mei

It must have been the moist air in this land that was making my thoughts wander. What might I have been were I not a wandering soul? Something inanimate, perhaps: stones or dust. Or what about a plant – a tree or a flower? They feel the elements: the wind, the sun and the rain. Through my gardening I had developed an empathy with them. To be a plant, you would need to know your place and be happy with it.

In her garden a fragrance stole up on me. It was a rose. I went to it like a bee. The air was damp and warm – the best for smelling roses. It was leaning on the brick wall, the dark purple of its petals bled with dew. I needed its fragrance for survival as I had needed his words then.

'This rose reminds me of you,' he had whispered one night in my ear. 'Fragrant, but without thorns.'

I had a weakness for flattery, and somehow words acquired a magic if they were taken from poems, which I suspected his were. Like a caress, they made me melt.

Jiao Mei was sitting in her room with a book by her side, calm, as she was the last time I saw her. I sat down on my usual chair, beside her, facing the window. I tried not to look at her body, all curves. The brown circles around her nipples had darkened and thickened. There was a pleasing glow about her.

She saw me and jumped up. 'Nainai, is that you?'

I had changed from my usual long *cheormgem* into a sleeveless red shirt and a knee-length blue skirt. My long hair flowed down in a plait, tied with a piece of red ribbon. The outfit was far ahead of my time – I had copied it from a poster in my memory.

'Oh, Nainai, Nainai.' She stood squarely before me, her toes placed evenly on the carpet, unashamed and lively. 'I wish I could hug you. Tie Mei.' She cocked her head to one side: 'May I call you Tie Mei?'

I was shocked to hear her use my name, but pleased too. I nodded slowly. It was one thing to match my clothes to hers, but quite another to change my attitudes.

'In my day girls were not meant to read and write.' I pointed at her book. 'Housework and motherhood were what we aspired to.' I was still using the old preaching tone, but I couldn't help it – I didn't think it would come between us now. 'I learned to read and write because of a special man.'

'Who?' She sat down on the mattress.

'A friend of my husband, a teacher. The man who taught me how to write my name. I tried to persuade Wen Ting and my parents-in-law to let me go to the school. My mother-in-law agreed, on condition that I caught up with the housework every night after I got home.'

I remembered my first day of school. I had felt as if I had wings and that if I flapped them I would fly. I was not only going to a place I revered, I was getting away from my mother-in-law. I changed into a plain blue student's dress and put on a large pair of shoes, even though my feet swam inside them. I held my head high but I must have looked old: all the other girls were much younger. They giggled and pointed at me but I didn't care.

They put me in the elementary group with the youngest. I put my hands behind my back like the little ones and watched the words being written on the board by the teacher, who was the man who had taught me to write my name. Tears came into my eyes. I loved his voice, I loved his hands moving delicately across the board.

'Tie Mei?' Mei said, and added, 'You were miles away.'

'Tie Mei . . . that was how my teacher addressed me, "Tie Mei", the same emphasis on Tie, the same gentle, expectant tone, as if he'd known me all his life.'

'And this man, your . . . teacher, did you love him?'

Shocked, I nodded, but I couldn't say more. Love was not the word we used then.

She waited, and when I still didn't say anything, she shuffled closer to me. 'The first English book I read was called *Stories from India*. It was a present from Barbara.' She said the name hesitantly, as if it might upset me.

But I was in a good mood. 'That must have been after I left you. Was she around much?'

'Yes. It was at the park where Baba worked. I wasn't sure of her at first – in fact, I made life hard for her to start with – but she taught me English whenever she was there. Baba taught her *t'ai chi chuan*. Then they fell in love. Oh, Nainai, I never believed then that he loved her, but now . . .' She stopped mid-sentence to gauge my reaction. Part of me was pleased with this reverence, the other part regretted it: I just wanted her to chat with me. I smiled encouragingly.

'Barbara was naughty. She made a garden behind Baba's back and when he found out he was furious. They'd criticised him again, and he screamed at her.' I could well imagine his fury – he'd been a bad-tempered child: their only grandson, my parents-in-law had spoiled him. The Englishwoman must have cared for him to put up with that.

'Wait a minute – the garden the Englishwoman made, where was it?'

'At the western end of the park, by an old well.'

'And a ginkgo tree?'

'Yes – how do you know?'

'Just a guess,' I said. Now I knew I had been right.

'It was a funny place. Barbara loved it – she said it was a paradise for her. But I never dared go near it at night. When the wind blew the bamboos made a sound that was almost like someone crying.'

My little girl crying.

'It was hard work for her, so many wild bamboos to uproot by herself, because Baba refused to help her – to begin with, anyway. He lectured her instead.'

The Englishwoman sweating in my garden. 'What happened to it?' I asked anxiously.

'It died after she left as Baba refused to touch it. The bamboos must have long grown back.'

That was better. I couldn't bear the thought of my garden being tampered with by that foreign woman. A ruin was how I had left it, a ruin was how it should remain.

Jiaojiao rattled on: 'Anyway, Baba would lecture her so. He could be so self-righteous. He was better at lecturing than you, Tie Mei – or, rather, much worse.' We both laughed. 'Baba loved an audience, especially an adoring one. He thought he was the Zhugeliang, the clever strategist, but there was no Liu Bei to spot his talent. He was a jade buried in the snow.'

'What did he boast about?'

'You know the sort of thing that interested Baba. The

glories of Chinese culture, how China once had an empire, what an accomplished civilisation it was.'

We were two giggly girls laughing at a man: my son and her father. The years had disappeared, we were friends, my granddaughter and I. I was amazed by how easy it was to tell her about the part of me no one else knew of, the part of me that the Lord of Hell condemned as unfaithful and wicked.

But later, as I stood in the Englishwoman's garden recalling our conversation, I realised there was much that I could not bear to tell her . . . not yet.

10: *Xiao Shu* – Small Heat

7 July

———◈———

Jiao Mei

Peckham, south London – another country, according to Barbara. I was on my way to meet Ken at Xiao Lin's wedding party. I hadn't seen him for a week. I wondered what his mother had said about us. On that side of the bridge the views were not as pretty and the buildings not as pristine. Even the sun dimmed after I had crossed the Thames.

The party was at Andy's new house. His first wife was there, too, with his son and daughter: she was a middle-aged woman with plucked eyebrows and golden earrings. Andy was handing round Chinese sweets, which I gathered was a wedding custom Xiao Lin had introduced.

'Andy, come and meet my friends Jiao Mei and Ken,' Xiao Lin shouted. Despite the heavy makeup, which made her face shine, she looked tired and drawn. She sneezed frequently. Allergies, she had told me, the afflictions that came upon Chinese immigrants after six years of living in England. 'It's my body telling me I should go home. I don't know why I'm still here.'

After six years abroad? I laughed it off. You could never entirely believe what Xiao Lin said. And I would be different. I didn't know where my sense of superiority over Xiao Lin came from but it was as stubborn and natural a conviction as Xiao Lin's that she should stay in England at whatever cost.

Andy and I had met once but he did not remember me.

'Ah, Xiao Lin's friend, excuse me,' he said, and thought for a while. Then, 'Knee how, is that "hello", or have I said something rude? I'm afraid my Chinese could do with improvement.'

'Congratulations,' Ken said, and shook his hand.

We squeezed through the crowded kitchen to get a drink and pick at a plateful of spring rolls and dumplings, all made by Xiao Lin, as Andy proudly proclaimed, then went to the garden.

'I wouldn't let my fiancée do the cooking for our wedding party,' Ken said to me.

'But Xiao Lin probably insisted.'

'I think he's exploiting her.'

'I'm sure she doesn't mind. She's getting the most out of him in her own way. Let's not argue about it.' Ken should have heard how Xiao Lin talked about Andy. Now they were married, it was her money they were saving, but I did not know how to tell him this.

'So, what did your mother say about us?' I asked. We were sitting on the lawn, which was filled with people. A few red lanterns hung, startling, against the brown fence. Xiao Lin's equally startling red silk dress clung to her curvy body.

'She wants to meet you.' Ken gulped his drink and frowned. 'Is this Chinese wine? So sweet.'

'Wine should be sweet. Why should you want to drink bitter things? Life is bitter enough already.'

'Sometimes, Mei, I don't know whether you're joking or not. Do you mean you're not happy?'

'I never felt better.'

'But you are happy, aren't you?' And he added hesitantly, 'With me?'

You are the truest and most solid thing in my life, Ken, I thought, but didn't say.

Xiao Lin's shrieking laughter made us both look at her. She stood next to a much taller man, gesticulating, wrapped in her red dress like a ball of fire. She leaned close to the man, who bent backwards, perhaps to avoid her, but smiled at her. Her words reached our ears: 'You bad, you bad.' She rolled her

136

eyes at him and her hands twisted his arms in accusation.

We all used body language when we were not sure of our English, but Xiao Lin seemed to do it more than most. Her language was childish when she talked with men. She could speak better English than she sometimes chose to.

Ken hugged me quickly and whispered, 'I'm so glad you're not like her.' I didn't reply.

In late afternoon we got off the bus at Waterloo, tempted by the light on the river, and walked along the South Bank. We sat on a bench. A few feet away the pavement was engraved with a poem. The creamy-coloured buildings opposite caught the dusty light. I didn't know much about them, all I could articulate were impressions, and even those were vague: grand, foreign, magnificent and, above all, open.

'Whoever said London was at its best in rain was wrong,' I said. 'Look at the light on those glorious buildings.'

Ken nodded enthusiastically. 'Some of our real heroes have been architects and engineers. We had the best engineer in the world, Isambard Kingdom Brunel, the man who built the Great Western and Eastern Railways, and designed the Clifton Suspension Bridge.' He explained patiently to me the principles of suspension bridges, and turned the conversation to the smaller bridge he was building. He had a surprise for me, he said.

We crossed to the north side of the river and I discovered that, close up, the buildings that had glistened from over the water no longer looked so magical. I was disappointed – reluctantly, secretly. I wanted this new world I was entering to be perfect and I was finding fault with it already.

'What are the public spaces like in China? There must be quite a lot of them.' Ken was curious about my country. His eyes rested briefly on the buildings we passed, but I knew he wasn't really looking at them – they were too familiar. 'Mei, did you hear me?' He nudged me.

I laughed. 'Public spaces in China? I should know all about them. I lived in a park, remember.'

'I was forgetting. So when the park was shut you had it all

to yourself. It must have been heaven.'

'Not really. In fact, it was rather frightening. In China you're used to seeing people everywhere. It is the places without them that make you feel strange. The Chinese for "park" is *gong yuan*, public garden, but it didn't feel like a garden to me.'

'I must see it. We must go there together. Let's spend our honeymoon in China.'

'I wouldn't want to go to China for my honeymoon. It's not a light-hearted place for me. I'd rather go to Europe, some-where new and peaceful.'

'But it's where you come from, and I'm interested.' He looked at me. 'You're making it seem less magical than I want it to be.'

'I have to remind you that it can be tough.'

'You forget that I'm a Londoner.'

In the windiest corner at Embankment we said goodbye and headed our separate ways. Sitting alone in one of the old, worn carriages of the Northern Line I remembered the last words he had whispered to me: 'Take the right-hand lift up in Hampstead.' Or had he said left? One of the two was nearer to the entrance and I never remembered which. He was a careful man who noticed details, I thought, as I had many times before. Something to do with his professional training. I liked his ability to separate real life from things that were less tangible. I needed a sceptic like him, I needed him, solid and trustworthy, like water and rice, to sustain me.

At Leicester Square a middle-aged Chinese woman got on, laden with shopping from Chinatown. Something in the way she moved reminded me of my mother, although I was sure Mama would have been insulted had I told her that. Why hadn't she written to me? The more I thought about it, the more sure I was that the divorce had had nothing to do with the 'clash of characters' cited in the documents, as even Tie Mei agreed. In those early years we had all been so close. If I was with my mother I'd be looking for my father, if with him I'd want her. That must have had something to do with my premonition that we were to be separated, and that I must be the glue that held us together. Then, they were teachers at the agricultural college, always in the greenhouse, so hot and humid, full of plants as tall as or even taller than me. I had wished then that I could grow faster and taller so that I could see what they were looking at, their heads almost touching, and hear what they were whispering. I couldn't believe there had been any lack of affection between them.

'Gone out for dinner, don't wait,' said the note in Barbara's handwriting on the fridge. I ate quickly. What would I do in a long summer evening without Ken? It was still light outside so I took a book down from the shelf and headed outdoors.

I stood in the middle of the garden, and breathed in deeply: honeysuckle – how much could Barbara capture? A bird called loudly. I looked up to see where it was perched. Things would get better. I'd asked for the mirror and she'd promised to give it to me. And I was reassured by the thought that my father might be watching over her, too.

I went into the pavilion and sat down on the wicker chair, with a blanket round my legs. I picked up the book but read erratically, distracted by the sounds around me. Was someone calling my name? I straightened up and listened, but hesitated before I replied. Nainai had warned me against answering the calls of strangers – wandering spirits call the names of the living because they want their souls. If you are foolish enough to answer, yours will be taken.

I was mistaken. Someone was walking their dog in the street: I heard the dog yap and a man's voice respond. He spoke in a low murmur, and he used words I hadn't heard before. I puzzled over them, repeating the familiar ones: had I heard this word before – here or in China? Perhaps Barbara had taught it to me in Sichuan.

When I looked up again darkness was gathering in the trees, and the flowers around me were blurred. A cool breeze made me gather the blanket tighter round me. This was the dangerous time when I was on a threshold, when my English world bordered on the Chinese, my world of night, of dreams.

This was the world of Tie Mei, who had let me glimpse her

youth. Once again I saw the girl in the red shirt and blue skirt, who revered the written word and had fallen in love with her teacher. She was like a tree, whose shade was the love I had taken for granted. Now I had got to know her. But my mind was troubled. How could she be any more than a product of my paranoid mind, born of homesickness, loneliness and yearning? No one else had seen her, and though the fragrance seemed real enough, it was hardly proof of her presence.

Tie Mei

'Jiaojiao,' I whispered, but she did not answer. I tried again, but still there was no response. She looked small wrapped in a blanket. So careless of her to fall asleep outside like this. But when I caught the fragrance of the flowers I understood why she had.

I went to check the rose, the Yueji, still in bloom. The Englishwoman was good with plants. I thought of Zhi Ying, a garden always reminded me of him. Once, on one of our class outings with him – sometimes we went out into 'nature', as he called it, to paint and draw – I fell into a ditch, full of spring mud. The others laughed at my clumsiness, but he jumped in to rescue me. 'Are you hurt?' he asked, and took off my socks to examine my feet – which even I was ashamed to look at. He turned on the giggling girls: 'Don't laugh at her! You don't know the pain she had endured. It's the custom you should ridicule – it tortured women. You don't know how lucky you are.'

No one had said anything like that before. Later, my parents-in-law and my husband criticised his dangerous Communist ideas. But that day his words to me were like music – he was talking about my suffering. I wanted to cry, but I never cried in front of other people so I struggled to stand up. For a moment I felt brave and special – I, who was twice the other girls' age, who sat at the back of the classroom with the tall and the misbehaved, and whose child had to be brought in for breastfeeding between lessons.

I worked harder. I worked at night. When I had done the washing-up, and mended all of the shirts and socks left out for me, I poured cold water on to my face to keep me awake. Then I went into the little room where the wood was kept and lit the oil lamp. I was careful not to make a sound or my mother-in-law would have scolded me: 'Don't waste precious oil, go to sleep. Whoever heard of a woman studying so hard, the daughter of a disgraced widow at that? Do you think you'll be chosen as a *xiucai*, the number-one scholar? Is our house too small for you? We have our reputation to think of!'

Then, I was bullied so easily. I felt inferior and unlucky. If it had not been for the encouragement of Zhi Ying and his books, I don't know how I would have pulled through. It seemed to me then that my only salvation was to learn, and this man was giving me the opportunity to do so.

The first letter I wrote to Zhi Ying was a sick note. I wanted to surprise him: 'Respected teacher,' I wrote, 'I am ill therefore I am asking for a day's leave.'

The next day he came to see me with some of my favourite prunes – I had no idea how he knew I liked them. As soon as he saw me he said, 'So, you are still alive.'

'Of course.'

He took out my sick note. 'Come here, Tie Mei, let me show you something.' I came closer. 'First, it was good calligraphy and I can see how hard you've been working, but . . . according to your note you have died of an illness and you're asking for leave for a day.'

'What do you mean?' I snatched it from him, frowning.

My husband, who was with us, took the note from me. 'You used *gu* in a position where it would mean "death" rather than "therefore", you silly girl.'

I had had no idea that *gu* had another meaning. For a long time my neck blushed red and I did not dare look up.

'Come, Tie Mei, don't be shy, it's quite funny, don't you think? We're glad you're still alive.' They laughed good-humouredly and finally I joined in with them.

Somewhere in my heart a stream of warmth had opened

up for Zhi Ying: he was like the father I'd lost all those years ago, kind, learned and witty. From then on, whenever he saw me, my teacher would clear his throat and say: 'I am ill, therefore . . .' I laughed with him and, in those days, my laughter was light.

I enjoyed those long, lonely nights in my garden, reading the books Zhi Ying gave me, tales of female warriors who were new to me. How different they were from the heroines I had learned about from my mother, who waited on their in-laws for years while their husbands went in search of fame and younger women, or cut flesh off themselves to feed their starving parents – filial daughters and devoted wives.

Zhi Ying's heroines were powerful in themselves. They fought to defend their honour and for their independence; they fought to defend the country against invaders. They fought injustice. Some were prostitutes, concubines, ghosts and spirits, despised and feared. I fell in love with the flower fairies, free spirits who dared to love and hate. I knew many of these stories by heart, but it was only with Jiaojiao that I'd shared them.

My thoughts turned back to her. 'Jiaojiao,' I called again.

Her eyes opened a crack. 'Nainai,' she whispered, 'it's story-time, isn't it?'

'All right,' I murmured. 'I want to tell you the story of the peony and camellia fairies. Once upon a time a young scholar called Huang Sheng was lodging in a monastery. The temple was surrounded by a garden with many peonies and a tall camellia tree. On looking up from his desk one day he thought he saw through the flowers a girl in white and another in red, but when he rushed outside there was no one to be seen. He was forlorn: for he had been so struck by the beauty of the girl in white that he had fallen in love with her and couldn't get her out of his mind. He thought of her all day and was overjoyed when, that evening, she strode into his room.

'She told him her name was Fragrance, and that the girl in red was Conquering Snow. When Huang Sheng expressed his admiration for her the girl confessed hers for him. Overjoyed, they embraced and swore never to be parted. From then on, she came every night. They composed poetry, played chess and did together all the things that lovers do.

'But one night Fragrance came with tears in her eyes. "I'm sad because we're about to be parted."

' "Why?" Huang Sheng asked.

' "It's our destiny. We can do nothing about it," Fragrance cried. When he pressed her, she shook her head and cried more. She left the next morning, distraught.

'Huang Sheng was puzzled. But later on that day a man visited the monastery, saw a white peony and fell in love with it. He dug it up and took it home with him. Only after he'd gone did Huang Sheng realise what Fragrance had meant: that she was the peony. He was desolate. Every day he prayed for her to come back, but soon he heard that the peony had withered and died.

'Heartbroken, Huang Sheng went to the hole where the peony had grown and wept as if it were her grave. He wrote sad poems and read them aloud, and his tears fell upon the earth.

'One day, as he paid his usual respects to his beloved he saw a girl in red weeping not far away from him. It was Conquering Snow. He turned her to him and they cried together.

'Night after night, when Huang Sheng could not bear his sorrow, he would only have to call and Conquering Snow would come to comfort him. But when he went home for the Spring Festival, he had a dream in which Conquering Snow pleaded, "Come quickly to save me. I'm about to suffer great misfortune. Come quickly before it's too late."

'So Huang Sheng abandoned his banquet, mounted his horse and hurried back to the monastery. It turned out that the monks were building a house and were about to chop down the camellia tree, which was blocking the way. This time, Huang Sheng knew what to do and stopped the carpenter, who was about to swing his axe.

'That night Conquering Snow came to thank him and

143

Huang Sheng said to her: "If only I had understood what Fragrance tried to warn me of that day. I could have saved her, too, but . . ." Conquering Snow suggested that they go to Fragrance's grave together to mourn her.

'Several nights later when Huang Sheng was alone in his study, Fragrance walked in. Overjoyed, Huang Sheng rushed to take her hand. He was puzzled because he grasped nothing. Fragrance told him that although once she had been a flower fairy, now she was a flower ghost. She told him of a secret mixture of herbs with which he must water her grave every day so that she might live again.

'The next day Huang Sheng went to the place the flower had been and saw a peony seed. He planted it, watered it with the mixture, and built a wooden fence to protect it.

'For a whole year he and Conquering Snow watered the peony seedling and watched it grow stronger. Then in the spring when he came to the garden he saw it had a new bud. In no time the flower had blossomed. Huang Sheng kept close watch over it, day and night. When it grew to the size of a plate a fairy was sitting right in the middle of it. Soon she flew down and grew to the size of a normal human. It was Fragrance.

'Huang Sheng was so delighted that he didn't want to go home. He decided to settle in the monastery and become a monk. By now the peony plant had already grown as strong and wide as an arm. Huang Sheng often pointed to it and said to Fragrance: "When I die, my soul will rest here, and grow to the left of you."

'Some years later, Huang Sheng suddenly became ill. His son came to cry at his bedside. Huang Sheng said to him, "Why are you so upset? This is the day of my birth, not my death. There is nothing to be sad about." He turned to the monks and said, "After I die, you will find a red seed beneath that white peony. Plant it for me. A plant will grow with five leaves."

'And by the next spring, there was indeed a strong seedling sprouting beneath the white peony. The number of leaves was exactly as Huang Sheng had predicted. The monks were greatly surprised and watered it diligently. Three years later the plant had reached a good height, but it never flowered. One by one, the older monks died, and the younger monks did not know the story of the plant. They chopped it down because it did not flower. Soon the white peony and the camellia had withered too.

'Jiaojiao?' But again she'd gone back to sleep, just like the old days.

On my way out, I caught sight of a small clump of flowers I recognised. We called them *fengxian hua*, Flower of the Phoenix Fairies. The flower was full of blood-red juice, and in China we had squeezed out the juice to paint our fingernails. There were a few in my garden, and I remembered once painting my nails before going to meet Zhi Ying. What a surprise to find them there! They were well tended. How careful the Englishwoman was.

I was falling in love with her garden, in spite of myself. People are different, but plants do not change.

11: *Da Shu* – Big Heat

23 July

Jiao Mei

'You should have come ages ago,' the young female doctor scolded. I lay meekly on the narrow bed and stared at the startling posters on the wall, warning of diseases. On the shelves behind her there was an orderly display of bottles and boxes. A photograph of a young boy with a missing tooth beamed at me.

'You are well into the second trimester. I'll arrange a scan and we'll have to do some blood tests.' She frowned and wrote something down. Trimester, scan and test: it all seemed so impersonal, but instead of feeling alienated, I felt safe and snug. I was being properly maintained, like a new car.

Later I joined the rush-hour traffic. I was wearing Ken's T-shirt and wished he had been with me to see the scan. Seeing the pumping heart of the little life on the screen had made it all the more real. I had asked the technician whether it was a girl or a boy: 'I'm not meant to tell you because we can't be sure,' she said, 'but between you and me I think it's a boy.'

I knew she was right. Tie Mei had predicted that.

Had she really come last night, or had I dreamed it? In my dream she had told me the story of the peonies and the camellias. The first time I heard that story I had cried because everyone died but now I appreciated the friendship between Huang Sheng and the fairies, and I was happy for the lovers,

147

for the strength and endurance of their love, which even death could not destroy.

When I saw Bill bending down in the front garden I slowed my steps. He'd taken a week off to be with Barbara, whose health had taken a turn for the worse. She wasn't in pain – well, she said she wasn't – but seemed lethargic and unusually quiet.

It had not been easy living with Bill's constant, silent presence. At times I felt as if I shouldn't be there. With Barbara mostly in bed, the two of us spent our days avoiding each other, me in the back garden and he in the front. We were only together for meals.

'Hello,' I muttered, as I passed him. He was concentrating on a strange new tool, a long, spiky implement with which he was poking the already lush, tidy lawn. A cigarette dangled from his mouth.

Barbara was nowhere to be seen so I started preparing lunch. What day was it? Wednesday? No, Tuesday. Bill would be here for another five days. Perhaps I should go to stay with Ken. I bent down to get at the potatoes and heard his footsteps, first to the shed, heavy with the tools, then returning, lighter, towards the house. He'd go straight up the stairs, as usual, I hoped. But, 'Jiao Mei.' His voice echoed in the empty house. 'Are you cooking again?'

'Yes.' I faced him.

'It was delicious what we had last night. What was it, that soft squidgy stuff?'

'Tofu – beancurd,' I said, surprised and flattered.

'What are you cooking today?' He was by the sink now, washing his hands.

'I think I'll stir-fry some potatoes with cabbage, a little chilli and soy sauce,' I said.

'Do you use potatoes a lot in your country?' He turned: his eyes were as calm as his voice.

'In the north, yes, especially in winter. Potatoes and cabbages are comfort food for me. I was brought up with them.'

'I had a lot of them when I was a child.'

'Where did you grow up?'

'In the Midlands. Do you know where that is?'

I nodded as I peeled the potatoes. He leaned by the sink, watching but not offering to help. 'My mother used to grow vegetables in her backyard. She grew a lot of potatoes,' he said, staring at the pile of peel. 'You're right about potatoes being comfort food. After the factory I worked for closed down I got fat eating potatoes all the time. It was Mother's fault, feeding me like that.'

When he'd stopped speaking I realised that his voice had captivated me. The tone in which he usually addressed me was sarcastic, but this low, confiding whisper was more like the way he spoke to Barbara. His voice was a small window through which I had glimpsed something of Bill's past.

'But what happened then?' I asked gently, touched by his show of vulnerability. I rinsed the potatoes in the sink, and he sat at the table.

'Well, I trained as an engineer. I was the oldest in my class at uni.' He was defensive now.

'And how did you meet Barbara?'

'At one of her portrait exhibitions, after my wife divorced me,' he said simply.

'When was that?'

'Three years ago – today is our anniversary. I'm taking her out tonight, and then on holiday to Spain for a change of scene. Don't tell her, it's a surprise.' He leaned forward and put a finger to his lips conspiratorially. 'I'm sure she's forgotten again.'

So that was why he was in such a good mood. He was more romantic than I'd thought.

'But some of my friends then never stopped eating potatoes, never got their lives back on track.' For some reason he had returned to our original subject.

I threw the potatoes into the hot oil. 'But mine are different, they're stir-fried, not deep-fried.' I turned to him. 'So they won't make you fat.'

'Jiao Mei.' I glanced up and saw Barbara standing on the stairs. She looked as if she'd just got out of bed.

'Darling,' Bill said, going to her, 'come and have some lunch. Doesn't it smell delicious?'

She shook her head slowly. 'I don't feel like eating. Mei, you can eat for me – eat for three today.' She headed back up the stairs.

We ate in silence. Bill gobbled down a mountain of food – eating for two himself. Then he sighed and stared at what remained. 'I'll take that up to her, try to tempt her.' At the stairs he turned back: 'That was delicious, very wholesome. It would do her good to eat some.'

I went out to the back garden and weeded. I enjoyed the work in the garden more as my pregnancy advanced. The urge to bend down was strong – apparently it prepared you for labour. My legs got stronger, like big bamboos rooted deeply in the soil. When I was sweating so much that my face was dripping, I sat down before the rosebush. I thought of my conversation with Bill.

Divorce, unemployment. I had thought he'd led a charmed life. Through the open door I could hear him on the front lawn, coughing gently, sending a waft of cigarettes in my direction. The man who trimmed his hedges ruler-straight to mark out his territory was a man of mystery. I liked so many things about him: the scent of the cigarettes he smoked, the affection and devotion he showed to Barbara, but he was so hard to reach.

A new fragrance distracted me. I knew this garden too well now for it to escape me. It came from my left, near the studio. The lilies. I stepped cautiously towards them. The white of their petals was darker than the white door of the studio and vivid next to the red of the roses, their fragrance more open and flamboyant. After all those days of tending them, picking out the slugs and laying crushed eggshells at the base – Barbara had not wanted to use slug pellets – two had bloomed. I had to tell her. She had to see and smell them, especially today, her anniversary. On impulse, I leaned forward and plucked the smaller one.

Indoors, Bill looked up from his newspaper. 'You shouldn't have done that, she'll be upset.' He never mixed the outside and indoor worlds. You'd never catch him with a flower picked from the garden – there was hardly anything to pick in his bit anyway.

At her door I paused. There wasn't a sound. Was she asleep? Although I had chosen to ignore them, Bill's words had impressed themselves on me, and reminded me of her secret pain. Was it cruel to remind her of her loss?

I stepped inside the room. At first glance I was struck by the whiteness of her sheet, echoed in the petals of the flowers I carried.

She was frowning. 'Mei, you never change, do you, you naughty girl? You shouldn't have picked it.' But her tone told me she wasn't angry. I moved the flower away from her as she stretched out her hands for it. 'What's it called?' She was quiet for a moment. 'Baihe – oh, Jiao Mei, how could I ever forget?'

The lily had been the sign that I had accepted her as my father's lover, the new woman in his life.

The breakthrough in our relationship had come with that mud fight we had had in the park. She had played with me as if she was a friend of my own age. No Chinese auntie would ever have done that, and neither would many Chinese girls of my own age. Her spontaneity had won me over.

Then there had been the trip to Songpan, in the middle of the summer holiday. My father was assigned a business trip to this town, near the Tibetan border, to identify some local plants, and he took Barbara and me with him. It was a 'holiday', Barbara had said, and that was when I had learned the word in English.

We saw the lilies from the bus. At the sight of them she had screamed like a three-year-old, 'Lilies! My favourite flowers! They're everywhere.' She hugged me. 'I want them, I want all of them, heaps of them.' The bus followed the river Min, which became violent and joyful the further north-west we went. Clusters of villagers tempted us at each roadside stop with nuts and fruit – irresistible to a girl growing up in a town. My father scolded me for encouraging them, but Barbara got off the bus, bargained hard, and came back with their goods. We stuffed ourselves.

We had a business letter of introduction to the town's government official, who looked at Barbara curiously. 'A botanist sent from Beijing's Institute of Nationalities.' Baba had tried to sound casual, but he was not good at lying and blushed at his daring. When he mentioned Beijing, even I was impressed. In a small town, anyone from Beijing, even a street-cleaner, had the status of a local mayor.

It had puzzled me then that nobody suspected Barbara was a foreigner. It might have been because she spoke good Chinese, but later I realised that, in this border town, there were people of all kinds: Huis, Tibetans, Yis, Hans, even a Thai. Such was the racial mix that they must have thought Barbara was just another minority among them. Nobody there had ever seen a westerner before, or so I thought.

That night Barbara and I stayed in one dormitory room, segregated from my father, in the guest-house and chatted deep into the night. Later still as I watched her sleeping face next to mine I decided to make up for my hostility and give her a present. But I had no money.

The following day when we climbed the hills and saw the lilies all around us, I had an idea. I'd gather her an armful – she had said that they were her favourite flower. I set about plucking the lilies, which covered the hills like grass. I sweated, was stung and scratched, but was absorbed by my fragrant task. When I bent to breathe in their perfume, I decided they were my favourite flowers too. Then I looked for her to present her with my gift.

But Barbara and my father were nowhere to be found. I knew they were around somewhere, but I couldn't see them.

Then, suddenly, they seemed to spring out of the tall grass not far from me. I handed the lilies to her. She closed her eyes and inhaled. 'They're heavenly,' she said. 'What are they called?'

'Baihe,' I said. 'A Hundred Embraces.'

She hugged me. 'What a lovely name. I shall never forget it.'

'Baihe,' she murmured now. For a moment I almost believed she could smell it.

'Did you know I wasn't the first foreigner to go there?' She hauled herself out of the bed, clutching the lily in one hand and her dressing-gown with the other. Her eyes wandered round the room, looking for a vase.

'Where is your red belt?' I asked.

She looked down at herself and smiled apologetically at me. 'Oh, I don't know, I can't find it.'

'It's important you keep it on all the time.' I was suddenly cross with her.

'I will find it, I promise,' she replied, almost childishly, and swiftly changed the subject. 'Do you know about this foreigner who went to Songpan?'

'No.'

'He was an Englishman, E. H. Wilson, a botanist. He went there in 1856. They called him Chinese. He said Songpan was his favourite town in China. Regal lilies originated in China and it was near Songpan that Wilson picked his samples. We have him to thank for bringing them to England.' She laid the flower tenderly in her palm.

As the fragrance wafted to me, it had a cold edge. I thought once more of the curse of the mirror. It was not always a good idea to delve into the past.

Tie Mei

There was a new scent in the house. It came from the Englishwoman's room, a mix of flowers and sweaty bodies. The air had moved violently there just before I came in. I smelt the strong odour of the man, the lingering sweetness of the woman but there was something in her smell that was not sexual – something submissive, a surrender. I no longer confused her scent with Jiaojiao's, but I was surprised by how acceptable, even pleasant at times, her scent was to me.

I found my girl upstairs, her fragrance young and everlasting. She was holding something transparent. 'Tie Mei, come and look at this. Can you see? This is his head, and this, according to the technician, is his finger. He's sucking it.' She pointed at the blurred image. 'Do you know what this is? It's a picture of my baby inside me. They told me it's a boy, as if I didn't know it myself.' A pause, then: 'I wonder what he'll be like.'

I looked closely at the picture. To think of being able to see that! How different her world was from mine.

I'll never forget the first time I saw electricity. It was that late-summer afternoon when I first visited Chengdu with my teacher. I cannot remember how I persuaded my parents-in-law to agree to let me go. Perhaps I told them it was another study trip. I felt reckless and my heart beat fast like that of a young bird. This was the most daring thing I'd ever done, going out alone with a man who was not my husband. I felt like one of the characters in the books he'd lent me. We sat in his favourite tea-house: it was not one of the ordinary ones, filled with men, the people here were young couples, like us, vibrant, excited – and in love, I thought.

The tea-house was perched on a stone bridge and we were in the upstairs room. The window was open and we could see boats on the river. Immediately below us, labourers sipped their tea, squatting on low bamboo stools. They held huge fans, which sent the whiff of their sweaty bodies up to me. Boys zigzagged through the crowd bearing baskets of water-melon seeds, peanuts and cigarettes. I peeped at the young girl students nearer to us, dressed simply in blue cotton skirts and no makeup, but with a look of independence on their faces that I admired. I took all this in greedily, as if these sights were part of the treat he'd arranged for me. He belonged to this world, which I could not reach, shut away in the house of my in-laws. I moved towards him, but Zhi Ying gestured to the centre of the room.

A blind man in a long grey robe and a pair of dark glasses appeared, his hand held by a small boy. The glasses drew my eyes to him, but it was impossible to read his expression. He hunched his back slightly. When they reached the middle of the room, the small boy let go of his hand and left the blind man alone. The tea-house was still bustling and I thought I was the only one watching him so closely. Maybe the others had seen him before but it was all so new to me.

He sat down on a stool and picked up a bamboo *erhu*, the Chinese violin, in one hand and a pair of thin pieces of bamboo, the size of Zhi Ying's palm, in the other. He coughed and straightened. All sound around us ceased. In the silence he opened his mouth and I heard a sound, like a stream of water entering a vast, dry valley. It grew bigger and bigger, and soon filled the valley with its welcoming, liquid embrace. It was a story he sang, about how a girl was sold as a prostitute when she was young, and how she fell in love with a young scholar who had promised to marry her and treat her well. She trusted him but he betrayed her and she killed herself. Afterwards she came back to haunt him and his new wife.

I was not conscious of the tears falling down my cheeks until they wet my hands. The clapping of the pieces of bamboo had taken the rhythm of my heart with them. Now I saw that the singer's face was lit with emotion. It was a sad story, but somehow I felt uplifted. How could a stranger articulate so well how I felt? It was as if he understood me, and was saying to me that my suffering was not in vain.

The world downstairs disappeared, the world of my in-laws too, and that of my husband. There was only my teacher and I, and the story the blind man was weaving around us. It was dark outside and in the tea-house, and in the story as well, for the girl was in hell, being tortured.

Then, suddenly, all was brightness. I was blinded for a second, as if the light had hit me, and looked up at a tube on the ceiling. I had not noticed it before. I ran outside to check that it was indeed dark, then back inside to stare at the tube again. My teacher smiled and shook his head. Young couples were pointing at me, giggling, but the blind man carried on singing – the brightness meant nothing to him. Embarrassed, I sat down. I felt like holding the singer's hand and describing the light to him. I wanted to tell him how beautiful it was, like his story. I wanted life to be as bright.

Of course I had heard of this new thing called electricity, but it was the first time I had seen it. I held my teacher's hand tight and felt that we must be invincible in our bright new world. Nothing could separate us, nothing could harm us. He was my electricity: in teaching me to read and write, he had brought light to the darkness of my life.

'Tie Mei, you're away in your thoughts again.'

I turned towards where her voice had come from in the darkness. 'It feels to me as though something has changed in this house. There's a new fragrance.'

'The lilies?'

'Maybe it's not a smell, but a change in the atmosphere.'

'Aha! It'll be the truce between me and Bill.' She laughed. 'He's a strange man. But for Barbara our paths would not have crossed.'

'He'd better learn not to upset you.' And he'd better be prepared for what's to come, I had been about to add, but I stopped myself. I didn't want to upset her again.

'Poor man,' she said, almost motherly. 'He just envies my closeness with Barbara.'

12: *Li Qiu* – Autumn Starts

8 August

Jiao Mei

Half of the world seemed to have left London: Xiao Lin and her new husband for China, Taro and his wife for Japan, and Barbara and Bill for their holiday in Spain. They'd all be back of course, even Taro, who was going to look for work in London. For the time being, I haunted the half-deserted streets of Hampstead and the empty house. I understood now Ken's obsession with space. Buildings had personalities of their own, and this one had responded to its inhabitants. I sat down quietly to listen to the silence and heard what I had wanted to hear – that it had accepted me. Its wooden floors sustained my heavy steps, the ceilings absorbed my sighs and the stairs bore my pain. And the garden . . . I thought affectionately of the plants. The garden rested my restless heart.

It was nice to be alone, especially since Bill had been around so much lately. But now, from a distance, I could think of him as a welcome guest. I didn't understand him but somehow I couldn't totally give up on him either. He and Barbara had been away for a week, but it was only since yesterday that I had been in a calmer frame of mind: after all, how could words, however ill their intent, cause someone to die? The week before they left, Barbara had seemed well again and spent all her time gardening. There was even a flush on her cheek as she bent down. 'Weed and water,

157

otherwise enjoy!' she had said, before she left.

Behind her Bill had shouted, 'Control the dandelions.'

Dandelions. I went out to the garden to dig. It was a task I loved, partly because it was so hard to get them out. Barbara would clear the ones around her rosebush and the lilies, but elsewhere she let them grow. I delighted in spotting their hiding-places and plucking them out. I knew they'd grow back before she returned.

When it started raining I went inside and picked up the post. I stared at the stained, torn airmail envelope that contained the letter I'd posted to my mother nearly two months ago. It had been returned to me with the words 'Not known here' scrawled across it in Chinese. It was torn at the edges, which meant someone must have read it – perhaps even her. It was maddening not to know if she had read it, stuffed it back into the envelope, and returned it as if she was no longer at that address. I reread it and hoped she hadn't received it. It was too detached, as if she were a distant aunt. But it was so hard to know what tone to use to a mother I had not been close to for so long.

When the rain stopped I went back to the garden to resume the weeding. The thyme between the paving-stones leading to the pavilion released its scent from beneath my feet. Behind me, the roses were fragrant even as they lay rotten on the ground. The waterlily Barbara had planted in May had blossomed, its dark green foliage setting off the delicate pink flowers.

The door of the studio was ajar and I wandered in. It was like another kitchen, full of tools, pots, knives, cloths, aprons and brushes. Barbara seemed almost not to distinguish between the studio and the kitchen, so the apron in here was covered with flour, and the tea towels in the kitchen smelt of turpentine. Beneath the turps, other scents made my mouth water – walnut and lavender oil. Tubs of different pigments were lined up on the shelves, like spice boxes. Lower down my hand encountered a box of eggs, some tea leaves and even a piece of chocolate. I had once seen Barbara smear chocolate on a painting, then lick off the excess. In describing the texture of a particular mix of paint, she would say it was between single and double cream.

Her life had no boundaries: art did not end where life began, nor dreams cease where reality set in. The studio and her garden were her real world, not the big house she shared with me and Bill. An old sun-hat fell from its hook on the wall, and I jumped.

When Ken arrived I was sweating over a stubborn dandelion. He tried and failed, then I tried and failed, then he tried again and succeeded. We were both exhausted and worked up about it. 'Look! Look!' I said excitedly. He was puzzled. 'Can you see any dandelions?' I crowed.

'None whatsoever. Is that all your doing?'

I gestured at the pile of dandelions I had dug up. They had lost their sheen now. He looked at them, then his gaze returned to the one he'd just pulled up. 'What a shame. I think they're quite pretty.' He was the only person I knew, apart from Barbara, who had admitted to liking them. But then, he was no gardener.

'Yes, but they take over. Anyway, they'll grow back in no time.'

'Really?' He laughed. 'I believe you – you're a magician, I know that. Come, I'll show you something.'

We went indoors. He spread out a few rolls of thin, almost transparent paper. 'Your bridge!' I said.

'Yes. These are just the plans, but they've started building it.'

I looked at the incomprehensible drawings and warmed to his neat writing. 'So your doodles were practice for these curves. Aren't they beautiful?' I said, although the plans resembled a sophisticated bird's nest rather than a bridge.

In bed I asked him to draw on me. 'Arches here, curves here and here,' I directed, and he responded. We were two intertwining bridges. My desire came from inside me now: in the past he had aroused it. The sweet smell of our bodies filled the room.

When I woke up again it was as if from a nightmare. Where was she? I smelt something damp and heavy, but it was not in our room. I tiptoed downstairs, following the scent, and found the dark form huddled in the small box space. 'Tie Mei, is that you?' I whispered.

'Just leave me alone a moment, I'll be all right.'

Tie Mei

I had had a narrow escape.

The devils ambushed me on my way to see my old garden. I shouldn't have gone but I could not help it. I had feared they lay in wait for me there, but since I'd learned of the Englishwoman's interference, I could hold back no longer. The garden was still a ruin, Jiaojiao had assured me, but I needed to see it for myself. I wanted to make sure that my other little girl was still singing among the flowers.

Cursed devils! Were it not for the mercy of the Moon Goddess, they'd have had me. I escaped, weakened but furious at what they represented. I struggled to get to the Englishwoman's garden and collapsed. The scent of the roses revived me.

I gathered my strength and went inside the house, but could only manage one flight of stairs. 'Nainai, are you all right?' Jiaojiao bent over me, her voice full of concern. Her usually welcome smell was almost overpowering. Had the fighting weakened me so much? I told her what had happened.

She was confused. 'Accident? Which Moon Goddess? What do you mean?'

I was too exhausted. 'I can't say more now,' I said. 'Don't come too near.'

'What can I do?' Her face hovered over me.

'It's all right now,' I wanted to say, but I lost consciousness.

13: *Chu Shu* – Heat Evades

23 August

Jiao Mei

'Mei.' Barbara's dragging footsteps reached my ears. I looked up from my translation – instructions on how to fold guest-bedroom sheets, to be rendered in Chinese, for which I would be paid sixty pounds. She was dressed in just a T-shirt and shorts, but I was wearing a jumper and still felt cold.

'Call this summer?' She gestured to the window, and the cloudy grey sky beyond. Before I could reply she added, 'Don't you hate our weather sometimes?'

I didn't say anything. 'Drop that horrid hotel manual,' she ordered. 'Let's . . . let's go swimming.'

'Where?'

'To the ladies' pond on the Heath.'

'But . . .' I looked at the sky again: it was not my idea of a swimming day.

'Oh, it'll clear up.'

But when we were at the pond it rained. I'd been there for the first time the week I'd arrived in England. It had been what I'd learned to call an Indian summer. Barbara had stripped off quickly and was about to jump in when she was told by a woman attendant in a blue uniform, 'No nude bathing, please.'

Since then we'd been there several times. I had even recognised one of the regulars in the shop once, but I hadn't been able to think where I knew them from. There was nobody I recognised today. We changed in silence, with the ease of people who knew the rules. I waited for her when I was ready. When we got to the edge of the pond she stood over the water for a minute, hugging herself. A sound nearby distracted me and I looked back to see her splash into the water. The silent trail of ripples she left behind her reminded me of a swan gliding away. Whenever I was with Barbara she always took the lead.

There were only two other women in the pond, one clinging to a black tyre nearby and another further away in the middle, floating with her face to the sky. I sat on the bank and tested the water with my feet. Then, at the sight of Barbara moving steadily towards the middle, I plunged in. The dark green water felt cold, then heavy around me; long weed caressed my legs.

A radio played softly, and the woman attendant mopped up the water on the deck. Her presence reassured me. Barbara had taught me to swim, but I could not trust water as she did, although since I had been pregnant it had seemed more welcoming. My body felt light and the water, lulling, took the pressure off my aching back when I floated.

My mind drifted to Tie Mei. Her fragrance was weak. I had felt guilty over the last few weeks: I had realised how little I thought of her journey from that other world, what courage it took to make it. Did I deserve her sacrifice?

For lunch I cooked green pepper and aubergine with plenty of salt. I should have put in the aubergine first, but instead I threw in both together, so that the pepper was overcooked and the aubergine barely edible. I must have wanted her to criticise my cooking.

She crunched and shook her head. 'Mei, I think the aubergine is a little undercooked.'

'Sorry.' I hung my head.

'Never mind. What's Ken up to nowadays?'

'He's building a Chinese bridge, and he's been pestering me with questions.'

She raised her eyebrow, and put down her fork. 'But

Sichuan is full of bridges – your home town is practically the Venice of the Orient!' Her eyes went to the bookshelf on the wall opposite the cooker where she kept most of her Chinese books. 'I've never seen so many bridges. Beijing seemed so straightforward by comparison, less charming.' She was unusually animated. 'I remember not being able to buy a map in Sichuan. It drove me mad at first, but then I came to love being without one. You got lost all the time, and it was fun.'

She stood up, walked to the bookshelf and drew out a thick volume. 'There, Chinese bridges.'

We looked at the book together. Colourful photographs, yes, many of Sichuan. We were transported for a moment to the network of waterways in my home town, and its smells. 'So, what did you tell Ken?' she murmured, without looking up from the pages.

'I told him the story of the magpie bridge.'

'The magpie bridge. Is that the one with the shepherd?'

She knew it. Baba must have told her.

She closed the book suddenly and pushed it into my hand. 'You should show this to Ken – good luck to him. I'm sure he'll be a good bridge-builder – he's just the man for the job.'

I flipped through the book, glimpsed the inscription on the front page and recognised my father's script. 'To a foreign friend, to remember her stay in China,' he had written, in his elegant, rather affected style.

'Baba never liked the north, neither the climate nor the politics,' I said.

'But isn't your mother a northerner?'

'Yes.'

We regarded each other in silence and then she left, saying something about the garden. Still holding the book I went to the open doorway, where I smelt the thyme again. The shower had revived its scent. Last time it had been so strong was when Ken had helped me with the dandelions. I'd told him they'd grow again, and here they were, everywhere, showing their sunflower faces, tolerated – no, encouraged to grow in Barbara's part of the garden. She trod past the dandelions with the same care that she took to avoid stepping on her lilies. When she reached the lilies, she bent down, her head close to the paving stone where the thyme was planted. She would not be able to smell either plant. This was a familiar ritual now: it was as if she wasn't sure she'd completely lost the sense of smell, as if by constantly checking the flowers this way, she'd discover one day that it had returned.

When she straightened up I moved swiftly away from the door. But it wasn't long before I searched again for her figure in the garden. Now she was squatting, weeding, and her posture brought back memories of her at work in that other garden, her secret garden for my father.

She had planned it almost as soon as she met him, at the first sign of spring. His potted orchids were enough for him, he had insisted, but she had been defiant: 'This land used to belong to your family.'

'But now it is a park,' he said. 'I'm not allowed to spend time or resources on my own pursuits.'

'I'll be careful,' she said, and walked round the shed to scout for a good spot.

Behind our shed, beyond the old well, there was a thick forest of giant wild bamboos that had been used instead of a wall as the park boundary. Behind it was a tractor factory's junk heap. Nobody ever went there. 'Here,' she had said, and started digging.

'I would only grow vegetables,' my father said, relenting, but she brought flower seeds and shrubs to sow and plant. Eventually he left her to it, and even helped her. We both helped. We let the bamboo near the shed grow to shield the garden from intruders. But the fragrance threatened to give it away. I could tell, though, that the threat of discovery thrilled Barbara and my father – it enhanced their closeness. It united us all. Even I, a grumpy teenager, liked the whiff of defiance and secrecy about what they were doing. Father's mobile garden did not interest me half as much as Barbara's secret one. We had a summer of exuberant scents and colours, a small paradise on the edge of the bleak park. She left us and the garden reluctantly, as there were flowers yet to bloom whose fragrance she would miss. The garden died soon after she left because my father would not touch it. He liked ruins, he said. They were romantic.

I wondered whether he would explain his reluctance to plant flowers, or allow them to take root.

It had all begun on an outing to a mountain on the outskirts of Beijing when my parents took their students on a botany trip. I was about three, and it was like a family picnic. To me the young students were like uncles and aunts – that was how I addressed them. They all took turns to carry me. It was heaven. We stayed in peasants' houses. During the day the students collected plants and pressed them in special paper inside books. They laughed and joked, and occasional arguments broke out. I listened half-heartedly, playing with the insects I caught in a matchbox.

'I like daffodils,' one student had said.

'Yes, they are lovely, but they are nothing compared to an orchid,' my father said, looking over at Mama, pleased with his joke: Orchid was her name.

'But cabbages are so much more important,' said the bespectacled student who'd carried me most of the way. Everybody laughed. 'Cabbages are beautiful and they feed people. Orchids are beautiful and useless.'

'You can't mean that!' my father expostulated.

'Oh, but I do,' said the bespectacled student. 'It's a fault to admire such bourgeois flowers.'

'They're just plants. There's no need to get so worked up about them,' my mother said gently.

But the student had meant what he said. Soon afterwards the army marched into the nursery, uprooting all the tender young plants that my father had nurtured. In a matter of minutes, they had destroyed flowers and new varieties that he had been working on for years. 'You should plant cabbage and tea, food and drink for the masses,' they said. The bespectacled student looked on, nodding.

It was referred to as 'The Cabbage and Orchids Argument' in the big-character Letter of Denouncement that was pinned up outside the canteen. A black cross darkened Baba's name: rightist, élitist, enemy of the masses, enemy of the people.

165

The student who had spoken up for daffodils recanted and denounced my father. He made a list of Baba's other favourite flowers, which damned him further. My father could not see how a simple flower could be bourgeois, and was sent to the far north in punishment.

I learned this much later on from other people, my father's colleagues and former students. The daffodil lover had forgiven himself: 'That sort of thing happened all the time. I could do nothing about it,' he said. Baba had never breathed a word of it to me. The political movement at the agricultural college was one of the most active, they said. It seemed that botanists in China had a special interest in politics.

Had he explained this to Barbara? All he had allowed himself since then was his mobile garden. The evidence of his disobedience, a few prized specimens in pots, could easily have been destroyed if he found himself in trouble again. But he no longer had the satisfaction of producing a plant that could breathe and feed, and put down deep roots. How tempted he must have been to plant his favourite flowers on the soil his ancestors had sweated over for generations.

My eyes came to rest again on the figure squatting before me. I felt my father's sadness and Barbara's love for him. It had been the empathy of a fellow gardener. Was he watching over her now, when she needed him?

Tie Mei

E vening settled into the darkness I craved. I was impatient to be with her. My time with her had become precious now that I knew how easily it could be snatched away. I saw that it was I who needed her, not the other way round. I needed her like I needed the darkness, like I needed the mercy of the Moon Goddess.

Strange, then, that I should find myself in the English-woman's room when she was the last person in my thoughts. I stared into a pair of eyes, older than Jiaojiao's.

They did not blink. It seemed she had been staring into space for some time. She whispered something I couldn't understand. I stepped back but suddenly she was speaking Chinese: 'Who are you?'

I remained still.

'Are you here to tell me something?'

I did not answer.

'Poor soul, it's a comfort to know that you exist. Perhaps we shall meet again, and you'll explain this to me.'

I was robbed of speech. I couldn't get over the fact that she was talking to me, and in my language. I fled from her room. I had seen so many souls facing what she was facing now, but none so calm or as guiltless as she.

And then I heard my Jiaojiao.

'You said they caught you, and then . . . the Moon Goddess saved you?' she asked gently.

'Chang Er came to my aid. Otherwise I would not be here. I prayed to her. I thawed her frozen heart,' I replied. She looked doubtful. 'You do remember the story of the Moon Goddess, don't you?' I asked.

She nodded, then lifted her face towards me. I knew there was something she was impatient to tell me. I came closer. 'It's going to be my birthday soon. Next time you are here,' she said, 'I shall be older. And I've asked for . . .' She looked suddenly unsure. 'You did say the mirror had magic power?'

'Yes.'

Relieved, she held back. I waited but she said no more words.

'Your birthday. Of course, that makes you a Sheep?'

'Yes – like Barbara and my mother.'

'And my Xiao Yingzi. You never met her, but if she had not been killed by chicken-pox, she would have been your aunt.' I had resolved to share everything with her. I wanted her to know the truth. I spoke fast. 'Do you remember my Chinese teacher, I told you about? He arranged for me to go to the girls' school and encouraged me with my reading.'

She turned her face to the photograph of me on the wall. I

did not like myself in that picture: smug and satisfied, believing I had a good life. 'Under his guidance I changed. I became a spirited woman, he said. So spirited that one dark night when he came to see me, we . . . Mei, are you listening?'

She nodded. Her eyes moved from the photograph to me. I remembered the fragrance of the roses that night, and the sound of crickets. Otherwise the garden was silent, holding its breath, keeping our secret. 'You made love together,' she said softly.

I nodded. That was when I had first known the pleasure of love.

'Shortly after that night, I knew I was pregnant. And one day my husband came home to tell me that his colleague, my teacher, had fled. I asked him why and he said it was because the government suspected he was a Communist.

'I was heartbroken. The man who brought brightness into my life had left me. What had I to live for? But I struggled on. I had to be brave for the baby. When the child was born I was happy for a while. It was a girl, with his eyes. My husband didn't know, but I think he would soon have guessed. I didn't know what to do, but she solved the problem for me. She became terribly ill.

'I tried to save her. I called her soul. I laid her on the bed, took a lock of her hair and went to the four corners of the yard. "Come back, Yingzi," I whispered, each time rushing back to her side to check for signs of life. "Come back, Yingzi, your mother needs you." I turned to the west, where I saw a twinkling star through the window. She never returned.'

There was a soft sound, like fine silk being cut with sharp scissors. Was she sobbing for me?

I continued, 'There wasn't a single day that went past when I didn't mourn her in secret. I neglected my son and husband, but I kept her memory alive. When I saw a girl of her age I'd think of her. When I saw older girls I would imagine what she might have looked like. Then you were born and you were just like my little girl. I loved once more, and that love was for you.'

Her head was bent low. She didn't look up even as I left the

168

house. I did not mind. I'd taken her little pearl tears, and they were my comfort. I lingered in the garden, fragrant and prosperous. It was hard to imagine it as a ruin, and yet once the love inside me had died, my garden died with it. After Xiao Yingzi died, it was truly haunted. People heard a little girl crying at night among the flowers. They said she was crying for her mother, for someone to lead her home. 'I'm lost,' she wailed. People said I was a witch because I would wander at night looking for her, but she never spoke to me.

I paused by the mute Mei tree, and looked back up at the house where a dim light shone. I thought it was Jiaojiao, then realised it was the Englishwoman's. Still she was not sleeping.

How extraordinary that she should have made a garden on my land, and that I should find this tree on hers. I felt my beloved garden call me back.

14: *Bai Lu* – White Dew

8 September

Jiao Mei

What with Ken's car stalling and the inexplicably heavy traffic, by the time we got to his mother's terraced house we were nearly two hours late. A ramshackle grocery shop stood to the right. To the left a road sign read: 'To Brighton'.

'What shall I call her?' I whispered in panic. The bright sunshine paled the clean yellow door.

Ken pressed the bell, then scratched his scalp and spoke slowly: 'Her name is Daisy Johnson, and she'll tell you what to call her. My first girlfriend called her Daisy and she didn't like it. Oh, by the way, speak loudly to her. She's deaf but won't admit it.'

He had hardly finished the sentence when the door opened. A small, frail woman appeared, her shining silver hair short and sprightly. She wore a pair of purple slippers and a white cardigan. 'Hello, son.' She gave Ken a peck on the cheek.

'Mother, this is Mei,' Ken said loudly.

'Hello, Mei, call me Daisy.' She looked me up and down, then stretched out a hand.

We followed her down a narrow corridor that led to the sitting room. A strange smell made me want to cough. A white Persian cat, sitting in front of the fire, opened an eye and looked at us. 'Mother, it's boiling outside. If you're cold,

171

why don't you go and sit in the sun?'

'I don't like too much sun on me. Now, tea or coffee?' For a small person she had a strong voice.

'Tea, please,' I said quickly.

'Milk? Sugar?' She spoke slowly, emphasising each word.

'Black, no sugar, please.' My answer was as measured.

Daisy nodded, approving, and turned to Ken: 'The usual for you?' She lowered her voice for him. Ken followed her into the kitchen.

The sitting-room was cosy and tidy, with the gas fire flickering in the centre of the wall. At first I had thought it was a real fire, but the flame was too blue and the arrangement of the coal too neat. On the mantelpiece there were colour photos of Ken as a child, and black-and-white ones of him as a baby, and his proud-looking parents. I looked carefully at his father, a military man in uniform, handsome and young, with a slight stiffness about him. He looked as Ken might if he were acting in a film.

Teacups clattered. 'No, Sheila, you can't come into the sitting room. How many times have I told you?' I looked behind Daisy and Ken to see a sheep trying to barge through the doorway. 'Sheila, get back,' Daisy ordered, and pushed hard. Ken lent a hand and Sheila trotted back to the kitchen.

Daisy followed her and Ken said, 'That's another of Mum's pets.'

Daisy returned, somewhat breathless, and smiled for the first time. 'Sheila's stubborn. She thinks she owns the house.'

'May I see your garden, please?' I asked, perhaps too quickly.

'Yes, of course. Come, I'll show you.' We went out through the kitchen. The lawn was perfectly groomed, not a dandelion in sight – Bill would have been impressed. Small pretty flowers grew along the borders, and an apple tree stood at the end. A brick shed with a pretty pink door next to the house was laid with clean, soft straw. This was where Sheila lived. To left and right there were high fences. Daisy pointed to the right, and made no effort to lower her voice: 'They're such trouble, people coming and going at all hours. God knows what they're up to.'

'Mother, the man is perfectly decent,' Ken muttered. 'He runs a shop. Leave him alone.'

'He thinks I'm just a weak woman, but I'll show him what I'm made of. I might be a widow but my husband died defending this country.'

It felt odd to be drawn so quickly into a stranger's confidence. I'd never come across anyone like Daisy before. She seemed to have decided already that I could be trusted. She reminded me of someone – perhaps Tie Mei? I felt I had nothing to hide from her penetrating gaze.

Sheila came near and I caressed her wool. I was amazed by how tame she was. 'And he had the nerve to complain that Sheila smelt. He shouted at her! Horrible man, he gave her nightmares.' Daisy smiled at me. I tried to stop a giggle as Sheila nibbled my hand. Daisy sighed. 'Oh, I've just fed *you*.' Then she changed her mind: 'But it's a special day – we have visitors, so why not?' She went to the corner of the garden and came back with a bucket of dried nutty stuff. 'There.' She put some into my hand. 'Would you like to feed her?' I held it out to Sheila, who ate it heartily.

'Sheep are sensitive,' Daisy said, behind me. 'They're not brutes like cows, they're not hardy. Well, they can deal with cold weather, but they don't adapt well to change. And they certainly can't stand being shouted at!' Ken made faces at me behind his mother's back.

After the sheep-feeding we were all ravenous. 'Wash your hands thoroughly,' Daisy said. I turned to the sink and ran them under the tap. 'No, *thoroughly* – use soap,' she said sharply, pointing at my belly. 'I don't want you to get any disease.'

'From Sheila?' I asked. I liked being told what to do by her.

'That's right. You never know.' She was satisfied only after I had scrubbed myself. Then she said, 'I'll go and get changed.'

Ken and I had said hardly a word to each other before Daisy was down again like a swift wind. 'Into the car.' She made quick gestures.

'Where to?' Ken asked.

'Brighton, of course. Have you ever been, Mei?'

Following Daisy's directions, we found ourselves in a big hotel looking out to the pier. I had never seen such white walls and such high ceilings. White-gloved waiters brought us tea, scones and cakes. 'We shall have a proper English afternoon tea for Mei's birthday,' Daisy declared.

A cream tea. I let the soft thick cream melt in my mouth before I allowed it to slip down my throat. Meeting Daisy added a new dimension to my picture of Ken: the only son of a strict but affectionate mother. I imagined her rocking our baby. What a perfect granny she'd make. Strict parents make indulgent grandparents, they say, like Nainai.

Tie Mei . . . I'd see her tonight. If only I could turn back the clock and take away her suffering. No wonder she was bitter. But I did not have long to indulge in such thoughts before Daisy interrupted me with her offer of another scone, already filled with jam and cream. 'Eat more,' she said. 'It might be twins, you never know. We do have twins on Ken's father's side of the family.' I gobbled it down.

On the motorway heading for London, the mellow afternoon sunlight poured over the hills, like oils over a canvas I had once watched Barbara paint. My mouth remembered the taste of the cream. I felt content and at ease for the first time in a long while. Everything would be all right. It was my birthday, and I had asked for the mirror. Barbara would be cured. Daisy liked me; Ken loved me. Now he responded in monosyllables to my questions about his mother and his family, but I put it down to the drive. We made it back to Hampstead in time for dinner.

After we had eaten I opened my presents. Daisy's was wrapped in tissue paper, which smelt of lanolin. It was a brooch. 'It belonged to my grandmother,' Ken said. He'd been unusually quiet throughout dinner – this was about the only sentence he had uttered.

Barbara picked it up. 'Do you think it's intended as a wedding present?'

Bill took it from her and held it under the light. 'They're the real thing – diamonds,' he said. 'So, your future mother-in-law approves of you.' He gave it back to me and I pinned it on my dress.

'Daisy has a sheep called Sheila,' I said. 'She told me sheep are sensitive animals, and that they have nightmares if you frighten them.'

'She's right, you know,' Bill said. 'I used to help on a farm and I know a bit about them. They're more emotional than cows, and although they can stand any sort of weather, they lose their lambs, even die, from shock or stress.'

I was feeling Barbara's present. I tore off the wrapping-paper impatiently, ignoring the pair of scissors Bill offered me. Barbara's voice sounded distant: 'I'm sorry I didn't polish it, I wasn't sure what you wanted to do with it. You're lucky it's only Qing – if it had been older, I'd have had to donate it to a museum.'

'Thank you.' I felt the mirror's weight. Already my hands were sweating and the lives of the people around me faded as I thought of the stories this mirror could tell.

Tie Mei

E ven before I saw the mirror I felt its vibration. I burst in like a child impatient for her red New Year parcel. The mirror was in her hands. But there was something wrong with the way she held it, too casual, almost irreverent. I needed to show her how.

I went closer. My treasure. I smelt it like a warrior caressing his sword after a long, hard battle. For a moment I was transported back to those days of freedom and power: my rebellion in the underworld. Bound neither by the rules of hell nor by the shackles of shame, I had never felt more alive.

'Well done,' I said, feeling jealous as I watched her delicate finger caress the patterns on the metal. The mirror seemed heavy in her hands. Could I trust her with it?

The moon showered its cold beam on the bronze surface. I pondered the strange connection between the women in my family and this mirror, at once curse and blessing. It had brought lovers together but then it had also become part of us: when we lost it we had lost that part of ourselves. That was why we had fought tooth and nail to get it back. It represented so much of what my family meant to me: their genius and honour.

'At last,' I sighed, 'it's back in our hands. How you must have struggled for it.'

'What do you mean?' She seemed puzzled. 'I asked for it and Barbara gave it to me.'

I was speechless.

'You didn't imagine I'd snatched it from her, did you? It was hers, after all.'

'It never belonged to her! It was always ours.' My anger surprised even me. 'It's not just any mirror, it's our honour, our happiness, the fruits of our labour that were stolen from us. How can you say it belonged to her, and still have any respect for yourself?'

'I do respect myself, that's why I asked for it. And I got it,' she said calmly.

Her confident manner irritated me more than her words. She had asked for it and been given it. It had been as easy as that. But what of my struggle?

'Tie Mei,' she put down the mirror, 'I know how you feel and I know how you've suffered, but we live in different times now. Barbara and I are like family.'

Family? Family is flesh and blood. I looked up at her, tall like her mother, with the almond eyes that reminded me of my son. I had never felt close to him as an adult, but Jiaojiao felt closer than a granddaughter. Now she lived with the Englishwoman, ate with her and was more intimate with her than with her own mother.

'I think Barbara knew,' she added, after a few moments' silence.

'How?'

'I don't know, I just feel it.'

I thought of how I had mistaken one for the other the other night. Had I said something to the foreign woman?

I moved to the window, drawn by the voices of the night

drifters. It seemed only yesterday that I had first come in search of Jiaojiao and found the mirror's resting place. Why did I feel emptiness, dread, now that the mirror was back in our hands, instead of happiness and fulfilment? There was no sense of conclusion: it felt as though things had just begun.

'Now that the mirror is back in our hands,' she said cautiously, 'doesn't it mean that there will be peace, no more deaths?'

I almost wished it could be true. Things were happening too fast. I had never thought she would get the mirror so easily. What would happen to the Englishwoman?

15: *Qiu Fen* – Autumn Equinox

23 September

Jiao Mei

The damsons were ripe and soft – they slipped off the tree into my hands and the basket. Two weeks had gone by since Barbara had given me the mirror, during which I had prepared for today, the Full Moon Day. I visited florists, read and laid my plans, my preoccupation distancing me from the troubles of those around me. It felt good to be focused.

It was a grey day; the air was cool and indifferent. The leaves had begun to drop, green and brown, mixed on the ground with fallen fruit that had been squashed by passing cars. I wondered why nobody bothered to pick it up.

Barbara had been sitting on the ground and stood up now, her basket full to the brim. 'Since I came back from China, I have been picking the fruit, making jam and pies. China taught me that.'

'If you don't pick it, someone else will. Or it will be wasted.'

'Here we are, worried it might belong to someone. I think that's enough. Mei, you shouldn't exhaust yourself. The two of us can only eat so much.'

We headed home past the pond.

'Ken hasn't been round for a while,' she said. I'd thought she hadn't noticed.

'He's busy,' I said. She glanced back at the Heath and didn't ask more.

We followed the traffic down to the high street. 'How shall

179

we celebrate today, the mid-autumn festival, Mei?'

'Chrysanthemum wine, crabs and a poem to the moon?'

'I hate chrysanthemums. A poem to the moon, maybe.' A young man in a suit came out of an estate agent's and stared at Barbara. He had heard what she said.

We stood at the busy crossroads. She bought a paper from a man standing by the tube. So many people. We waited for the traffic lights to change so that we could cross the road. As red became amber, she said, 'It was on a Full Moon Day that I proposed to Yuan Shui, on my second visit to China.'

I stepped back from the road. A man behind me swerved to avoid bumping into me. I stared at her: what an awkward place to make such an announcement.

She crossed the road slowly, without looking back, so I followed. 'I fell for him at first sight, when I saw him at the park. That's always the way with me.' She might as well have been talking to the man walking almost beside her. I could only half hear her, and struggled to keep up. She glanced at me. 'But nothing happened until Songpan.'

'Songpan?' I smiled. 'You were waiting for my approval, weren't you? I've always known it.'

She stopped. 'Was I?' She seemed genuinely surprised.

'I'd thought . . . Didn't you know how much I resented you?'

'I never thought of it. Really? Oh, you silly girl.' She walked on.

Dumbfounded, I stood where I was, as if her words had pinned me there, but then I ran past her and up the hill to the house. I stopped, panting, at the door, and put my hands to my cheeks. She had told me so casually about her intimacy with my father, almost as though she was discussing a shopping list. How could she be so careless? I'd thought she'd cared how I felt. I'd thought she'd restrained herself with my father because of me. I watched her coming up the path.

From nowhere a sweetness came into my nostrils, soaking into my clothes. I turned, and saw the smoke billowing from our neighbour's garden. 'Smell that,' I said to Barbara when she stood next to me. I pointed at the smoke. 'I wonder what they're burning.'

She closed her eyes and breathed in deeply. I was satisfied by her look of uncertainty when she opened her eyes. 'Dead leaves?' she said.

'Maybe.' I fumbled for my key. I knew it was applewood, as far removed from the smell of dead leaves as I could imagine. 'Let's go in.' The scent was unbearable now.

The moon rose slowly and I cooked quickly. There was no salt tonight.

'What's for dessert?' she asked, licking her lips. I took out the mooncakes I had bought in Chinatown earlier that day. Xiao Lin had helped me choose them. They were the ones Barbara liked, with brown sugar, pinenuts and sesame seeds.

I peeped at the clock. She caught my eye. 'You look as though you're expecting someone. Ken?'

I shook my head. 'I'm waiting for the right time to serve my third course.'

She pushed aside her plate. 'I must say this is an excellent dinner. Very tasty.'

She did not know how much spice I had put into it.

'Where's the third course, then? Can I have it now?'

'You must wait.'

On my way upstairs I glanced into our neighbour's garden. Even here, indoors, I could smell the applewood. Now I knew for sure that she had entirely lost the sense of smell. I hadn't meant to punish her, but I regretted my moment of cruelty.

In my room everything was set up. I opened the window and sat down. The mirror rested reassuringly by the wall, reflecting the moon. So much depended on this. Tie Mei had seemed hesitant about the magic effect of the mirror, but I could not fail.

Two souls to console. Only magic could heal them. I owed them both so much. But how do you help one so bitter and another so oblivious of her own pain?

I picked up the thin piece of paper I'd prepared earlier: on it I had written a couplet in black ink, my best calligraphy, a poem for the Moon Goddess Chang Er. I lit a match, burned it, and murmured: '*Chang Er ying hui to ling yao, bi hai qing tian ye ye xin*. Chang Er must regret stealing the secret lotion, her lonely heart bled night after night in the big blue sky.'

I had learned those lines in my Chinese-literature class, appreciated them as a fine example of classical poetry. I had never imagined I'd use them to pray. Would it work? I could not afford to doubt. Blind faith was all I had now.

Facing the moon, I lit the incense, then closed my eyes. The magic mirror would attract the Moon Goddess. I chanted to the lady whose heart was frozen. Would it thaw for Barbara?

'You were a lover once yourself, lover of the hero Hou Yi who saved the people of the earth by shooting down the nine suns that scorched the land and caused men and cattle to burn to death. You had both been sent down from heaven to help the people of earth, so you learned the ways of the world. But soon Hou Yi had a new lover and you were bereft. You began to miss the heavenly life you'd left behind and wished you were back there – you had grown old, like all earthly women, and lost your beauty. You thought that was why Hou Yi had deserted you. Then you discovered his hidden pill of immortality and swallowed it.

'But Hou Yi came after you, shouting your name, and said he was still in love with you, you were his true love, and he had left his new lover to return to you. But it was too late, you were already in two different worlds. The tears of regret and resentment you shed froze the beautiful palace where you lived and made it a hostile place that killed those who approached it . . .'

I opened my eyes and saw the melancholy face of a young girl in the mirror. It was curious how she resembled me. 'Please, would you help Barbara? I thank you, Moon Goddess,' I heard myself say, almost in spite of myself. But once I started talking, I could not stop. 'And Tie Mei. You know her story, you helped her when she most needed you, rescuing her from the devils, but she suffered in life and still needs comfort, like you. You must help them both, for if you can't help Nainai, if she cannot learn to forgive, Barbara will never be cured and I will never be free.'

I bowed deeply to the moon, three times, then went downstairs.

Barbara was waiting for me quietly. 'Follow me.' I led her to the garden. Her hand felt small in mine, reminding me of a kitten I had once held, whose heartbeat made me feel protective.

The moon was full and bright, so we could see the path clearly. The dew wet our shoes and the raised steps to the studio were moist and slippery. A drum started beating inside me, becoming faster and harder. Had I gone mad? It was bad enough that I had hallucinations at all, but now I was dragging Barbara into it. A cold sweat made me shudder. Perhaps it was not too late to turn and say to her: 'Sorry, this has all been a mistake.'

But it *was* too late. She had brushed me aside, lifted the latch and gone in. I closed my eyes. Then I heard a cry at the same moment that a suffocating scent escaped from the room, making my head spin. Then her voice, like a flute echoing in an empty valley, wailed, 'Mei, what's happening to me? Where has this smell come from? It can't be – can it be lilies?'

'Yes,' I said, trembling at the door. 'You did smell lilies.' The magic had worked. But I could not move, I dared not enter.

'Mei,' she murmured, in a voice that sounded more like sorrow than joy. Finally I moved my legs and entered, steadying myself on the door. There was a switch by my hand, but the moon was so bright that I didn't need a light.

'Baihe. A Hundred Embraces,' she murmured like a creature of the night that had found its haven from the storm.

I thought of the places I had gone to search for the lilies, shops, parks and neighbours' houses. In September they were hard to get and expensive. My eyes drifted to the table where they lay.

But Barbara was flitting around the room like a trapped butterfly, sniffing in corners where I couldn't see anything, pawing at things when there was nothing to touch. The room was suffocating. I couldn't bear it any longer. I left her there, and ran down the path, through the house and into the quiet moon-bright street. Somebody help us, I screamed, but no sound came. How could I have such power?

I wanted to escape, but the moon followed me, the moon who had done all this. I ran up the hill to the pond, round the pond, down the darkened green path to the Heath, then up and on to the road. Still I could not shake off the moon – or that image of Barbara, arms flailing like the wings of a trapped butterfly.

The sight of people walking along the high street made me slow down. Cars drove past me, a homeless man in a sleeping-bag stirred as I stumbled past; his dog raised its head. The moon was still up but its force was waning now that I was in the brighter, artificial light.

Exhausted, I leaned against the wall by the crossroads, where I could look up at the fake Gothic clock. I watched the lights change, and stared at the spot where she had told me of her proposal to my father. How accidental everything had seemed, yet how fated it had turned out to be. Her second visit to China had taken place while I was away at university. My father had been compensated for having been wrongly labelled a rightist. The government had apologised, but he had refused to move out of his home in the park – he was used to his hermit's existence. But he had neglected his garden, had given away his pot plants now that they were no longer forbidden, and worked long hours in the greenhouse inventing new varieties of azalea for the park.

When I saw Barbara again it was during the Spring Festival. My father had looked thin, in the early stages of his cancer, although nobody had suspected it. They had sat together like an old couple, not looking at each other, but watching for each other's movements with an inward pair of eyes. I found her wandering sadly around the garden he had neglected, once her paradise. Why had she proposed to him then, when surely she had begun to see him in a different, more realistic light?

The homeless man was eyeing me curiously. My eyes drifted back to the clock. 'Mock Venetian.' Ken's voice echoed in me. It had always been such a comfort before, but now I felt sick.

'Be careful what you wish for,' Nainai had warned.

Tie Mei

H ow timely her gift of rose fragrance was! How it soothed me. I had needed it badly. Ever since I saw her with the mirror, I had felt odd, unfulfilled, when I should have been rejoicing. Now I felt dread and regret where I should have been happy. A new craving started in me, a craving I could not name, but which the fragrance of the roses seemed to answer.

The mirror was back in our hands. And, so far, no blood. A victory without battle. How easily I seemed to accept it, although fighting had been the only way I knew to get what I wanted. Now my granddaughter had shown me another way, a path I trod gingerly.

But among the fragrance I smelt also the cold sweat of anger, hers, not mine. 'Jiaojiao?' I said.

'Yes, Tie Mei.' Her voice came from a corner of a room and when she looked up her eyes glistened, like those of a hunted fox in the dark.

'Jiaojiao,' I said cautiously. 'Thank you for the roses, they were wonderful.'

Her hands smoothed the edges of the mirror, which she was holding. 'The magic, it worked.'

'So you have the power. What are you going to do with it?'

Now the light in her eyes startled me. 'Well, that's just it. I don't know what to do.'

'About what?'

'About Ken.'

'What happened to him?'

'He slept with an old girlfriend. He said he bumped into her when he was on the way back from seeing me that day when I told him I'd lied about my period. He said he was hurt and they both regretted it as soon as they'd done it.'

'When did he tell you this?'

'Last weekend when we were talking about our wedding. He said he wanted to come clean, and I said I'd forgive him anything.' She stood up abruptly. 'I knew something was wrong because he'd been acting strangely, but I had no idea it could be something like this.'

I didn't know what to say. I looked at the mirror she was holding, shining in the cold moonlight. Instead of reflecting powdered faces and lovers' smiles, it had witnessed blood and tears from too many women in my family.

'I want to hit him.' She dropped the mirror, knelt down and buried her face in the pillow.

Abandoned, the mirror lay on the fold of the sheet. The fragrance of the roses thickened around us. I steadied myself as excitement surged through me. Hitting back had felt good. But I said, 'Remember, you lied to him first.'

'Yes, but I did not mean to hurt him.'

'Do you think he meant to hurt you?'

'Why are you talking as though you're on his side?'

'I'm trying to get you to see sense. It's not a crime worth punishing.'

'But I want to make him suffer, as he made me.'

'Jiaojiao, think.'

After a while her head emerged from beneath the pillow. 'Tolerance, tolerance, damned tolerance,' she murmured. 'Oh, let him go to hell.'

I sat by her and didn't say any more. Whatever I said would be wrong – and it had been I who had spoken of revenge. I gazed at the photograph of myself on her wall. In that life of suffering I had swallowed the broken teeth instead of spitting them out. I knew how she felt. Hating is easier than loving. And now she had the power to do whatever she wanted.

16: *Han Lu* – Cold Dew

9 October

Jiao Mei

As I dragged myself up the hill I remembered hearing the baby's heartbeat at the clinic. 'It's like a galloping horse,' I said to the midwife. She smiled indulgently at me – she must have heard the same thing so many times.

A mother with a toddler in a pair of muddy blue wellingtons walked past me. 'Another puddle!' the child shouted. Something stirred in me, a memory of running after Mama when she left me at the nursery. Although I enjoyed playing with the other children, in the first moment after she left, I felt abandoned. I felt it again when she left my father and me for that man.

I'd still not had a letter from her. After the last one was returned I'd sent another, to her work address, which I was certain would reach her. Somehow, as the birth approached, my need for her to reply became more urgent. Perhaps today. I began to hurry.

Breathless, I rested against the sycamore outside the house. In the early-evening mist it stood tall and imposing, its unblinking stare like the truth. An earnest tourist with a notepad in his hand leaned close to the railings to admire the house and strained to read the blue plaque by the door. I closed my eyes.

Tie Mei's ghost visited fortnightly. Her tale of her life had moved me. No wonder she was bitter. But Tie Mei was not the only one haunting me. Ken and I were reconciled, but his betrayal plagued me – I could forgive but not forget. My only comfort was that it was another secret between us: intimacy, love, some of it had to do with keeping each other's secrets. Bill had returned from holiday three days ago, and I knew he had a different view of Barbara's rediscovery of her sense of smell. I didn't know what she had told him about the lilies and I did not dare to ask either of them. There were no more friendly overtures, and dandelions were growing in his front garden. It was hard to say where Barbara was. Since the lilies she had spent almost all her time in the studio, leaving it only to sleep and eat.

Back inside the house an official-looking envelope caught my eye. I recognised the logo of my university. I tore it open.

'Good news?' Bill's voice startled me. He was lying on the sofa by the bookshelf.

'Oh, yes. I passed.' I waved the paper at him. I supposed it was good news.

'Well done. You must be pleased.'

'Yes, I am.' It wasn't evening yet but he was already drinking. As he stood up the world inside his bloodshot eyes shook.

Nervous, I asked, 'Where is Barbara?'

'Where do you think?'

'In the studio? Still?'

'Do you know what all this painting is about?' His emphasis on 'you' was almost aggressive.

'No.' I wanted to escape the smell of alcohol, and slipped into the garden.

The wind had shaken the loose leaves off the tree and those that remained had changed colour. Gold, red, bright yellow, a fantastic display. If I were an artist I'd have wanted to paint it. I cut across the pebble path and went to the studio. I hesitated briefly, then tiptoed in.

The floral fragrance seeped out of the door, which was ajar. The lilies were clustered together, their white decaying to yellow, the collapsing flowers flesh-like. Then I saw Barbara, slumped before the white canvas. She appeared to be sleeping.

'So this was what she was making all the fuss about, this smell of decay.' I felt Bill's breath on my neck, and spun round.

But he had cornered me; we stared at each other, neither making a sound. Finally I asked, in a voice I barely recognised as my own, 'What do you want?' He stared down at me, expressionless. 'Let me go,' I shouted, but he wouldn't move. I waited for him to speak, for the accusations I thought were sure to come.

'What's it all about? This horrible smell, the obsession she has with the lilies? She speaks of nothing else.'

I remained silent.

'Don't you pretend to be an Oriental Buddha. I know it's your doing. There's something unnatural about . . . all this. Perhaps you'd care to explain to me what's going on in this house. She's even talking about a ghost.'

'You'd better ask her, not me.'

'No. I think I'd rather ask you. She's always been eccentric, but she was all right before you came here. You've changed her, you've made her unnatural, you've made her long for things that don't belong to her, and made her swallow guilt that is not hers.'

'Are you talking about her nostalgia for China?' The fresh air was clearing my head. 'You don't like me because of my father, do you?'

'I'm not jealous of a dead Chinaman.'

'What have you got against me, then? What have I done?'

He was silent. I could see lines on his face that I had not noticed before – I had always thought him remarkably young for his age. 'I know you're upset about her illness but, please, don't accuse me of things I haven't done,' I whispered.

'You think you can pull the wool over my eyes like you have over hers? You've already got what you wanted. You can stay here at our expense – why make her suffer? Is this how you show your gratitude? You twist your face and pretend you had a hard life. Do you think being Chinese exempts you from being judged? If you want something from life you have to earn it.'

The eloquence of his speech stunned me and tears came to my eyes. He was right. It *was* all my fault. If I hadn't been there, Tie Mei wouldn't have come, and perhaps the curse would never have been activated. But I hadn't asked for any of this to happen. Tell him! Tell him! a voice inside me said.

'Bill, it's not like you say. You know I care about her as much as you do. I just want to make her life—'

'Miserable?'

'As good as it can be. And I've tried.'

'How? She's . . . wasting away,' he choked out.

'No, no, no! She's recovering – she can smell now.' My voice rose in a desperate effort to convince him – and myself.

'What do you mean?'

'She lost her sense of smell for a long time, don't you remember? I tried to tell you.' I could see his bewilderment. 'I know you don't believe me but scent is important to her – that's why she never leaves the studio. She can smell the fragrance there.'

'Would you call that horrible stench fragrance?'

'Bill, you don't know the whole story. Perhaps I can explain.' But what *was* the whole story? I was frustrated, almost angry with Tie Mei. I could not share that with him.

As I went nearer he snapped, 'There's no bloody story! You've made it all up!'

'Bill,' I pleaded, and he retreated a step, shoulders drooping. I remained motionless, fearful that any small movement from me would provoke yet more anger.

He lowered his gaze, as if I didn't exist. 'Bill,' I murmured. 'Bill?'

'What do you know?' he whispered, and walked away.

I lingered in the garden. Relief was swiftly overcome by humiliation, then self-pity. He had been so unfair.

I walked back to the house, the cold sweat on my back making me shiver. As I thought over our conversation I gained a new perspective on my relationship with Barbara.

Something had never been quite right, and it had had nothing to do with her. I had wanted her to take responsibility for my life. Since my parents' divorce I had been looking for a mother, and in Barbara I'd found one. She'd brought me to England, but when she had failed to take charge of my next step after university, I had felt confused, lost, because this was not how I had expected her to behave. What an irony! The girl she thought the most independent of all the Chinese girls she had met wanted her to run her life for her. I had resented her for not fulfilling the role of a substitute mother. She could not have known it – I had hidden it too well. Until now I had fooled even myself.

I was ten times worse than Tie Mei, whose lust for blood I had scorned. She at least was honest about her hatred; I hid my resentment even from myself.

Tie Mei

I lingered in the Englishwoman's garden. The air stung with confrontation. The unexpected return of the mirror had changed Jiaojiao. For the first time I had glimpsed a vengeful side to my soft little girl.

I thought of the young man who was responsible for taking Jiaojiao from me, and felt not hatred but pity. He had behaved foolishly, but he had come back for her, unlike Zhi Ying.

I found her sitting on her bed with a piece of paper in her hand. When she saw me, she said, 'There, my graduation papers. I've done it. I'm a scholar now. Are you happy?' She sounded normal.

I went forward to examine the paper. A red seal, words in their language. Impressive. 'Congratulations,' I said.

'If only education could solve all our problems.'

'We must celebrate.'

'I don't feel like celebrating. It's only a piece of paper. I've been lucky – I don't think they should have passed me.'

'Don't be too hard on yourself. I'm sure they knew what they were doing.'

'I don't think people always know what they're doing. I don't always know what I'm doing. I . . . Bill . . . Sometimes I don't know who I am.'

'Bill? Barbara's man?'

She looked furtive. 'How did you know?'

'He'd better watch out if he gives you any trouble.'

'Tie Mei, it's all right, I can handle him. He's just upset about Barbara.' She paused and shot me a look of accusation. Then she said slowly, 'She's painting again. She can smell the lilies in the studio so she hardly ever leaves it.'

She wouldn't say any more and I felt we shouldn't discuss the Englishwoman. I looked around for the mirror, but couldn't see it. From the calmer atmosphere, I guessed things were better between her and her man than they had been last time I was there.

'I forgave him,' she said, as if she had read my thoughts, 'but it's hard for me to put it out of my mind.'

'So the wedding is going ahead?'

'Yes – if I don't give birth before then.' She laughed. 'Ken said he couldn't wait.' Her mouth twisted a little. 'I've been thinking,' she looked at me pensively, 'about revenge and forgiveness. I suppose we all get angry when we're hurt. I could have hit Ken for what he did, but I didn't. She spoke quickly, her gestures impatient. 'The will may be there to take revenge, but you don't always need to act upon it.'

I chose my words carefully. 'Sometimes you can't help yourself. Jiaojiao, you're young, there's so much you don't know.'

She looked almost offended. 'What is it you want to tell me, Tie Mei? I'm ready to hear it.'

'I will show you. But can't you see for yourself?' I pointed to the mirror. 'Search in the mirror, and you will find out what you need to know.'

17: *Shuang Jiang* – Frost Descends

24 October

Jiao Mei

It was seven o'clock in the morning and my husband had already gone to work. I heard the rush-hour traffic just outside the window. In Barbara's house you wouldn't have known you lived in London, but here each time a bus went past, the window vibrated, and the whole house shook with the clanking of a train. I had seen it over the wooden fence in the back garden.

I could still smell Ken's warmth next to me.

I'd have preferred a summer wedding and dancing outside. But now, a few days into my marriage, I lay alone in bed gazing at the cold mist outside.

I was glad that the wedding had jostled Barbara out of her dreams. She had left the studio to take me to a dressmaker, discussed, teased, threatened, and finally we left with a long red dress that flowed freely, concealing my bump. We had meant it to be a casual wedding, almost a formality, but with all of our friends there – Taro and his wife, back from Japan, Xiao Lin and Andy, Ken's mother and his colleagues – and the dress, designed and paid for by Barbara, it had been quite an occasion.

Most of my belongings were still in Hampstead. Ken had wanted us to move out so that we could be 'properly married', but Barbara had insisted that I stay there until after the birth – 'If anything happens, somebody will be around.'

Since the wedding, Barbara and I had discussed everything from nappies to the wallpaper for the baby's room. These were things any mother would have done for her daughter and I was happy that it took both our minds off other things.

Ken and I had reached a compromise on our living arrangements: we'd stay at his place for the first week of our married life, then he would stay with me in Hampstead until the baby was born. 'We'll have our honeymoon when the bridge is finished and I get paid. We'll go with the baby,' he had promised.

Contraction, pelvic floor, dilation: the terms were familiar now. I would be ready when the moment came.

When it started to get dark I listened for footsteps. After a few false alarms I pushed open the door impatiently: the mist had returned, and it was as if the day had never happened. It had been like this when Ken had left for work. The air was cold and heavy; the open door sucked in the smell of traffic.

Back in the house I rang Barbara for a chat. Something odd was going on, she said. There were lots of dandelions in the front garden.

'Yours just spread to Bill's lawn,' I said.

'You don't understand. There are so many the lawn is covered – almost made of them. Bill's very upset about it and he blamed you – as if you could have had anything to do with it when you're not even here.'

Tie Mei, I thought. At the other end of the line Barbara giggled. 'It's quite funny, actually. A man from the local paper called to look at the garden and Bill was so rude to him that it made headlines. We're famous.'

I laughed with her. 'You can make dandelion soup or whatever you always said you'd do if you had enough of them.'

'That's a good idea. Give Bill something to do.' She hung up.

This could only be Nainai's doing. Perhaps she had meant it as a joke. But what swift work. The way she picked up my feelings and thoughts, like radar, was frightening.

I fell asleep quickly, as I always did now.

Ken woke me: 'Mei, why is it so cold?' He shivered. 'Have you left a window open somewhere?'

I rubbed my eyes, sat up, stared at him, then remembered. 'No. It's not the wind, it's her.'

'Who?' I felt his warm hands stroke my belly, which woke me properly. This was not the best time to tell him about Nainai. I kissed him instead. 'Listen, darling, I need to be alone for a while. I'll be in the sitting room.'

I rose, and a cool fragrance followed me out of the room.

Tie Mei

It was darker inside than out. I sniffed at the unfamiliar smells around me. I'd not gone back on my word, and I was about to tell her of the deaths I'd witnessed.

I looked around me. I wasn't sure I was meant to be here, but I was grateful for this glimpse of her new life, her future. All I had to speak of was the past. So far she had listened patiently to my stories of loss, but I had no idea how she would react to these tales of revenge. But we needed to go through this together. Only then could I go in peace.

But hurry, Jiaojiao, the vibration of all these young lives has left me weakened.

I stood in the darkest corner facing her, away from the light. A train whistled by and I saw her emerge in a long dressing-gown, the mirror in her hand. Her face was fuller now – she'd put on weight. She stood before me, silent.

I didn't waste any time. 'Have you been looking at the mirror? Did you see anything?'

'I can't, Tie Mei . . . well, not exactly. I thought I could see things, but then I wasn't sure. I . . . I didn't try very hard. I see so many things I shouldn't anyway.'

I sat down next to her and together we gazed into the mirror. 'Look carefully. Here, see the young girl, dressed as a man, about to embark on a journey that will take her far from home. She is sad but she is comforted by the mirror because it reminds her of her home and her father. She knows, too, that the mirror will bring her luck, her man, her lover.'

Jiaojiao was staring hard. Could she see the girl? 'See how new and beautiful the mirror in her hand is. There was no blood then. She is in love now. Look at her making up her face, putting on rouge for her man. Now she is pregnant, radiant, but she is still working, carving beautiful things into the wood.'

Jiaojiao's face softened. Oh, she saw her, just as easily as she saw herself.

'Now look at her in agony. Hear the cry of the baby girl. Look at this man with a gun in his hand, robbing her of life and the mirror.' I paused. Anger rose in me as it had the first time I saw the scene.

'Look, Jiaojiao, look. This is how my great-grandmother was avenged. A few nights after the murder, here we are. See the rippling lakes, the majestic palaces. Imagine the scent of night blossoms, and burnt flesh. Yes, this is the palace, once the biggest palace, the most glorious garden in China, now trampled underfoot by foreigners who smelt of stale milk. They were hysterical with joy, drunk with greed. Look at how the floors were covered knee deep with silks and gowns thrown out of the cupboards as the devils made their progress from room to room. See that man smashing the jade cups that the emperor used to entertain his princes. The devils roared with laughter as each fell to the floor.

'It is too much to bear, isn't it, the murderers enjoying themselves? But now we're out at the Happiness Sea, the lake where the minister in charge of the garden had drowned himself. They said the drowned remained near the scene of their death, looking for men they could drag into the water so that they could be born again. But here comes the foreign devil who killed her, dressed like a clown in an imperial gown.'

Jiaojiao leaned forward. Her hand clasped the mirror.

'There – do you see her? The ghost of my great-grandmother? See that beautiful jewel-encrusted dress, how she tempts the devil. See how her eyes glisten. He gave no thought to who she was. It was the jewels he set his eyes on.

'The greed that had led him to kill also led him to the water, to his death. He drowned.'

18: *Li Dong* – Winter Begins

8 November

Jiao Mei

Watching fireworks had been one of my favourite childhood pleasures, a glorious contrast to my dull everyday existence. For a luxurious moment we could forget the careful counting of ration tickets. The only thing I didn't like was being stuck in a crowd, and there was always a crowd. I peed in my pants once.

The sky here wasn't ready for the show and it rained intermittently. It didn't distract me from thinking of Barbara. It seemed we had made almost all the preparations for the baby: the new blue wallpaper was up, nappies and tiny clothes had been bought, a cot stood in the corner of my room. Now Barbara had withdrawn to her shell of silence and reclaimed her studio. I'd stolen in there once: there were no lilies but on the canvas the pictures of them were fresh, the petals pinkish white as if they had bloomed only yesterday. Bill, convinced that she was suffering delusions, had asked her again to see someone, but she had refused. 'Why should I? Why do you all think I'm ill?' She included me in this, although I'd never said any such thing to her. 'I eat, I work, I'm not in pain. You say I imagine things, but I'm an artist, that's what I do.'

Since the wedding Bill had been with us almost every day. He and I still avoided each other. The weather had changed for the worse. Barbara shivered, and Bill seemed to shiver with her.

Ken rubbed his hands in the cold air. We were watching the fireworks from his colleague's balcony. 'This is nothing,' I murmured to him. 'You should come to China on October the first.'

'What is that?' he asked, his eyes still on the sky.

'Our national day, when there's a firework display in Tiananmen Square.'

'Oh, yes?'

'Compared to that, this is . . . what do you say? Baby's play?'

'Child's play.' He turned to me at last. 'It's really good, though, don't you think?'

I shrugged my shoulders.

There was a break in the show.

After a few minutes' silence, Ken laughed. 'Of course, you invented gunpowder.'

I laughed, too. 'But the skill went into making fireworks for the emperor's enjoyment.' I remembered the display in the story of the mirror.

'Lucky emperor,' Ken said dreamily, 'sitting there watching his concubines dancing around the Yellow Flower Maze. What a sight that must have been.'

'Cursed emperor,' I said. 'He deserted his garden.'

'Worse, though, to lose his empire!' Ken stared at me as if I were a five-year-old. I was surprised by the strength of his reaction. It had been such a long time since I had told him the story of the mirror that I wasn't sure he had remembered it, but it seemed he knew every detail.

'Who cares about his empire?' I said. 'I didn't know you'd listened so hard.'

'Of course I did, and I've thought about your story a lot. There's a lot of truth in it, and I'm ashamed of what my ancestors did – they've done much worse in other parts of the world. But that was a different time. It needn't have anything to do with us.' He turned impatiently from me to look up at the sky as the fireworks resumed.

My eyes drifted briefly towards the spectacle but my thoughts stayed on our exchange. The ruins of the Garden of Eternal Spring had stood next to my school. Our outings there had been so numerous that my response to it was blunted. It was not until much later, when I had started going there on my own, that I could appreciate the special beauty of the place, or what remained of it. Nostalgia was what I had felt most keenly, though, not anger or the desire for revenge.

But I felt differently now, after what Tie Mei had told me. She had awakened in me a strong sense of national shame and family pride. The burning of the Garden of Eternal Spring and the plundering of the treasures were no longer the stuff of propaganda – they felt personal. My ancestor had helped to build that paradise, and my ancestor was robbed and killed. It was my garden, as much as the emperor's, that they had destroyed.

What had impressed me so deeply was how vividly and powerfully Tie Mei had described the scene of revenge, as if she herself had been the avenger. She would have done it – I did not doubt that as I remembered the way she had relished the man's death. She had reminded me of the days when she had first come to me, enraged and saddened by the life I was leading. I had been appalled by that image then, but this time, picturing my ancestor's suffering, I had sympathised with Tie Mei.

But could luring someone to their death ever be justified? What happened in her other stories, and what did the curse mean? I still did not have the answers I was so desperately seeking.

An uproarious 'ohhh' drew my eyes back to the sky for the finale, as millions of shooting stars illuminated the heavens above the opposite bank. Suddenly Ken looked down at me. 'About that mirror story.'

'What about it?' I felt chilly.

'I think it sounds so romantic that the mirror could be the matchmaker.'

'Yes, but it's just a story.' I reached out a hand to his. 'I see my grandmother sometimes.'

'I know, darling,' he said slowly.

'What? Do you see her too?' I staggered, and had to steady myself on the wall.

'No, of course not. I know you . . . are seeing things, though. Mei,' he looked me in the eye, 'if this continues after the baby is born, I want you to go to a therapist, a counsellor.'

'You think I'm mad?' I leaned against the wall, trembling.

'No, no, that's not what I meant at all. I think . . . I don't know. You've been through such a hell of a lot, it must have something to do with it. The strain. But, Mei, I'm with you now, we're in it together.'

I looked away. My stomach contracted as the baby shifted position. He moved less often now that both of us were so big – there was less room for him. I put Ken's hand on my belly and the movement stopped.

We were the only people left on the balcony. Inside we joined Ken's colleagues for drinks. 'How's the bridge coming along?' someone asked.

'Slowly,' Ken said, in a deep, steady voice as he poured juice for me without looking up.

'And the family?' another shouted.

'Soon.' Ken looked at me. 'Any time now.'

Later that night we went to a club with some friends. Xiao Lin had advised me to move about as much as possible. 'The sooner you have it, now you are nearly nine months, the better. You don't want to be overdue, oh, no. Dance as much as you can, that's how I got mine down.'

I shook my body. But there was no movement inside. I was meant to count the baby's kicks every day, and had been given a chart to record them. I had made a mess of it. Did one ripple of kicking count as one or several kicks? In the end I gave up: it was alive, of that there was no doubt. And now it was fast asleep – rocking always did that. I already knew how to handle it – I would be a good mum.

We wandered from one tube-like room to another. The ceilings were low. Artificial smoke billowed around us and flashing, colourful lights winked at me, with a million fleeting thoughts. Ken's eyes were closed. Taro's face, unblemished and smooth like a child's, made me want to stroke it.

'You shouldn't be here.' A woman, her head shaven, pointed at my belly with the end of her cigarette.

'I'm trying to induce labour,' I said.

She laughed, and her single earring shook. 'Good luck.'

Ken put his hand round me protectively. I noticed he'd put on a little weight, as if in sympathy with me. He would protect me with his body, if need be, I thought proudly. Power could be a wonderful thing. It depended on how you used it. I looked at my watch: twelve thirty. I motioned to Ken that I was going outside, and sneaked away.

He had known all the time, and he'd been good about it, although I didn't feel apologetic about my relationship with Tie Mei. I had never shared with him my fears about Barbara, but my feelings for her were now so tied up with my thoughts about the birth. Pain was part of the process, just as what was going to happen to Barbara was part of something bigger. I could not bear to think of what that might mean, just as I could not imagine what the pain of labour would be like. But both were inevitable and that certainty was strangely reassuring. Blind faith was all that could help me – I had to trust that things would unfold in a way that would ultimately make sense.

The street was still well lit. A few people were hanging around the door, one holding on to a rail, vomiting. A homeless man with a blanket sat motionless opposite an antiques shop, from which a giant wooden African head stared at him. Empty taxis passed by in both directions. In the distance a siren rang. The night's hand reached out to soothe our pain.

I stepped over the long limbs of the homeless man and walked straight through to a green space beyond a big supermarket, just next to the antiques shop. The gate wasn't locked. There were trees on both sides, and a clearing in the middle, a bench. I walked to it and sat down. Above me the London sky was pink.

Gradually, her smell came to me, as though my faith was summoning it. She seemed pale in the strong London light. I pitied her, this fragile visitor from another world. I'll hang on to you, with the same determination that helped you find me across the great divide.

Tie Mei

I was barely more than a fragrance. I knew what this weakness meant: the time remaining to me there was short. I tried to concentrate, but it was getting harder.

'You've got the mirror?'

She reached for her bag with some effort, turning slowly. Her eyes, which had been on me like a hawk's since I'd appeared, lingered on me, then dropped. When she looked up again I saw that they were greedy, the look of a mother already. How quickly she was changing.

I pointed at the mirror. 'See this room of treasures? Where do you think this Japanese had got them? There were some shoes, did you see? Chinese women's shoes. He looked bored. Was that why he was drinking? Anyway, he had the mirror.'

She murmured something I couldn't hear. But I wasn't listening, because of what I saw.

'Look behind him, look – my poor mother, with her hair loose and her clothes torn. She was still beautiful, even then.'

'How could you tell it was him?' she whispered.

'He wore the military uniform. I knew it too well – I'd recognise it anywhere. In my childhood it was a sign of terror.' I paused, and willed her to see the scenes in the mirror as I did. 'Look, he sees her. See how he stares, then runs to the corner of the room to escape. See the way he shakes his head, his face ashen. Now he's run to the door, and is trying to get out into the street. But wherever he runs, she's there before him. Wherever he goes, she follows.'

I stood behind her shoulder, breathing down her neck. 'Look carefully now, and you should see my mother. I've always wanted to show you how beautiful and gentle she

204

was.' She stared at me instead of at the mirror, her eyes streaming with tears – tears I could no longer shed. 'Damn the curse,' I said. 'Who cares about revenge? I just want my mother back. I just want my own life back, the life I had with her, and the life I had with you.'

19: *Xiao Xue* – Snow Begins

23 November

Jiao Mei

Ted's house was in the middle of nowhere, full of cold dusty draughts and thick dog's breath. Like his sister's place in Hampstead this was another big echoey house, with neglected corners where cobwebs grew. There were toys everywhere. My hosts left me alone – I was used to this now: it was the English way, apparently. I knew to ask for drinks and even food when I needed them. Ted was adding more wood to the open fire. Then he went to draw the curtain, and I felt a whiff of damp air that made me cough. The wooden floor was uncarpeted but it was warm where I sat near the fire. The dog lay drowsily next to me, its white and grey fur wet and muddy from the walk. With each crackle of the flames it raised its head half-heartedly, then dozed again.

I sipped tea and watched Ted. He resembled Barbara, same broad shoulders, same straightforward yet hesitant smile, curly brown hair. Now he sank down on to a well-worn armchair, eyes half closed; he didn't attempt conversation. His size reminded me of Bill but, unlike Bill, his silence was not oppressive. I felt he was just lost in his thoughts, or a little shy. It helped that he was mostly silent, even with Barbara, whom he obviously loved. Soon he was going to the village pub, which he always did after dinner. When he stood up to get his boots, the dog's tail wagged: he knew it was time for another outing.

'You must forgive him, he's never seen a foreigner before.' The sister-in-law, a pale, tired-looking woman, bent forward with a bath towel in her hand. I turned to find a little boy with wet hair staring at me. 'Matthew, this lady came from China, a faraway place. Do you want to know where it is? I'll show you on the map.' She took him away.

'I thought she was talking about the dog,' I whispered after they'd gone. Ted chuckled and the dog's ears pricked. Barbara was nowhere to be seen.

We had walked for two hours, the final stretch in darkness. It had felt like for ever to me. The woods seemed to have remained untouched for hundreds of years. Lying by the path, a large tree reminded us that this was an island, exposed and vulnerable to the elements. Only three of us had gone out for the walk: Barbara led, Ted followed, and I trailed behind, panting, trying to catch up.

'It might snow,' Ted said – his feet seemed to know where they were going.

'Snow?' Barbara exclaimed. 'That would be wonderful. I haven't seen snow for years.'

'You should come down more often.'

'You'd love some snow, wouldn't you?' Barbara called back to me.

'Yes,' I said quickly, not wanting to disappoint, but I didn't mean it. In Beijing it always snowed. I remembered the red blossom of the Mei flower dotted around in a white world, so pretty. I used to love it, but one winter everything changed. I remembered the freezing wind as I stood with my mother in front of a strange man's house waiting for him to come out to talk to her. 'I'm cold, Mama, I want to go home.'

She had picked me up. 'Be patient, my child,' she said, hugging me. 'This man can help Baba, so Mama has to talk to him.'

'Why don't we knock on his door? He's at home, I can see him.'

'No, child, we mustn't intrude.'

But the man didn't let us in, and the snow with the red blossom in his yard had imprinted itself so vividly on my

208

mind that even now I could picture the moment when he drew the curtain with the lights on inside. I recognised him as the bespectacled student who had carried me at the botanists' outing, and had spoken out in favour of cabbages. 'He's seen us,' I shouted excitedly, but he did not emerge. I was confused: why wouldn't he come out and speak to us? He'd seemed to like me at the outing.

Now I heard Barbara telling Ted about the dandelion lawn, giggling softly. 'But that's what I love about him – he's such a perfectionist, unlike me,' she said.

At the end of the wood we came across a small church on a high cliff, exposed to the wind from the sea below. Barbara took me to where her parents were buried in the church-yard. Ted stood by the gate. As we walked past him he said, 'You look like the Chinese girl in the picture book Barbara had when we were kids. She had already decided to go to China.'

I asked him what Barbara was like as a child and they exchanged the mysterious glances that siblings reserve for each other. 'I remember her picking Grandma's roses, grinding the petals to make rose-water to drink. Weren't you sick?' he said.

She laughed. 'I don't remember that.'

I glimpsed the sea below.

'Want to go down? I'll take you,' she said.

Ted waved and took a short-cut home to make tea.

The path was narrow and we kept close. I hadn't wanted to come on the walk, but now I could not turn back. As I started behind Barbara, however, I realised I didn't feel tired any more: my steps had become almost automatic. We didn't talk and I lost track of time. Then, suddenly, it dawned on me how normally she had been behaving since we had been away. This trip was just for the two of us, she had said, a girls' weekend away. She wanted to show me the sea. I said I had seen the sea with Ken, but she insisted: this was her bit of the sea, where she'd grown up.

I remembered the sparkle in her eyes on the train, her infectious anticipation. She had joked and giggled, a complete change from the last few weeks when she had been elusive, keeping to her room, eating snacks rather than meals. It was as if she was playing hide and seek, and all of us were in the dark.

Now it felt like none of that had ever happened. Even Tie Mei seemed distant here. Maybe we had both needed a change of scene. Oh, the pleasure of this walk – it had come not a day too soon.

A well-wrapped woman came up the path with her dog and nodded to us, the sky behind her dark and gloomy. Almost as soon as she had passed us, rain began to pour. We trudged along, the chalky soil sticky and heavy under our feet. Suddenly I felt exhausted again.

Fortunately we had reached the end of the path. I looked but could not see where the sea began and the sky ended. Barbara's voice broke the wetness around us, like the flight of the seagulls zigzagging across the sky: 'I took Yuan Shui to the sea, the East China Sea. Our last trip together.' She faced the sea, her back to me. I stood behind her. 'We had planned it so well, we were so excited. It was to be an adventure for both of us. I wanted to show him the sea, to open him up, and he . . .' she turned back to me and I was alarmed to see that the dreaminess had returned '. . . he had wanted to show me the gardens in Suzhou.'

They were his idea of heaven. He had often described them to me, and I knew he and my mother had gone there for their honeymoon. For him, they epitomised Chinese culture: art, tranquillity, poetry, beauty. I could picture the gardens in my mind, though I'd never set foot in them – they had been copied all over China. I imagined my father and Barbara holding hands there, alone in the dark, counting the moons as the ancient poets he admired had done with their lovers.

Pavilions, spring blossoms, winding paths and arrangements of rocks. I was sure I would never warm to those gardens: they were less about plants and flowers, scents and colours, than about concepts and ideas. They did not appeal to my senses.

But they had spoken eloquently to my father. The position

of a particular plant, its name which might pun with something else – osmanthus (*gui*) for nobility, or hibiscus (*furong*) for honour – the way plants and other features were combined in a view, would bring to his mind a poem or a story and excite him or draw him into the past. He knew by heart all the stories to which the gardens alluded, and never tired of telling them to me.

He must have shared them with Barbara, too.

Seagulls flew madly in the sky. I was wet, she was wetter, but we stood still. I was eager to hear what had happened on their trip. 'So did he see the sea?' I asked.

She nodded slowly. 'But he clammed up like an oyster. I think he was frightened. He withdrew deeper into himself. He was a valley man, and the sea was too much for him. There was a chill in him that I couldn't warm.' She stepped closer to me and I saw the feverish burning in her eyes. I wished I hadn't encouraged her to confide. 'You must have held his hands – did you notice how cold they were? Somehow he could only get close to inanimate things, or abstractions – past glory, historical figures, plants . . .'

You knew him better than any of us, his mother, his daughter – perhaps even his wife. You made love to him, maybe even when I was sleeping in the next bed. But it seemed that the better you knew him, the more difficult it was for you to let him go. Perhaps you knew him so well that you saw beyond his failings to his potential. You knew what he might have been had he been able to tell you. But it had been a doomed journey.

'He loved you,' I said, partly to convince myself. But I knew he must have. He had taken risks to be with her.

'He was attracted to me, I know that. I tempted him. I was exotic, I adored him, I played disciple to his ideals. He was flattered, perhaps even touched.' She turned away. 'But I don't think he loved me. Well, not the way I wanted him to.'

'But he did, I know he did,' I insisted.

'I wanted us to be together like two normal people, but he hid too many things. It was as if he didn't believe in his own worth.'

211

Baba's wounded pride. After so many public humiliations he had no face to save, even at home. From botany lecturer to gardener, from happily married father to divorced class enemy, he had suffered a terrible fall. No wonder he had lacked faith in himself.

She'd gone from my side. I followed her into the thick mist. Soon our shoes were wet and the waves were beneath us. We were in the sea but we still couldn't see it. She walked too fast, and I was frightened that she would disappear into the mist. I grabbed her. 'Let's go back,' I said. 'I've been in the sea now.' She did not move. 'Let's go,' I urged again. 'I'm worried about the baby.'

This worked instantly. We hurried back, the wind behind us and the rain upon us.

I picked my way carefully, tired and increasingly alarmed. What if I went into labour there and then? She put more distance between us, as though she wanted to run away from me. I tried to catch up, but it was getting harder. Whispers in the darkening woods set me on edge.

Back at the house the scones and cream I craved failed to materialise, but I wolfed down six digestive biscuits with two mugs of tea. Dinner was roast lamb, but Barbara did not appear.

I went to bed late after I had read numerous stories to Matthew, who was too excited to sleep. My bedroom was a cold, damp little room that had once belonged to Barbara. There was an old teddy-bear that I clutched to my chest. My body was tired after an afternoon's walking, but my mind was active. On that bed, I felt Barbara and I were inextricably linked on a path that would take us both to our destiny. Getting off it was out of the question, and there was comfort in the knowledge. But where would it lead? I was too tired to follow the thought through. The sea roared, and I was transported back to our garden in Hampstead. We were only away for a weekend but I was homesick. Before we had left, we had planted lily bulbs and I was impatient to watch them grow. I knew nothing could be seen above ground yet, but I imagined them soaking up the nutrients in the earth. I missed the house, which felt less big and gloomy now that I was going to make a nest in it. I tossed and turned, but could not find a comfortable position.

It was a long time before I realised there was a new smell in the room – Tie Mei's fragrance. Soon, in that special realm between sleeping and wakefulness, I saw her through half-closed eyes, faint, willowy. 'Tie Mei.' I roused myself and spoke aloud to bring her into focus, to pull her into my world. With one hand, I felt for the mirror resting next to me.

She came nearer, her fragrance stronger. I sat up, and a feeling of helplessness came over me. Somehow I felt she was going to disappear, that I was powerless to do anything about it.

'Tie Mei?' I called again, and held the mirror before her. Slowly she looked down at it, her fingers caressing it. We sat close and it was a sign of her weakness that her scent was no stronger, but I felt nearer to her than I'd ever been. Last time she'd been here, I had shed her tears for her, but this time, my heart beat for her, its rhythm that of her voice, slow, slow, rise and fall. Then I saw, for the first time, the image in the mirror. 'It was a good-looking face,' she began, 'not particularly young, not smooth like my husband's, but rugged. It was the ruggedness I loved – it suggested a life more daring, more vital than mine.'

'Zhi Ying?' I whispered.

She turned reluctantly from the mirror to me. 'But he was a coward. He had a weak heart and a weak mind. He couldn't face the consequences of his own actions.'

'Tie Mei?'

'His was the only murder I committed,' she said.

I examined her face in the moonlight. How much it had changed from the first night when she'd appeared to me. It was now calm without any trace of rage or tension, or even remorse.

'You found him at last,' I said.

'Oh, yes. I knew I would.' She nodded slowly. 'I found him with the mirror. I killed the old man in him. He died in my

213

arms. What more would he want?' she said, a gentle smile on her face.

It was her gentleness that accompanied me to sleep that night.

Tie Mei

It was a wonderful night, with a full moon. I followed its light into a comfortable-looking flat. From the objects scattered about I pieced together a picture of his life after he left me. A propaganda cadre with the Communist army, he must have done well through the Liberation years. There were photographs of him smiling, decorated with medals, and of his children, with his cheekbones and his wife's skin.

He must have been given the mirror as a bribe, or a gift: the plate that held it bore the words 'Jing-lin Museum'. There were other antiques scattered around, and I saw he had remained a man of taste.

But I smelt death in his room. I had heard his cough, which pained me, before I saw him. He emerged along a dark corridor, much smaller than I remembered him, hand on the switch about to turn on the light. 'Zhi Ying,' I whispered. He looked up, as though he had expected to see something strange.

'Tie Mei, is that you?' He waited. I didn't move. He shook his head and walked on.

He stumbled down the corridor, coughing, looking back over his shoulder. In his bedroom he reached for a small blue bottle. His unsteady hands missed and it fell to the floor. He stopped to pick it up, catching my eye. What was in that look? Relief? Recognition? There was no alarm. I held his hands: they felt stiff and cold. I smoothed them and as I did so the flesh became supple. I leaned forward and sat on his lap – this was how we had used to sit. He started shivering but he didn't shake me off. I smoothed his face, feeling the bones beneath the now loose skin that I had known so well. I kissed his lips and felt not the dry mouth of an old man but the sweetness of our youth.

I whispered to him, just as he used to whisper to me years before: 'This rose now has thorns.' I drew out his *yang* as he lay in ecstasy in my arms. Death gave me power I had never had in life, and I wanted him to pay. But this was not punishment: it was as though I had released him.

The second before he died, Zhi Ying had tried to say something. Once, I had told him the story of the mirror, but I didn't know whether he'd registered it. Had he thought of me when he'd asked for it? In the years after he disappeared, I had thought of him often. As the Communists won victory after victory and eventually took over China, I had harboured hopes that he would come to me, but I never heard from him.

When his life ebbed away I felt a part of me also die. In my heart there had always been a place for him, I realised. I had kept his memory alive – even my resentment had etched him deeper into my soul. Afterwards it was a long time before the emptiness left me. He was the only man I had loved. I thought I'd never get over it. But in a sense now I, too, was free. Nobody could have released me from him except myself.

Telling Jiaojiao about it reminded me how far I'd gone. 'I'm free now, really free,' I murmured, my eyes on the Mei blossom in the Englishwoman's garden. How had I ended up here? It was like . . . I was returning home. I smelt the two of them strongly here. It was nearly time to leave Jiaojiao, and this garden.

'I shall hate to leave,' I said, to the mute tree.

The wind had a melancholy sound, and the branches reached out, as if urging me to stay.

20: *Da Xue* – Big Snow

7 December

Jiao Mei

Three days after my official due date I received a letter
from my mother. The sight of the stained envelope with
its blue and red airmail ridges made me leap to snatch it
from Bill. It could only be from her. Clutching it tightly in
my hand, I rushed to the doctor's appointment. Part of me
wanted to tear open the envelope, another part wanted to
save it for later. My preoccupation meant I missed half of
what the consultant said to me but I heard, 'If you don't go
into labour by next Wednesday we might induce you.'
Sobering words.

When I came out of the hospital the world seemed to be in
a spin. Men on motorbikes sped along the road, taxis squealed
past, a woman with a ponytail jogged along, her bosom rising
and falling rhythmically. Even the air seemed to move to a
beat of its own.

I sat on the pavement and tore open the letter.

Jiaojiao

Your letter arrived this morning and I have dropped
everything to write back to you. I hope this will get to
you before the baby arrives – from what you said in your
letter your due date must be soon.

There's so much to tell you, I don't know where to
begin. I feel as if you're at once distant, and so near to

217

me. I'm talking to a photo of you that I have kept with me all these years, the one of you standing between us, clasping us, your lovely face smiling.

Your letter made me think so much of your child-hood. I didn't have much milk when you were born and in those times it was hard to get powdered milk, let alone fresh. We lived near the zoo and every dusk I heard the tigers roar. In my idle, depressed state, I would spend a lot of time wandering there. One day I saw the keeper walk past me with a bucket of white liquid. 'What is that?' I asked.

'Milk.'

'Milk?' I couldn't believe my ears. 'Fresh milk?'

'Fresh milk.' My nipples hurt at the words. 'It's for the tigress who's just given birth.'

I knew what to do. The next night I stole into the zoo, tiptoed past the dozing keeper and went for the bucket. The tigress peered at me through the bars of her cage and our eyes met briefly. I quaked as I approached her. I'm sorry to take your milk – I am a mother like you and I need to feed my baby. Suddenly she roared and I knocked down a gourd next to the bucket. The keeper woke and shouted at me. Desper-ate, I told him what I had come for. He took pity on me. 'Come every night after dark, and I'll spare some for you,' he said.

You owe your life to the tigress. Nainai used to say you were blessed with good fortune and I have always believed that. You've always been a brave girl and I know where your courage came from. You drank the milk that was meant to be for the tiger cub. How could you not be brave?

How could I not be brave? She was the tigress. I had been loved, so fiercely loved, from the very beginning. I'd always known it. I held the letter to my heart as though it was my mother, and saw her face in front of me, young, smiling, the face I saw in my dreams. When I looked up the rain had

218

started again: cars, shops, people, everything was blurred and my face was wet. Then a hand touched my elbow and a voice from another world, this English world, whispered, 'Are you all right? Do you need a doctor?' I blinked and looked up into the face of a concerned passer-by. My tears must have alarmed him. 'I'm fine,' I said, and got up hastily. I smiled to myself all the way home. When I saw the house, I raced up the hill.

I seemed to end up in the back garden by the pond without having to walk there. I opened the letter again, my eyes feasting on the words like a hungry wolf's:

We loved each other, Yuan Shui and I. I thought there was nobody else who loved each other as much as we did. We were inseparable. But after the orchid-and-cabbage incident we were cast into complete darkness. He had been such a well-liked and a good man, how could he be a rightist, a class enemy, simply because he loved beautiful flowers? A few months later, after several humiliating public rallies, where he refused to repent, he was sent to the far north, to work on a forest farm. It was so remote, and the letters took months to arrive. At first I refused to believe it would last, I kept hoping someone would realise this was a mistake, and release him soon. But you know as well as I now that tens of thousands of people were in a similar plight. Who were we but small cogs in a big wheel that crushed us mercilessly? When I realised he was not to return I became so depressed. My sole thought was to get him released, whatever the cost.

I was told the man who could intervene in his case was the student who had denounced him: he had now become the movement leader. I went to plead with him. Before this happened he had been quite friendly, and even, I suspected, had a secret desire for me. I had returned his friendship, but no more. But now that I was begging him for a favour he refused to see me. Do you remember standing in the snow waiting for him to come out of his house?

I knew what she was going to say next, I knew it with dread and the thrill of discovery.

Eventually he agreed to meet me, and he promised that if I married him he would see to it that your father was returned. He didn't force me. I was desperate for your father to be freed. I said yes.

Everybody turned against me, family and friends. But I knew I had done the right thing. Sacrifice was the most I had to offer your father, I decided. For his happiness I would give mine away.

You know the rest, don't you, now? Once he returned, your father readily granted me a divorce. He called me a whore, and said I was not the woman he knew and loved. That I was free to do whatever I wanted. Then he said he wished I was dead. I would have preferred that, but what good would it have done you or him? I divorced the movement leader five years after we were married. By that time you and your father had already gone to the south.

I don't know what your father said about our divorce. I was a cruel woman and a bad mother. But I would have been a worse mother if I hadn't left you. Do you understand? Now that you're about to be a mother, I hope you might. You know what life was like for a family of rightists in those days. If I had not done it, your father would not have been released, and you would always have been the child of a bad element.

I'm living on my own now, I have been for a few years, which is why the letter you mentioned didn't reach me. I have more time for myself, which is good, but it's hard not to spend it all dwelling on the past. Now that you are back in touch, now that you know the truth, will you forgive me? I dare not hope for love as I deserted you and have no right to ask for that, but things have turned out well for you, it seems. You are the best scholar this family has ever produced, and you're doing a degree in a foreign language. To think that my sacrifice might have helped to contribute to that is a huge comfort to me.

It's been so hard not being in touch. You were too young to understand but I thought your father would eventually forgive me. I waited in vain. I don't hate him, but I'd hoped he'd let you know the truth. When they told me you were going abroad I thought that was the end of the world for me. That night you left I almost didn't come to see you. I felt doomed either way: to see you off to such a distant place, without you having forgiven me, was unbearable; to miss the chance of seeing you for possibly the last time was unthinkable. I went in the end, telling myself I'd be as cold as a stone when I saw you, that that way I wouldn't hurt you.

Oh, Jiaojiao, if you've understood all this, if you've forgiven me, will you call me Mama again? I will hear you despite the distance between us.

'Mama,' I said, but I could not hear my own voice. I wanted to shout but a tight knot was forming in my throat, suffocating me. How alien, small and insignificant everything around me seemed now. I longed for the square yard in Beijing where my happiness lay, where my mother was smiling and I was indulged. How cold the wind was here. Forgiveness was the wrong word. What would I have done if I were her? What did it take to be a mother? A tentative pull inside me made me put my hands to my belly. My baby, helpless, dependent. In a flash I realised I would have done everything for the baby inside me that she had.

'How many moons?' A voice spoke and made me jump. I turned to see Barbara, pale and indifferent, as if she hadn't seen me. She squatted down, and repeated, 'How many moons do you see?'

'What do you mean?'

'Ah, you're even more stupid than I am.' She pointed at the water. 'There's one in the pond, one up there in the sky.' She waved a hand in the air, her eyes fixed on the water. I looked up and, sure enough, there was a pale moon against the blue sky. I would never have thought to look for it at ten o'clock in the morning but there it was.

'And there's the moon in the teacup I am holding.' She winked at me, then put down the cup and held her head in both hands as if she was trying to pull something out of it. 'Oh, my head,' she murmured, and stood up slowly. 'Now, where is the other moon? Ah, yes, the moon face of you, my lovely one.' She stared at me. 'Oh, you look so like him – keep away from me.' I stepped back but stayed near, and caught her just before she stumbled at the edge of the pond. I saw that her eyes were half closed and felt the full weight of her resting on me as though she were a baby, unable to support herself. I looked around – I needed help, I couldn't hold her like this for long.

She was gripping me hard as her eyes followed something in the distance that I couldn't see. Then, suddenly, she struggled free with such strength that I fell back a few steps. Her face opened into a smile, as if someone was telling her the happiest news she could hear. 'Barbara?'

She put a finger to her lips. 'Look.'

'What?' I followed her gaze to the space next to the pavilion. 'Look.' She was staring at the earth there, unblinking.

'But what am I looking at?'

'Can't you see it? Let's go nearer, then.' She dragged me forward, around the pond, up the pebbled path and towards the pavilion.

We stood before an empty patch of earth, hard and frosty. I remembered the digging we'd had to do to clear the space for the lilies, whose bulbs were now sleeping underground, getting ready for next summer. She squatted down and closed her eyes, her head tilted backwards. 'Oh, fresh, fresh fragrance,' she said. Then she opened her eyes and whispered, 'I don't want to sound ungrateful but the ones that are growing smell even better than those you gave me at the studio.'

I held her hands and shook them. 'Barbara, there are no lilies yet. They're still bulbs.'

'What do you mean?' She looked at me as if I had said something ridiculous. 'Look, here, right here, smell – no, feel them.' She bent forward and scooped air into her hands, the fingers moving as if they were puppets. 'Feel them, so cool, so delicate.'

I stepped back and looked around me. We were in deepest winter, two weeks before Christmas. The ground was hard and frost-sealed. Trees bowed their heads and waited patiently for spring.

'How have I missed all these?' she exclaimed. 'The orchids, in bloom already, and the jasmine, I should have planted more. But what's this?' She walked towards the crabapple tree, whose branches still bore small red fruits. 'Did I plant this osmanthus, or did the scent come from the park? No, this one is too young to blossom yet, but I could swear I smelt osmanthus. Look, we must do something about those bamboos – they're killing the poor honeysuckle.'

Half-way through her monologue I realised she was back in the garden she had created for my father. She had left too early in the season to see all of the flowers in bloom, but now, years later, she'd finally gone back.

I did not have the heart to correct her. Let her dream. My only concern was how to react when she woke up.

'I'm glad I insisted on it, don't you agree? If we had listened to Yuan Shui we would never have had all these. I do worry a little, though.' She turned to me. 'I hadn't imagined the blossoms would be so spectacular – and the fragrance! What if we're discovered?' She looked at me, radiant; the fear of retribution could not diminish her pleasure in the scent. 'But let's enjoy it while it's there, shall we? Breathe deeply,' she ordered. I obliged – and smelt a fragrance, too.

'Oh, look, here he comes!' She pointed at a figure emerging from beyond the pond.

It was Bill. I called to him urgently, but she seemed confused. 'Bill?' she murmured, puzzled. I had never been more relieved to see him.

As he came nearer she looked back at me quickly, as if to

find a way of escape. 'Hello, darling, what are you doing here?' Bill said, reaching out for her. But she shrank away from him with a howl of pain, and covered her eyes with her hands. 'Darling, darling,' Bill embraced her, 'let's go in.' She struggled weakly, but it didn't take him long to overcome her. 'Let's go in,' he said again, gently. Sobbing, she let herself be led away.

I had no doubt what was happening. The equilibrium I had found suddenly collapsed. There was not a moment to lose. 'Call the doctor,' I said to Bill, who had sat Barbara on the sofa and suggested a cup of tea to calm her down.

He frowned as he reached for the kettle. 'What are you on about? She's just a bit emotional.'

'Believe me, Bill, she's very sick. Call the doctor.'

He looked at her intently. She stared past him, as if he didn't exist. Finally he, too, grew alarmed. 'Are you sure?'

'Yes. Hurry,' I said.

Bill's hand was on the phone as he said, 'I think it's best to go up to A and E. I'll get the car.'

I waited in the empty house. Half an hour, two hours, the whole afternoon. It was getting dark. A spasm pulled at my lower back. Was this it? I wasn't ready. Where was Ken? I gripped my mother's letter and paced around restlessly. When the spasm had passed I sat down.

Why didn't Bill ring? Which hospital had he taken her to? My head spun like a wheel, with thoughts of labour, my mother and Barbara.

My mother had been so matter-of-fact about her suffering, almost as though she had absolved the guilt of those who had tried to ruin her. That was typical of her generation. They did not blame anyone. And Barbara: didn't she blame anyone for her unhappiness in the past, and her pain now?

Tie Mei, my mother and Barbara: my family of passionate women. For all their failings, they had accepted their responsibilities: Tie Mei, for my ancestors' honour; my mother, for protecting my father and me; and Barbara, whose love embraced not just my father's vanity but my insecurity. I felt pale beside them. How I had lectured Tie

Mei on her vengefulness, condemned my mother for her disgrace and patronised Barbara for her carelessness. Bill was right: I was the guilty one – guilty of lacking passion, guilty of selfishness. While these women had given themselves up to their passion, I had thought the promise of a new life here in this land justified lying to and hurting Ken, the man I claimed to love.

My belly pulled. I waited for the spasm to die away as it had before but, like a strong current, it continued until I cried out. Should I ring the midwife?

It subsided, and I went listlessly into the garden. Close to the Mei tree, against the fast fading light, I found new buds, delicate pink wrapped in worn brown. It was nearly time for it to bloom. A Chinese poet had once adopted a Mei as his wife, such was his love for it. Its blossom braved the cold. I knew how much endurance its beauty required.

Another wave of pain forced me down.

Tie Mei

Finally I was back in my garden, but it was no longer a ruin. The heady scent of the night blossoms was just as I had remembered it, but someone was walking the path I used to tread. The flowers nodded at her as if she was the gardener. Like me, she had no shadow under the moonlight, but she could not see me yet.

It was the Englishwoman. How pleasing her body seemed, half buried among the flowers. Where her height had made her look clumsy in the big house, now she blended in, as if she herself was one of the plants she tended. She reminded me of myself when she bent down to talk to the roses.

A fellow gardener, but I had done her wrong.

Then she straightened and smiled. No, I'd made her happy – she wanted to be here. This had become her garden.

Suddenly I felt something calling me to the other garden that spoke to me with intimacy. I heard a cry from inside the house. Jiaojiao. Was it time?

21: *Dong Zhi* – Winter Solstice

22 December

Jiao Mei

'What a fat baby he is! This is what happens when you are overdue. You should have listened to me.' Xiao Lin put down the pot of fish soup she had made.

'Give me some of that soup now. I'm starving.' My mouth watered at the smell.

'Go and heat it up.' Xiao Lin gestured to her big husband. She was getting big herself: married life became her. He frowned, and she added, 'Please,' impatiently. When he was gone she asked, 'How old is the baby?'

'Twelve days.'

'And Ken's already left you to go to work? He's meant to look after you for a whole month. Have you forgotten about the *zuo yuezi*, the month's rest?'

I smiled at my baby, who was suckling. It didn't hurt any more.

'I wanted to visit you earlier, but Andy said we should leave you alone for a while, what with Barbara and the baby. He didn't realise you'd need looking after, now that Barbara's gone and Ken's back at work.'

'I'm all right, really.'

'Did it hurt?' She sucked her teeth as if even the thought of it was painful.

'A bit.'

' "A bit," she said!' She spoke in English so that her

husband could hear. 'A bit – you heard that? How English she's become! Don't try to be brave with me – it bloody well hurt! I know! Like a butcher's shop, down there.' Her husband retreated to the furthest corner of the room and picked up yesterday's newspaper.

'The soup! The soup!' Xiao Lin shouted at him, then rushed to the cooker to rescue it.

I drank the soup as the baby drank my milk.

'What black hair – he's got your lips, but definitely Ken's eyes,' Xiao Lin murmured. Thomas opened one eye and had a good look at her. 'Do you want me to stay? I am on Christmas holiday now. I'll make you fish soup every day,' she promised. She was still working, even though she was married, but in an office now.

'Ken's mother is coming for Christmas – perhaps afterwards when she's gone.'

She nodded. 'All right. You just let me know. The foreigners do not know how to look after you, do they? There, you're tired. Do you need anything before I go?'

'Could you make me a cup of tea?'

When she brought it, I was lying down with Thomas. 'Drink your tea. We're going,' she whispered, and tiptoed out.

The room grew quiet as Thomas fell asleep. I was woken by a sound that at first I took to be his whimpering, but when I opened my eyes I saw that Oscar had been wailing. 'Where is she?' he seemed to ask.

'Oscar.' I called him to me. I would get used to stroking a cat, I would.

I didn't miss her yet.

I was in a new life now, with new memories. Thomas was my life. Thomas and I were one. I smelt Xiao Lin's perfume. This new life had changed me. Xiao Lin is not flashy, she's warm and caring. Her husband is not awkward and cold, he's considerate and kind, I thought. How had I got it so wrong before?

When darkness fell I didn't want to turn on the light. I heard Ken's footsteps. He lingered outside Barbara's room.

Could he smell cigarettes in there? I couldn't smell Barbara at all now. He used to greet me first, but nowadays it was Thomas. 'Oh, Thomas, my Thomas,' he cooed.

'Plenty of fish soup. Xiao Lin has been,' I said. He gave me a peck on the cheek and went downstairs.

We slept early. New parents do not need much sleep, they say, but we could never get enough. I slept whenever I could. But my sleep was shallow – I woke at the slightest sound. Soon I heard Bill's footsteps, slow and heavy, dragging up to Barbara's bedroom. For the last few nights he had just crawled into the bed and slept. The darkness suited him and us. We were a herd of lost animals stranded together in a cave during a storm.

Ken sighed. 'The poor man. I don't know how he's going to live through this.'

I closed my eyes. I was not mourning her yet.

Tie Mei

Her face had changed: she'd lost the childish look. In labour her whole body was distorted, when she bore down, when she pushed, when she was on all fours. Her man was there, supportive and strong until the last moment when he saw blood. I was impressed none the less: when I had given birth the men were miles away. Women's blood, birth, menstruation were unclean, to be shunned. The maids and the midwife, gentle and powerful, looked after me.

I could not help her, I murmured to her. She asked for the Englishwoman who had died almost the moment the child was delivered. The balance of the souls: one freed, the other trapped – no, briefly attached.

Hers was a seductive place, the smell of her milk, the smell of a being half-way between soul and flesh. Thomas, a foreign name, but I liked it. He whimpered and she opened her eyes. After she'd changed his nappy she sniffed: 'Nainai, are you there?' She looked straight through me. How quickly the smell of the baby had overwhelmed hers.

'Nainai?' she asked again, and her hands stretched out before her.

Could she not see me? Was that a sign? I went closer to her. Her eyes strained as she tried to locate me. 'I know you're here, Nainai, but I can't see you.' After a while she brightened. 'I knew you were at the delivery too. I could smell you.' In the moonlight I could see the lines forming at the corners of her lips.

The mirror was beside her, placed casually on her dressing-table. Her hair was thinner now, but longer, falling over her shoulders. 'You should cover the mirror when you're not using it,' I said.

She laughed. 'Well, it has survived the last few hundred years, I don't suppose not covering it will hurt it that much.'

'It's not that, it's . . . Thomas. The souls of little ones are still lucid. If he sees himself in the mirror, his soul might be tempted away.' I dispensed my last piece of grandmotherly advice with authority, smiling inwardly at such superstition.

She seemed horrified, and she reached to turn over the mirror. Thomas opened his eyes. 'Look,' she said, 'it's that look again! He sees right into me, as if I had known him before.'

'I think he did know you.'

She smiled down at him, not taking in the full meaning of my words as he closed his eyes again. 'Well, we knew each other for nine months.' She leaned over him. 'Oh, my Thomas.'

While she was admiring the baby, I took in everything in the room. First I looked at the wall. My photograph had been replaced by pictures of the baby in various people's arms. The room was littered with toys, baby clothes and bedding. A big pair of man's shoes stood grotesquely next to her slippers. Already it was a homely room, not the bare, tidy girl's room I had been used to. The young man slept on with one arm stretched out to her, snoring gently with his mouth open. Fatherhood must have exhausted him. I had got used to his presence now that it was time to go. Finally I held her face, no longer round with exhaustion, in my gaze. Now that she could not see me I could stare into it for as long as I liked. I would take this image with me as I went. We'd been through a lot together, my granddaughter and I. She had grown and matured before my eyes, And I, too, had changed through knowing her. It was hard to say goodbye, but I needed to rid myself of bitter memories. But how to tell her?

'Nainai,' she whispered, a note of panic in her voice. My silence must have alarmed her. 'Why is it that I can't see you any more? Is it something to do with Thomas?'

It's better to have a short pain than a lingering one. 'Because I'm leaving you.'

'Not just as I'm starting to get used to you! What about Thomas? He needs you.'

'He needs *you*. You are his mother.'

'It's too sudden. Don't.'

'I won't be far away, I can't tell you where yet, but you will know soon.'

'What do you mean? Tell me.'

'You will see in time. Look, the baby's just woken up.' I directed her attention to Thomas. She responded promptly.

I went outside to the back garden – and was shocked by what I saw. No weeds, no clinging dry twigs to shield my beloved Mei blossom, which was shivering in the wind. I recognised the sharpness of the style: it had been the Englishman. No wonder his bit, the front garden, was entangled and green and full of weeds. As I had passed it earlier on, I had noticed how much better it looked and how warm it made me feel.

But he couldn't eliminate the fragrance of Mei, which I held deep inside me. I went to it, and felt the contentment of having resolved something. In the distance London twinkled with what Jiaojiao had told me were Christmas lights. They reminded me of the lanterns we put up for the Lantern Festival. The candles glowed inside red silk.

22: *Xiao Han* – Small Chill

6 January

Jiao Mei

The drizzle outside the car window reminded me of the day of the funeral. Ken had turned the heating right up and Thomas slept soundly in my arms in the back seat. Daisy kept turning round to check on her first grandson. In no time at all the car was like a sauna.

At the funeral I had seen Ted again. His short haircut and thinner face emphasised his similarity to Barbara. I avoided him for fear that memory would invade him the way it pierced me like a dagger.

Afterwards we went back to the house for drinks. Ted sat in her old place. Bigger than her, he made the chair seem too small, just as Bill did. He said it had snowed over Christmas, that she would have loved it. The way he talked about it, the way everyone stood and chatted, with glasses and plates of food, it was as if she had merely gone for a nap and would soon wake up to rejoin us. I could not get used to the English way of mourning.

I sat down and stared out at the front garden, which Bill had finally tackled. I looked around me: it was a complex crowd. An Indian woman, a gardener from Sussex whose fingernails were black with earth, a charity worker who had once been Barbara's lover, and the ex-husband who was a businessman.

A brain tumour had caused her death, the doctors had informed us.

Nobody cried at the funeral, nobody cried at the reception at home. I caught a tear or two here and there, and a suppressed sob, but none of the loud weeping you hear at Chinese funerals, which helped to drown the loss. Barbara had done well in accustoming me to English ways – even in death. I was full of tears, but couldn't let them out as no one else was crying. I kept the sea inside me locked and carefully guarded. I watched the other guests from the sidelines, haunting the gathering. Gradually rage dried the tears and burned through me, another feeling I could not show. It was worse than grief: grief could be comforted and shared, but not this.

'Do you know what her brother does?' Ken asked. He had talked to more people than I at the funeral.

'Did you talk to Barbara's ex-husband?' I asked, instead of answering.

'Yes. He lived in India with her, you know, for nearly five years.'

What had she been like then? Younger, more idealistic. I pictured her fetching water from the river Ganges, a scene I vaguely remembered from a picture book.

'She had a nervous breakdown when she came back to England. Culture shock, he said, and they split up shortly afterwards.'

'Was he Indian?' Daisy, who had been silent most of the journey, frowned: this conversation was full of people and names she did not know and it bothered her.

I looked into the shop windows as we waited at traffic lights, watched the men in the sandwich shops carefully putting all the ingredients inside the pieces of bread, more lives to feed. One looked up blandly at the traffic. Our eyes met. His didn't blink. He said something – 'Next', probably.

'No,' I said. 'He's English.'

'She sounds quite posh, this Barbara, big house in Hampstead, rich husband. What was she like?'

I hoped Ken would think this question was directed at him so that I could sit back and watch the view. Outside, a man put up his newspaper to shield himself from the drizzle. What *was* she like? How to sum up a personality.

'She was an artist. A bit eccentric, I suppose,' Ken said slowly, after a long silence.

'That's what my neighbours think of me,' said Daisy, evidently having decided that Barbara must have been all right.

We stopped for a quick lunch at a Little Chef, which lasted for nearly two hours by the time we had changed Thomas's nappy and fed him. Endless motorways. A change in speed woke me from a doze. The rain had stopped. We drove to the edge of a small, neat town.

There was nobody else in the park. The ground was hard, the air cold and moist. Red and yellow signs with exclamation marks warned that it was not officially open. Red and white cordons marked out the boundaries of a space we were forbidden to enter. Ken stepped over the line, Thomas on his arm, with the assured step of a man who knew where he was going, and stretched out a hand to Daisy. I followed gingerly behind. It was a surprise, he had said. I don't need any more surprises, I had thought.

We went across a vast expanse of wasteland to a newly built rockery with some green on a raised-up slope. Daisy exclaimed, 'My dear, is that it?'

Then I saw it: the bridge.

It was not very big, not as big as I'd thought, but pretty, just the right size for the park, arched, wooden, with carved lions. The wood was naked, no paint on it yet.

Daisy went to it and I turned to Ken, smiling proudly. He'd been talking bridges, dreaming bridges for months. I thought of the pile of doodles and plans littered about the house. While I had been making a baby, he had made a bridge.

'What are these creatures?' Daisy ran her fingers over them.

'Lions,' I said, without looking. I shouldn't have presumed.

'But do Chinese lions have wings?' She was sharper than me.

Ken gave Thomas a kiss.

'Wings?' I went to stand next to her. But these were not lions: they were birds. 'Magpies!' I said, looking at Ken.

'Why magpies?' Daisy was curious.

'Ask Mei. She gave me the idea. There is a story behind it.'

So I told her of the fairy and the shepherd, and the magpies building a bridge for them.

'And it's four for a boy!' Daisy exclaimed.

It rained after we'd gone to bed. I got up in the dark to feed Thomas and couldn't sleep after that. All was quiet around me. Something was missing, I thought, as I listened to the familiar pitter-pattering. No sound of the radio to accompany the rain; no Barbara.

A feeling of hollowness rose inside me. It emerged as the sea of tears that had never found an outlet. Now they came in waves.

She had been taken away. She could no longer smell lilies, drink coffee, eat my stir-fry. I could no longer touch her. She had never seen Thomas.

I should have known about losing parents – I'd been through it – but it hurt as much as it had the first time. And the uncertainty made it worse. To this day I still don't know what killed her: the curse or the illness. I will always wonder.

Ken woke, and saw my eyes wide open in the darkness. He knew what was going round in my head, and tried to comfort me. 'Don't be like Barbara, feeling guilty when you shouldn't. I don't believe in curses, but even if there was one, it had nothing to do with you.'

'But it's all so unfair. Why her?'

'Darling, life is unfair. Think of it as an accident.'

'What?' I didn't follow.

'Life is a series of accidents. I suppose you could just as well ask, why him?' He leaned over to Thomas's cot and stroked his head. 'This precious little thing.'

I kissed the man who built bridges.

Tie Mei

My last trip to see Mei. I didn't wake her, I entered her dream.

She asked me if I had come to say goodbye, and where I

was going. I said I was going to another life. That startled her and she almost woke. I told her to remember all the times we had shared together, and that after tonight I wouldn't be able to come and go as I pleased, but I would be there for her, for ever, a bit of her family in this foreign soil.

She cried. Would she know where I'd gone? Would she recognise me? Would she be happy?

I said, yes, she would recognise me and, yes, I would be happy, that she should come and see me, and bring Thomas with her whenever she could. She should keep me entertained by reading the stories I had told her, the fox stories, the fairy stories and the flower fairies. That way I would remember her.

Then I entered the darkness down below. Beloved twin of my soul, here I come.

23: *Da Han* – Big Chill

21 January

Jiao Mei

I was packing. It's amazing how much stuff a baby can generate. We had decided to move out at the weekend.

When I told Bill we were leaving, his bloodshot eyes opened wide. 'No, don't, you can't. You can't live at Ken's, it's too small.'

'We've found a new place – in Balham. Or is it Peckham? One of the two.'

'Oh, no, not South London.' He winced as if we'd been sent to Siberia.

During the sunny patch in the afternoon when Thomas had fallen asleep, I went to have another look at the garden. The icy path led me towards the studio. Somehow the path felt longer, the garden bigger, emptier. The view to the nearby houses had never been clearer. I must have been away from it for longer than I had realised. When I looked closely at the trees and plants, they were not where I expected them to be. I recognised the sharp neatness as Bill's hallmark. So that was what he'd been busy doing: rescuing it from decay, he would say. Killing it, she would have said. At the thought of her I turned and found the studio door tightly shut with a rusty lock on it. I smelt the damp, the turps, and a trail of lavender oil that could not be locked in.

I peeped through the murky window and saw piles of papers and the canvases on which she'd painted the lilies.

Were they lilies? Were lilies so colourful? There was such a riot of colour, I couldn't be sure. I leaned back – at least he hadn't burned them.

Again I faced the desolate garden. I was stocktaking, starting the inevitable farewell. When I'd covered the whole garden, I stood next to the Mei tree. All the leaves had fallen, but the pink buds were ready to burst.

The smell of tobacco broke my contemplative mood, and I heard Bill approaching. Silently his hand reached out to touch the trunk. 'You saved it,' I said, with mixed feelings.

'Sometimes you wonder why you bother,' he said. 'You clean it up, it gets messy again.'

It didn't stop him tidying the garden, his way of remembering her. The space around the studio was empty, the soil turned, the bulbs beneath waiting for next year, for the cycle to begin again, to grow, to bloom. It felt like only yesterday that Bill, Barbara and I had planted them. I looked at his dirty fingernails, and unshaven cheeks. In my mind I reached out a hand to him. A surprising thought occurred to me: I would miss him.

'I'm going abroad for a while,' he said.

'Where to?' I asked casually.

'Sunny Spain.' He laughed bitterly.

Alone, I thought.

'You and Ken can stay here and look after the garden. I might be away for a long time.'

'But . . .'

'The back garden is yours, and the studio,' he said slowly.

'What do you mean?'

'I mean that she left you the garden and the studio. It's in her will.'

'I don't want the garden. What would I do with it? It's too big and I'm not a gardener.' My voice shook.

'How can you say that? She wanted you to have it and you know you want it. Take it. You can do what you like with it. Sleep in it, for all I care.'

Indoors Thomas cried and I went in to him. When I came down it was darker and I couldn't see Bill but I smelt a fragrance. A fragrance that had visited me many times over the last year.

It came from where Bill was standing.

'The Mei has blossomed,' he said, and turned to me. I went nearer and saw the smudge of tears on his face.

Tie Mei

I am a blossom. I have five petals, stretching out. I am in a garden. A man is bending over me: behind him is a young woman. I smelt her strongest although she was further away. She is special.

I have no idea how long I have been asleep. When I woke up this was what I saw. Fragments of dreams stayed with me, but as each new petal opened, they disintegrated. There was an ocean, big and wild, a young girl asleep, suspicious-looking souls, a mirror, and many blossoms.

I like the sunshine. I hate water. I should be somewhere hot and sunny. But I have to be here because my root is here.

I feel pain, all over, especially in the joints. I long to stretch and grow.

I shake gently, and they breathe deeply.

24: *Li Chun* – Spring Begins

4 February

Jiao Mei

I didn't realise they'd display it so quickly. Thomas shuddered at the cold wind and I hugged him tightly. 'We're going to see Grandmother's mirror,' I whispered to him.

The mirror was in a glass case, along with the other bronze objects, in an obscure corner of the museum. It was shown decorated side up, so that I could not see my face reflected in it. 'Bronze Mirror, Tang Dynasty, China, *circa* 722–4,' it said. We had both believed it was Qing. 'Had it been older I would have had to donate it to a museum,' she had said. Things might have been so different. I stared at the mirror, feeling its unaccustomed distance from me. The fluorescent light made it seem almost surgical, more green than it already was.

Two Chinese men sauntered over and bent down to look at it, whispering between themselves. From their badges I knew they were from a Chinese university, here for a conference.

An Englishman I recognised vaguely as one of the professors from my college came over and bent down with them. 'As you can see, taken from China at the time of the opium wars, it's a bit of an embarrassment.' He shrugged his shoulders as the two Chinese smiled politely.

It was raining as I stepped out of the warmth of the museum. At home there was a postcard, and a letter from my mother. I tore it open quickly. She was posting a jumper she had knitted for Thomas, would I look out for it? 'I had no

243

measurements so took a rough guess at the size of a newborn, though I thought he might be a little bigger, being half English, so I was generous with it.' I waved the letter in front of Thomas. 'What do you think? Are you a big boy for Granny?'

The postcard was from Bill in Spain. 'Make sure you don't water the Mei blossom. In fact, I think it would like it here.'

I put down the card, and went to the window. In the front garden, I saw the dandelions, washed by the rain, growing fast.

'Be a gardener. You know that's what she'd have wanted.' Those were the last words on Bill's card.

Author's note

People often ask me why I write in English. It's a long story.

England is a garden – that was my first thought when I set eyes on it as a fresh-eyed student, fourteen years ago. Now I have written a novel about it. This book is my fruit, nurtured by the all too generous rain and not so generous English sun.

England is not my garden, I did not make it: I simply came here to enjoy the bloom and blossom. And yet I have always considered it to be mine. It's hard to say when that feeling began: perhaps when Uncle Gao, an old man in my father's factory, told me my first story in English, 'Snow White'. Formerly one of the country's most prominent automobile engineers, when I first met him he was relegated to sweeping the corridor floor. Dad whispered to me, 'I want you to show respect to this kind and clever man.'

The combination of an earthquake and a political movement meant that, along with all the other children, I was off school for a whole term. My parents, fearing for my education, were delighted that Uncle Gao lent me English books to read, and would chat to me in English while we waited for the bus in the snow, drawing strange looks from all around us.

He had opened a door to a magic world. As I grew older I grew bolder, reading more ambitious English books, tumbling over new words as if they were mere stepping stones in my eagerness to reach the end of the story.

I started to keep a diary in English.

Imagine a language that is musical to the ear, that is not (to the Chinese) tarnished by imperial overtones, that your parents cannot understand, in which you can totally immerse yourself and be free. That was what English meant to me. I entered the garden and the view was promising.

In my university in southern China I met native speakers for the first time, above all my English teachers, from Australia, New Zealand, America and England, and my two special English girlfriends. I grew more and more curious about this new world. Unknown, exciting, I felt it was my future. I fell in love communicating in this language.

I've never written a book in Chinese. To you native English speakers, I apologise – I've hijacked your language, but I could not help it: it has always been my own private language of freedom.